Valerie Kershaw was born in Lancashire. She was a journalist with the *Manchester Evening News* and later worked in BBC local radio for ten years. She has written three other novels, *The Snowman*, *Rosa* and *The Bank Manager's Wife*, which was made into a play by Central Television. Valerie Kershaw now lives in Staffordshire where *Rockabye* is set. *Rockabye* was the first winner of the Lichfield Prize.

Paperback
Exchange
12/13 St. Peters Street
Hereford HR1 2LF

·····················
NON RETURNABLE

Acclaim for *The Snowman*

'A remarkable achievement'
Guardian

'An impressively taut debut'
Listener

'Consistently interesting, well-shaped, exciting'
Bernard Levin

Acclaim for *The Bank Manager's Wife*

'Wickedly well done'
Guardian

'A stylish chille[...]
Daily Telegraph

CW01496661

ROCKABYE

Valerie Kershaw

CORGI BOOKS

All of the characters in this book are fictitious, and any resemblance to actual persons, living or dead, is purely coincidental.

ROCKABYE
A CORGI BOOK 0 552 13676 X

Originally published in Great Britain by
Bantam Press,
a division of Transworld Publishers Ltd

PRINTING HISTORY
Bantam Press edition published 1990
Corgi edition published 1991

Copyright © Valerie Kershaw 1991

The right of Valerie Kershaw to be identified as author of this work has been asserted in accordance with sections 77 and 78 of the Copyright Designs and Patents Act 1988.

Conditions of sale
1. This book is sold subject to the condition that it shall not, by way of trade *or otherwise*, be lent, re-sold, hired out or otherwise circulated in any form of binding or cover other than that in which it is published *and without a similar condition including this condition being imposed on the subsequent purchaser.*
2. This book is sold subject to the Standard Conditions of Sale of Net Books and may not be re-sold in the UK below the net price fixed by the publishers for the book.

This book is set in 11/13 California
by Colset Private Limited, Singapore.

Corgi Books are published by Transworld Publishers Ltd., 61–63 Uxbridge Road, Ealing, London W5 5SA, in Australia by Transworld Publishers (Australia) Pty. Ltd., 15–23 Helles Avenue, Moorebank, NSW 2170, and in New Zealand by Transworld Publishers (N.Z.) Ltd., Cnr. Moselle and Waipareira Avenues, Henderson, Auckland.

Printed and bound in Great Britain by
Cox & Wyman Ltd., Reading, Berks.

To Karl

ONE

The remains of the meal lay between them on the plastic-topped table. Neither smoked. Very few people in the building smoked now. Isobel was looking out of the seventh floor window to the Birmingham University tower a mile away. Haloed in the neon glow of the city, the landmark was defined precisely by what it was not, a black rectangular hole in the November tea-time sky.

Fanny Wragg, who was fifteen years younger than Isobel and still had puppy bright eyes, looked up from the organization's news sheet. 'There's an attachment going for an arts producer at Radio Avon.'

'Why don't you apply?' Isobel produced and presented Radio Brum's arts programme; one of the ways she had of defending her job was to encourage eager youngsters to try their luck elsewhere.

'Do you think I'd stand a chance?'

'I'm sure you would. You've done some very good interviews for me.'

'Even that big dick in the front office liked that package I did on David Lodge,' said Fanny.

'I'd put in for the job if I were you.' Isobel was

7

again looking over the city. Suddenly the tower floated away. 'It's getting foggy.'

Fanny folded the paper and passed it to her. 'There're one or two things you might be interested in. An attachment to network radio. A television job at Southampton. It's you who should be thinking of moving, duckie. You've been here three years.'

Isobel knew that to Fanny three years was a lifetime. She also knew that if she didn't make a move soon, the weight of her thirty-eight years would start to run her into the ground. A broadcaster began to be regarded as no longer young – no longer exciting? – at thirty. 'I suppose you're right, Fanny. In fact I know you are. But it would mean selling the cottage.'

'So what?' Fanny began to stand up. She was a leggy youngster, dressed in a bat-winged cotton sweater and baggy zebra-striped pants. Mickey Mouse earrings jangled as she turned her head and looked across the canteen. 'I bet Vernon goes and sits with our beloved programme organizer. The newsroom reckons that Hilary Winstan isn't quite the macho guy he pretends to be. They say our Vernon's forever following Hilary into the loo.'

'Oh, Fanny. You should know better than to believe a newsroom story,' Isobel said as she rose. She, too, watched Vernon Strutt-Walker trip towards Hilary Winstan's table.

'There he goes with his chicken vindaloo,' said Fanny. 'Did you hear Vernon's Simon Rattle package?'

'No.'

8

'Honestly, darling, he was practically licking that poor man's bum. Well, I suppose we'd better make tracks. The fog will be worse out of town. It's never bad in the centre.'

'It's very good of you to give me a lift.'

'When's your car ready?'

'Saturday.'

'Haven't you got Friday off? I wish I had. I've a frightful day tomorrow. I'm doing a piece for Jacko with the Sports Minister. What's-his-name? Didn't you once interview the guy for the breakfast show?'

'Gerald Hogg. He used to be an England cricketer.'

'I don't know anything about cricket.'

'I think I've still got Hogg's autobiography, *Forty Not Out*. I interviewed him when he was on the publicity circus promoting it. Do you want to borrow it? Just read the beginning and the end. The middle's a blow by blow account of the matches he starred in. I couldn't understand a word.'

'You're an angel. I've got some stuff on him from News Information, but it's all a bit predictable. Is he a good talker?'

'All politicians are.'

Very few people were in the canteen at this time in the evening; even the bar, which had now been moved to a new building outside the broadcasting centre, would be thinly populated. Fanny's generation of media people were public Puritans. When they drank immoderately they did so at private addresses, holding parties to which, at thirty-eight, Isobel was too old to be invited. She was only indignant about this in principle; such apartheism was monstrous, of course, but it did save her the task of wriggling out of going.

The broadcasting centre was designed like a squared Q, built round a courtyard with a tail sticking out to the east. It was a mile from the city centre, set in playing fields with a stream winding through the grounds. The radio station's management offices were on the first floor at the front of the building. A corridor, carpeted in Tory blue and filled with the station's output, noisily divided the offices from an operations room and three studios. These overlooked the courtyard. The patch of green was often turned into an extra television studio, providing the local radio station's guests with some light entertainment while they waited to be interviewed.

Radio Brum's production offices and engineers' rooms were tucked into the broadcasting centre's tail, down the corridor from television's regional newsroom. The two women made their way to this part of the building to collect their hats and coats. Now, at half past six, the main production office was deserted. Pools of tape dribbled over the floor, discarded press releases overflowed from metal waste-paper bins. One of the dozen phones was ringing. Neither took any notice of it. They collected their belongings, Fanny adjusted her makeup, and then they made for the ground floor. They went out by the back entrance, passing cages of props as they made their way to the car park.

Like everything else she did, Fanny Wragg

drove well. Isobel, who had sudden and terrifying lapses of confidence, looked on enviously as the girl easily manoeuvred the old Ford out of the street across the on-coming traffic on the A38.

She tried to relax. 'Will you marry Geoff?'

'He hasn't asked me,' said Fanny.

'Would you? If he did?'

'Rather not. There're a lot of things I want to do before I get myself tied down.' Fanny was batting along. The city centre was already clear of rush-hour traffic and visibility was good.

'Does he own the house in Lichfield?'

'We bought it between us. Double mortgage relief.'

'But what happens if you get a job elsewhere?'

'We'll probably sell and split the profits. Do you think you'll marry again?'

'No.'

'You can't be sure.'

'Fairly sure.'

'Mind if I switch the radio on? I've a package coming up on Jacko's show.'

'Of course not.' But nevertheless Isobel was irritated. She never listened to the output in her non-working hours if she could help it. She felt this was the only way to keep reasonably sane.

'It's the first time I've done any nuns,' Fanny told her. 'Oh, duckie, they wore short skirts. It wasn't a bit like *The Nun's Story*.'

Isobel grunted and, with an expertise which came from long practice, managed not to hear a word of Fanny's piece.

The car was now speeding through Spaghetti Junction. 'I know it's fashionable to sneer about Birmingham, but you can drive a car through it, which is more than you can say about London or Manchester,' Charlie, her ex-husband and a Brummie born, had told her when he'd first brought her to the West Midlands. 'And what's more we grow the best trees in the country.' Isobel, to her surprise, had found he was right.

They were at the Lichfield fork in the Tyburn Road when she became aware of a lack of noise. Fanny had turned off the radio. An unspoken question was filling ever more space between them.

'What a good piece.' Isobel had found that if she really attacked her words people tended to believe her.

'Too much Mother Agnes?'

'Oh no. Well judged I'd say.'

'The bloody woman was so . . . unworldly. Honestly darling. Not a clue. I'd to chop her to bits to lift out one or two decent quotes. But I thought the actuality worked quite well.'

'Very well.' She leaned further back in her seat. Tower of Babel, she was thinking sleepily. Mile after mile of chat and back-to-back play listed music; recipes, advice, nuns, cricketers, politicians, book pushers, transvestites, hernias, tomato blight, AIDS, antiques, God spots, Sinn Fein and the greenhouse effect . . .

She came to with a start to find the car deep in yellowish cotton wool. 'Woken up? Even the fog lights aren't much use. I knew it would come down as soon as we left the city. It always does. I was all right when I had tail lights to follow.'

'Where are we?'

'About a mile from Lichfield. We'll come to the Burton roundabout at any moment, I hope. There'll be overhead lighting there. Alrewas is between Lichfield and Burton, isn't it?'

'Just short of halfway. This is really so good of you. I'll do the same for you, I promise.'

'I'll keep you to that,' Fanny warned. 'How long have you lived in Alrewas?'

'Ever since I came down to the West Midlands. That was just after Charlie and I got wed. He'd got a job at a comprehensive school in Lichfield. Let me see. Lord, it must be twelve years ago now.'

The fog frayed apart and they saw the round-about ahead.

'Thank God for that. I just take the A38 towards Burton?'

'Yes. There's a slip road off it which leads into the village.'

'What happened? Tell me to mind my own business if you want to.'

'Between me and Charlie? The usual. He ran off with another woman. Sandra Tiptree. She was sports mistress at the school he taught at. The divorce came through about four years ago.'

'I'm sorry, duckie.'

'I'm afraid it was my own fault.'

'How do you mean?'

'Charlie's a born womanizer. You know the

type. Anything in skirts. And I knew that before I married him. But I married the bastard all the same.'

'Why, for God's sake?'

Isobel laughed. 'I can see you've never been in love.'

'I think an awful lot about Geoff. Really. We're very fond of each other. I wouldn't shack up with a guy just for the double mortgage relief.'

'Oh, come off it, Fanny. I didn't mean it like that. Anyway, I don't think it's a good idea to be in love with the man you marry.'

'Why?'

'Well, you're not marrying him at all. You're marrying Mr Dreamboat. God knows who I thought I was wed to. Certainly not Mr Charlie Maccabee. I'm afraid that man turned me on something rotten.'

'Have you seen him since?'

'I got a letter from him about two years ago. He's living near Blackpool now. He wrote to tell me his new address. I can't think why. I think he really wrote to tell me that Sandra was going to have a baby.'

'The shit.'

'I wish I hadn't given up smoking,' Isobel fretted.

'It's my fault. Talking about your ex-husband. Laying on the stress. Sorry.'

'When I first stopped smoking, I couldn't wait to get to bed and go to sleep. And then I'd dream I was sitting at a bar on a high stool, smoking my head off. I even felt guilty in the dream.'

14

'I suppose he was marvellously good looking.'

'Who?'

'Charlie.'

'Yes. Now let's shut up about him.'

'Are you quite positive there wasn't too much Mother Agnes?'

'Just about right I thought.'

'Such a shame nuns chop off their skirts nowadays. It's so unromantic,' said Fanny. 'They all seem to have fat calves. What do you think your next move will be?'

'What?'

'In your career?'

'What indeed?' It was a question which troubled Isobel; most of all she was troubled by the growing conviction that radio work was not for her. She didn't feel drawn back to print journalism either. Just what do I want to do? she asked herself for the hundredth time. And then: Isn't it enough to keep a roof over my head and get enough money to pay for the groceries?

And it was, she told herself, glancing at the darkened form of the young girl sitting beside her. Fanny was edging the car off the dual carriageway on to the Alrewas slip road; she drove the old banger to within an inch of its capabilities. She wondered if she'd been like that at Fanny's age. Oh yes, she dimly remembered. She'd been a spunky kid too; cocky, full of herself, crackling with life.

'I'll tell you one thing for nothing,' said Fanny. 'If I haven't made it to network producer by the time I'm thirty I'll jack it in.'

'Good!' laughed Isobel. 'Turn left up Main Street. Just before we get to the top there's a bridge over the canal. We make a left just before there. But perhaps you'd better park in Main Street. Samson Cottage is down an alley and I really mean an alley. No room to manoeuvre.'

'Do you like living alone?'

'Yes. That's one thing I really like.'

'I don't think I'd ever feel really comfortable without someone else's dirty socks lying around.'

'You're a masochist.'

'How long have you had the cottage?'

'We bought it when we first came down from the north. It was a complete wreck, but cheap so we had enough money to do it up.'

'I'd have thought you'd have wanted to sell after you and he split up. A fresh start and all that.'

'There's only one fresh start. And that's when you leave your mother's womb.'

'That's a sobering philosophy, duckie.'

'It's a sobering world,' Isobel said.

A thick yellowish pall eddied over Main Street. The car's fog lights picked out the sweating gleam of tarmac pavements. Isobel said: 'Cinery urns containing bits of human bones have been found in villages near here. Axes and flint tools have been dug up in Alrewas. There are traces of at least twelve barrows in the village and some mysterious prehistoric circles. This and other Staffordshire villages along the banks of the Trent and Tame go back to the Iron Age and earlier.'

'It's got a very funny name. Alrewas.'

'I think it just means alder marsh. And it can certainly get pretty wet. Some of the village was flooded last year. Kids were paddling down the streets on lilos. Pull up here, just beyond the off-licence. Come and see the cottage and I'll get you the Hogg book.'

When they got out of the car they both looked ahead of them. Fog was creeping over the top of the small hump-backed bridge, sliding down black scales of tar. 'I hope it clears by morning,' said Fanny. 'It's all right for you. You can stay in bed.'

'The cottage is just down here.' Isobel led Fanny past the blank gable end of a Victorian terraced house.

'My God. It is narrow.'

'You can get a car down, but it's better to make your first attempt in daylight,' said Isobel. The tarmac was squeezed between the house and the side of a derelict Victorian building. Pointing to it Isobel said: 'It's empty now, of course, but I think it was once living quarters and warehousing for goods hauled to the village by canal barges.' Just beyond, swirling in vapour illuminated by a sodium street lamp, was a thatched cottage. The front door was to one side and, tucked under wetly gleaming reed, was a second-floor window not more than eighteen inches high.

'It's just like a gingerbread house,' said Fanny. 'But what do you do with your car?'

'Oh, there's a wide piece of land to the side between the cottage and what was once a chapel. It's empty now and the Sunday school behind it has been turned into a house. A surgeon lives there. We both have canal frontage. That's why we bought the cottage. Charlie used to sit and fish from the bottom of our garden.'

'You're certainly tucked away. No-one would ever know you are here. Where does the alley lead?'

'The village playing-fields. But the cottage is not as secluded as you might suppose. There's a tow-path on the other side of the canal and everyone and his dog uses that. If my washing's not whiter than white the whole village would hear about it by the evening.' Isobel got out her key.

'Where does the Samson bit come from?'

'No romantic story I'm afraid. In Victorian times it belonged to a village tailor called Matthias Samson. Of course the cottage is much older than that. Seventeenth century.' As she walked in, Isobel listened out as she always did for the tick of the grandfather clock; for her it replaced the lick of a welcoming dog's tongue.

The front door opened straight into the square-beamed living-room. Stairs were tucked into one side of the inglenook. The room was rigorously neat and besides the grandfather clock, there was the base of an oak dresser and two chintz-covered armchairs. A cricket table by one of the chairs doubled up as a place for the telephone and a surface on which to put down drinks. Book shelves were built under the window which faced the alley. 'Let me take your coat. The cottage is warm. The central heating works by timer. What about a gin and tonic? And I'll give you a quick tour of the rest of the house.'

'It's lovely, duckie.'

'The kitchen's the same size,' said Isobel going through to get the gin.

'I can see why you wouldn't want to give the place up.' Fanny followed her and hitched herself up on the kitchen table. She pointed to another door. 'What's through there?'

Silently Isobel opened the door and switched on the light. In contrast to the living-room and kitchen, this room was such a jumble that Fanny was slow to realize it was an artist's studio.

'I do botanical paintings mostly. I'm afraid I've such a small talent that perhaps it would be merciful if I had no talent at all. Still, it keeps me out of mischief. And I can look at plants for long periods and not feel completely silly.'

'You're full of surprises. I'd no idea,' said Fanny. 'Really. I'd never have guessed. You always seem so . . . efficient. So business-like.'

'Do I?' Isobel was startled. 'I try and make myself shape up. Be efficient. That's because deep down there's a very messy creature always trying to get out.'

'And this is your messy room?'

Isobel laughed. 'Yes.'

'The canvases seem frightfully good. But of course, I don't know anything about it. I'm no judge.'

'This part of the cottage was built after the Second World War. It's supposed to be the dining-room, but

I eat in the kitchen. A bathroom was built above it.'

'That must be rather large.'

'Part of it was turned into wardrobes and linen cupboards. A cottage like this has no storage space you know. Come on, I'll show you. Your book should be upstairs. I use the second bedroom as a study. Do bring your drink.'

'You're so lucky to have a place like this.'

'Yes. I think so. Though I very nearly lost it, because I was pretty ill at the time of the divorce. Too ill to stand up to Charlie. But my solicitor, Mr Drago, fought him tooth and nail for me. Mr Drago turned out to be a tiger. Watch your head. My bedroom is over the living-room.'

'It makes me quite hate my modern box,' and Fanny's hand strayed to touch one of the great cruck beams.

'I'm afraid a cottage like this is full of small inconveniences. You have to go through the second bedroom to get to the bathroom and linen cupboards. But that doesn't matter because there's only me,' said Isobel. She stopped to draw the curtains in her bedroom before taking Fanny across the landing. 'Duck your head.'

The bedrooms were built into the roof of the cottage. In each, two walls sloped down to almost floor level; the gable ends were sturdy triangles. Thick oak beams were joined by mortise and tenon, half-inch pegs of wood providing extra pinning.

Besides books, Isobel's study contained a single bed which also served as a couch and a tall cheval mirror. Her desk was under a lattice window in the gable end. Track lighting mounted on two horizontal beams illustrated this working area.

She led the way across a floor which sloped steeply from the rear to the front of the cottage. 'The building is listed and the Council wouldn't let us put in a new floor,' she said. 'It's gypsum. Apparently one of the few in Staffordshire. I'm not at all sure what's so worthwhile about preserving a gypsum floor. I always thought that and plaster of Paris were the same thing. The door to the bathroom is tucked behind the chimney stack. See?' She pointed before kneeling down in front of a row of books. 'Ah. Here's our Hogg.' She put down her glass of gin and tonic and pulled it out. As she did so, she caught a glimpse of a furry face in the cheval mirror. Startled, she turned her head.

Paddington Bear was standing in his red Wellington boots on the rush-seated Victorian rocking-chair. One of the toggles on his black duffle coat was hanging loose. There was a tear at the top of the left sleeve. His very bright, very glassy eyes winked at her.

Cold touched the nape of her neck. The chill spread through her. Shivering, she rose.

She was immediately aware of other eyes on her, those of Fanny Wragg. 'What's wrong?' The girl mirrored Isobel's shock. Her long clever head was starting from her shoulders.

Isobel opened her mouth to speak, to reassure Fanny. 'I'm perfectly all right,' she wanted to say. But the words remained unspoken. Fanny's face was becoming a blur.

'Isobel!'

Isobel sighed; the sound came from so deep within her that it had to break through little bits and pieces of her to escape.

'Are you all right? Are you ill?'

'It was my daughter's,' said Isobel.

'I don't understand.'

'My daughter's Paddington bear.'

'I didn't know you had a child.'

'She's dead.'

TWO

The offices of Pipkin and Drago were in a square at the bottom of Dam Street. The narrow medieval thoroughfare was shadowed by Lichfield Cathedral, which stood on rising ground above it. In the square itself crowds surged through the city's Friday market. Isobel, her gloved hand tightening on the strap of her shoulder bag, stood hesitantly. Though she was haunted by the image of the bear on the rocking-chair, she also felt a sense of disbelief. She understood this to be an unwillingness to accept what had happened. She felt her uncertain body being pushed backwards by the swell of the crowd.

'It really is quite extraordinary that you should choose this moment to ring up,' the appointment secretary at Pipkin and Drago had told her on the phone. 'Mr James Drago's eleven o'clock client has just this minute cancelled.'

'I'm afraid my affairs are dealt with by Mr Henry Drago.'

'Mr James' father has been retired for over a year now, my dear. But if you would care to see Mr James, I could slip you in. You did say it was urgent?'

'Very urgent.'

'And you are willing to see our Mr James?'

'Yes. Certainly.'

'Very well, my dear. We'll see you at eleven.'

But now Isobel was not at all sure she was doing the right thing. She found herself almost willing to believe she'd imagined the bear. Suddenly, drawing herself upright, she purposefully pushed her way through the shoppers. The market was held in the lee of a church, which had been turned into a day centre for the elderly; after almost knocking an old man down she slowed and moved more cautiously. She'd become so anxious that the palms of her hands began to sweat. She crossed to Dam Street, pulling off her gloves as she went.

Arriving at Pipkin and Drago's offices, located in a discreet two storey Georgian building, she was shown into a ground-floor waiting-room. Net curtains veiled her from the street. A two-bar electric fire gave off a sawing buzz of heat.

When the door of the room was quietly closed behind her, she immediately went to the mirror on the wall. She felt so frayed she was sure her hair must be in disarray, her lipstick awry. But the short glossy cap of black hair neatly framed her small boned face and her eyes, an inky blue, were so dark they concealed much of her agitation. Contrary to how she felt, she saw she looked perfectly calm and collected.

But I'm dressed in blue, she noted. A blue lady. That thought hadn't occurred to her when she'd chosen to wear the matching crêpe wool jacket and trousers. She'd decided on the outfit because it had just come back from the cleaners.

She moved away from the mirror. If only I hadn't given up smoking, she thought, plucking at the edge of the waist-length jacket. She began to pace the waiting-room.

'Mrs Maccabee? Mr James can see you now. First floor, first right. His name's on the door. You can't miss it.'

James Drago's office was at the front of the building, overlooking the market square. The man didn't at all resemble his father; Henry Drago had certainly been tall, too, but with a simian cast to his features which his son hadn't inherited. He'd also been thin. James Drago was built like a prop forward; his eyes were disconcertingly boyish. She found herself wondering if he were old enough to understand her problems.

'How do you do?' The grasp of his hand was enthusiastic. 'Please sit down.'

She made a conscious effort not to sit bolt upright on the edge of the chair. But then she found she'd hunched her limbs about her as if to protect herself against hostile elements. Though Henry Drago had fought hard and well for her, her previous experience of being in a lawyer's office had been traumatic. Finding herself in the same position didn't bring back memories, rather intimations of dread.

Sitting behind his desk, James Drago took up a pencil and began tapping it against a pad of paper. The mannerism was an exact replica of one of his father's. She still found it annoying. She averted her gaze. 'Now, what can we do for you, Mrs Maccabee?'

'Your father dealt with my divorce four years ago.' She came to an abrupt halt. She didn't know how to go on.

'Are you having trouble with your ex-husband?'

'I'm not sure.'

'Perhaps it would be better if you began at the beginning. If you could fill in the background for me and move on from there to what's troubling you.'

Now she experienced an overwhelming sense of dread, as if she were bodily being pulled back into a void. Her hands clutched on to the arms of the chair.

He waited for her to begin.

'Charlie Maccabee and I were married in Manchester and came down here to live when he got a job as a French teacher at a local school. I'm a journalist and I managed to get a job on a paper in Birmingham. Three years after we were married we had a daughter. We called her Anne-Marie.'

She shifted slightly, turning herself further from him. 'During Anne-Marie's first term at school, I got a call to say she wasn't very well. It didn't seem to be anything serious. Just cold-like symptoms. Two days later she died of meningitis in Good Hope Hospital.'

'I'm sorry.'

'Charlie was in a pitiful state. He really was. But I couldn't feel anything at all. It was as though Anne-Marie were still alive and this was in spite of the fact that I had been at her funeral and had seen her buried. It was awful. I didn't have the least inclination to cry. It didn't seemed to have happened. Part of me knew she was dead. But I couldn't feel she was dead. I found I had to fake grief. People expected me to be devastated. Charlie did.

'I got a job again on a newspaper and then about six months later I became ill. I had a nervous breakdown. I was in St Matthew's for three months. They had me on modified insulin to start with – to build up my appetite I think. I went down to under five stone.

'Charlie was marvellous while I was in hospital. But of course . . . Charlie is, how shall I put it? . . . a light weight. I mean, a chap like that isn't cut out to cope with tragedy. He rose to the occasion for a short while, but of course I was still pretty ill when I came out of hospital. Charlie just took off with the games mistress.'

'Did he marry her after your divorce?'

'Yes. I got our cottage and Charlie was pretty cut up about that. But there was no maintenance. That was a good thing in its way. It made me have to get well enough to go back to work. A job came up at a local radio station in Birmingham for a publicity assistant. It was only for three days a week at first, but at the time I found that ideal. I seemed to sleep most of the days in between. And then I began to learn broadcasting techniques and now I produce and present the arts show and do bits and pieces for other programmes. I work full time.'

'Has your ex-husband been in touch with you since the divorce?'

'First of all he and Sandra Tiptree – his second wife – lived in London, but he got in touch with me when they moved to Squire's Gate. That's between St Anne's and Blackpool. Sandra's parents live in St Anne's. He wrote with his new address.'

'Then you were still friends of sorts?'

'Hardly. That was the first time I'd heard from him since the divorce. Sandra was to have a baby. Charlie was cock-a-hoop. He probably wanted to tell the whole world. The man's a rotten husband, but I have to admit he's a wonderful father. Anne-Marie adored him. And he was absolutely mad about her.'

'When I asked you if you were having trouble with him you said you weren't sure?'

'Last night when I got back home from work—' she stopped, trying to reorganize her thoughts, my car's having a new clutch put in – and a colleague gave me a lift home from work. I'd promised to lend her a book, so we went upstairs to a room I use as a study to get it.' She felt the hairs at the nape of her neck begin to waft upwards. 'Anne-Marie's Paddington bear was on the rocking-chair.'

'Are you saying that your ex-husband entered your house illegally and put your daughter's bear in the chair? Look here, Mrs Maccabee, would you say your divorce was pretty acrimonious?' Then to himself: 'I'm afraid all divorces tend to be that—', but continued, 'Let me put it this way. What leads you to believe your husband would do this? Are you going by his past behaviour to you?'

'No. I'm not. I think that probably, in spite of

the arguments over the cottage, our divorce was less acrimonious than many. Partly that was because I was ill. Certainly too ill to kick up a great fuss. I – how can I explain? – it was as though a plate-glass window existed between me and the world. I . . . well, I'd pinch myself to try and see if I were there. I didn't feel real. I felt like a ghost. I didn't feel there.'

'Are you telling me that at the time of the divorce you were too ill to appreciate what was happening?'

'No. I knew what was happening all right. I knew everything that was going on. But I was incapable of responding to it. There was no-one there to respond to Charlie except your father. So you see, Charlie and I didn't have any fights or throw things at each other or say terrible things to each other. It was a very civilized divorce in its own way. I can think of no reason whatsoever why Charlie would suddenly . . . do such a thing. It's a bolt from the blue.'

'There's been no trouble at all since your divorce?'

'None.'

'What about your daughter's toys? You are absolutely sure the bear wasn't in the house before you came home last night?'

'Of course not.'

'Why are you sure?'

'The head of Charlie's department was a Frenchman called Bruno Seuret, who was married to an Englishwoman. The day before I came out of the psychiatric hospital, Bruno and Caroline went to the cottage and cleared out all of my daughter's things. Charlie found he couldn't do it himself and asked his department head to do it for him. The Seurets had a large house, you see, with a stable block. I understand Anne-Marie's clothes and toys were stored in the stables and then taken down to a charity shop in Lichfield.'

'You asked your husband – your ex-husband – to do this?'

'No. Charlie just got it into his head that it would be better for me if my daughter's things were taken away. To be honest, I was too ill to be upset by the sight of Anne-Marie's belongings.'

'And none of your daughter's things were left at the cottage?'

'None.'

'And you are absolutely sure of this?'

'Absolutely sure.'

'How did you know that the bear you found on the rocker was your daughter's bear?'

'There's a tear in the arm of the bear's duffle coat and a toggle is loose. It had no hat on. A friend's puppy chewed its hat up. I'd know that bear anywhere. It was Anne-Marie's.'

'Then all your daughter's toys couldn't have been given away?'

'No. I can only suppose Charlie decided to keep one or two. But I can tell you that he didn't keep them at the cottage.'

'Does your ex-husband still have a key to the cottage?'

'I really don't know. It's possible. I don't

remember him returning any of his keys. But no-one else has a key to the cottage. Of that I am sure.'

'Have you no idea *why* your husband would suddenly do such a thing? Is he, for instance, a cruel man? Vindictive?'

'He wrote to tell me Sandra was having a baby. Many might consider that a cruel thing to do in the circumstances. But basically it's as I told you. He's a light weight. A ladies' man. He likes to have things easy. I mean he'd lead the rats deserting a sinking ship, but even so, I would never have described him as bitter or twisted. He's the sort to take all he can wheedle and if there's no more for good old Charlie, he's the type to shrug his shoulders and try his luck elsewhere. I've been up most of the night thinking about it. It simply makes no sense to me, Mr Drago. Charlie was certainly a bastard. And he was cruel to me in his way. But not in that way.'

'How do you mean? That way?'

'Well. It was a bizarre thing to do. That's how it seems to me. Quite bizarre.'

'Perhaps the death of his daughter affected him in ways not apparent to you. You did say he was very fond of the child. Did he at any time blame you for Anne-Marie's death?'

'How could he? She died of meningitis.'

'People aren't always rational.'

'No. I know.'

'You said someone was with you when you discovered the bear?'

31

'Fanny Wragg. She's a station assistant at Radio Brum.'

'Did you say anything to her?'

'She could see I was distressed. I told her the cleaner must have been tidying up and left the bear on the rocking-chair by mistake. Of course I don't have a cleaner, but Fanny doesn't know that.'

'Why did you tell her that?'

'The station is a very gossipy place. On the whole, I like to keep my private affairs private. I don't like being talked about.' She hesitated and then said: 'I'm not a staff member, Mr Drago. I'm employed on a free-lance basis, so I don't have to tell them anything. There are some things I'd much prefer my employers didn't know about. My medical history, for one. I don't say it would jeopardize my position there, but it might.' She hesitated again. 'If they thought I was in any kind of trouble, they might think I wasn't capable of giving my all as a broadcaster. You can gather, I'm sure, that I don't regard my position there as at all secure and it's not. A new manager, a new programme organizer, a few wrong words or not fitting in to a reworked programme schedule – and I'm out on my ear. Not just me, of course. Most of us broadcasters are on short-term contracts. It's a very precarious trade.'

'I see.' James Drago formed his hands into a steeple.

He was silent for so long that Isobel said: 'I do assure you, I'm fully recovered from my breakdown. I'm not using you as a pawn in some sick fantasy. But I can't wonder every time I open my front door—' she stopped. 'Why is he persecuting me like this?'

'I don't know, Mrs Maccabee, but we'll put a stop to it. I was just deciding on the best course of action. We can't be absolutely certain, of course, that it was your husband who gained access and planted the bear. But I have to say I think it's a 90 per cent certainty. The first thing you must do, and you must do this immediately, is to have all your locks changed. As to Mr Maccabee, we'll begin by writing to him. That's usually enough.'

'Does this sort of thing happen often?'

'No. But I do assure you that if the harassment goes on, we'll have him in court before his feet touch the ground. Try not to worry.'

'You don't happen to know anyone who could change my locks?' As she rose she discovered her knees were trembling.

'Of course. I'll ring now if you like. It's a Mr Rose. Hang on a minute. We'll try and get it done today for you.'

Isobel sat down again.

When I get home Annie's bear will be waiting for me.

'He can fit you in at two. He's a good chap. Samson Cottage, Alrewas?' He was glancing at a piece of paper in front of him.

'Tell him to go down Main Street to the off-licence. The cottage is in an alley just past there.'

He relayed her instructions and put the phone down. She rose again. 'You are in a hurry to get away. You haven't given me your husband's address yet. Ex-husband's address, I should say.'

'Sorry—' She opened her handbag and brought out Charlie's letter.

'Can I keep it?'

'Of course.'

'Did he play with other women all the time he was married to you?'

'More than likely. Looking back I can see I was very careful not to know.'

'You're lucky to be free of him.' The solicitor got up to escort her to the door.

'But am I free of him, Mr Drago?'

'Yes, you are, Mrs Maccabee.' James Drago shook her hand. 'We'll soon put a stop to his games. Your bag. Don't forget it.'

Outside once more, Isobel at first drifted towards the market stalls. Suddenly she shrank from coming into close bodily contact with the surge of shoppers. She turned back up Dam Street towards the cathedral. Everyone else is all right, she told herself, alarmed at the implications of her flight. It's only Charlie.

Charlie took the skin off my back.

I can't even cry about Charlie.

Why is he doing this to me?

He'd seen Annie's coffin, hadn't he? He'd seen the pale spring sun twinkle on the gilded handles.

She came to the end of Dam Street. A child's lost glove was displayed on railings which enclosed Minster Pool. On the far side of the water, Georgian houses climbed the bank; above soared the three

34

spires of the thirteenth-century cathedral.

Isobel walked up to the cathedral; pop music blared down from parapets of dark red sandstone. The stonemasons were working on scaffolding shrouded in sheets of black plastic. Strolling down The Close, she rounded the south wall of the building. The west front rose before her with its stone frieze of St Chad and twenty-four kings carved above three great wooden doors.

Lichfield, Licetfield, she remembered, meaning place of the dead. It was said that a thousand Christians were slaughtered here in Emperor Diocletian's reign and very likely many more were murdered when, a thousand years before the birth of Christ, pagans practised their rites on an immense stone buried immediately behind the high altar. More blood had run in the Civil War when the precincts became a battlefield and the great central spire was smashed by canon balls.

But even though she knew of the violent past of this place, the sheer monumental calm of the stone brought some peace to her.

She entered through one of the doors into the nave. The great dim structure lay before and about her; there was a discreet scurrying as sightseers plied like mice across the stone floor. In the distance the wrought brasswork of the choir screen winked in the gloom.

'*All things bright and beautiful,*' the words tripped along in her head. '*All creatures great and small—*' and she was a child again singing in the classroom and a great blue sky bowling past the

35

windows. '*All things wise and wonderful—*' Not a lot older than Anne-Marie.

Annie's little bear is waiting for me.

She knew then she was in danger of remembering everything she'd taken great care to forget. There was her daughter's hand. An exact replica of Charlie Maccabee's hand.

Abruptly Isobel turned and left the cathedral. It was a long time since she'd had faith in anything. She walked quickly away from the west front towards the town. She was busy finding the pins to nail down the reality of her life. Butter. Bags for the hoover. Light bulbs. Remembering more and more shopping as she went along, she almost missed the bus back to the village.

When she got home she found herself looking carefully round the living-room. Looking for what?

Angry with herself, she hauled her shopping through to the kitchen. She made herself a cup of tea and wandered out through the French window of the studio into the garden. The lawn, which sloped slightly on its way to the canal, was bordered on one side by the back of the two storey warehouse and on the other by the boundary wall of the derelict chapel. Beyond that wall, she could hear the shouts of one of the boys who lived in the converted Sunday School. 'Z-z-z-z!' he yelled as though he were a saw and not flesh and blood at all. 'Z-z-z-z-z!'

Mallard ducks, taking no notice of her, shook their feathers as they climbed out of the canal into her garden. They paraded along the bank in a line, water dripping from their tail feathers.

Warming her hands round the mug, she walked towards them. A fisherman, perhaps not believing in the November sunshine, was sitting under his green umbrella on the other bank, his carbon-fibre rod stretching back across the towpath.

She turned as a narrow boat chugged under the hump-backed bridge. The man at the tiller saluted her gravely; just as gravely, she acknowledged the gesture. Slowly the gold and black of the boat hazed over as it retreated from her on its way to Fradley Junction. As she turned back to the cottage, she looked at the old fashioned roses she grew against the warehouse wall; Gloire de Dijon, Etoile de Holland, Aimée Vibert, Zephirine Drouhin, Lady Hillingdon. She had, she realized now, won back some peace in the four years since Charlie had left her. I can't let him destroy it, she thought.

She'd almost reached the French door when she heard the phone ringing.

Charlie? She found herself thinking.

Her heart squeezed away from her protecting ribs.

'Where were you, my dear?' asked Drue Lycett-Green.

'Oh Lord. I'm so sorry. Something cropped up and I had to go down to the solicitors. I really am sorry, Drue. It went right out of my head.' Isobel had promised to have coffee with the old lady that morning.

'Has something awful happened?'

'Something unpleasant. Yes.'

'Why not come over to Mickleholme Villa later this afternoon? We'll have a sherry. Or some of my sloe gin. I won't pry. I promise.'

'It'll be after three. Would that be all right? I've someone coming earlier to do some work in the house. I really am sorry. It was unforgivable of me.'

'I'll forgive you straight away if you'll give me a game of cribbage.'

'Of course I will.'

'Mrs Bennett has made some saffron cake. That'll be nice, won't it?' said Drue.

Later, after she'd had her lunch, Isobel climbed the stairs. Since she'd found the bear she'd visited it at intervals. It was like a loose tooth; she felt the need to keep touching it in spite of the spurts of pain.

She lifted the latch and crept into the room which had once been Anne-Marie's.

She waited a moment before turning to gaze into the great black glassy pupils of those perfectly round toy eyes.

'What are you doing here?' she asked softly.

'Sharn't tell,' said Paddington, though the embroidered down strokes of his mouth remained primly closed. 'You can't make me.'

THREE

Isobel showed her identity card to the security guard on the gate and then drove her red Golf into the car park at the back of the broadcasting centre. The tarmac was icy. The grass on the surrounding verges stood in starched quills.

She parked her car with care, picked up her bag and tape recorder and locked the car door. The interview she'd just done with Godiva Tormey, in Birmingham to talk to a literary workshop about the job of a publisher, had been a disaster.

'The publisher is the writer's hieratic other, the one whose needful *aperçus* are wrested out of the material by an array of diagnostic tools that are expert, methodical and flexible enough to perceive in each thickness of homogeneous substance the dermal and internal systems embodying orthodox narrative fiction. He is exhaustive, lucid, non-restrictive in prescriptions, moving beyond the functions of gustancy to the piquant pleas of salivancy and yes, we do finally demand of him that he plunge his big toe into the crashing sea surf of art itself.'

Godiva Tormey launched her head forward, emphasizing her point with a loosening lash of thick brown hair, causing Isobel to swerve. Isobel automatically realigned her Uher's microphone.

'Salivancy is at the core of prudent prelibation and prelibation is the initial moment in that deed we label art.'

Isobel stopped her Uher. 'What does dermal mean, Ms Tarrant?'

'Tormey.'

'Tormey.'

'Derma. Derma. Skin.'

Isobel turned the tape over and spooled it back. 'Prelibation?'

'Foretaste. I can see you aren't of a literary turn of mind, Ms Maccabee.'

'Gustancy?' She ceased to be kind. 'Wind. Windy? Now if we could take it again. Pretend you are explaining the job to B-stream ten-year-olds. This is local radio, Ms Torment.'

'Tormey. It's always a mistake to underestimate the intelligence of your audience, don't you think? May I call you Isobel? Issy? Godiva is a bit off-putting, isn't it? Do call me God. One must expect more from people. If one expects it one gets it.'

'Unfortunately radio audiences aren't students Mrs . . . Ms—'

'God. Godsie if you like.'

'They have at their command a button marked off. Please could we try again? I'm afraid I didn't understand a word Miss Tar . . . Torm . . . Godiva. Remember. We're B-stream ten-year-olds.'

But Godiva Tormey had no conception of what

a ten-year-old could be. It was quite probable, Isobel thought later, that she'd never been one herself, but had leapt with one bound on to the workshop circuit, forever moving from one polytechnic to the next in homogeneous substances whose internal systems were never quite mastered by British Rail.

Isobel was in despair as she heaved the strap of the Uher over her shoulder and set off back to the broadcasting centre. And it wasn't just on account of Godiva Tormey. The night before, her programme *Brum Arts* had crashed about her ears. Her live guest, who had talked so well off microphone, had become paralysed with terror when the red light went on. 'Yes,' he said in answer to her question. 'No.' 'Yes.' 'No.' 'No.' 'No.' And no other word did he utter. A note of outright farce had been added when a non-English speaking Asian cleaner had barged into the studio with her hoover going full blast. The West Midlands poet Darren Lovejay, reading from his selected verses, had had to screech above the noise.

> '*We are the old shoes*
> *The mender sadly chucks away*
> *The shoes that wore-away-wore . . .*'

'It sounded like the mating yells of a demented tyrannosaur,' said the station assistant in the ops room later. 'My ear drums almost packed up.'

Isobel, still shuddering as she recalled the fiasco, climbed the stairs to Radio Brum's first-

41

floor offices. 'Bums and knickers,' she muttered to herself.

'What's that?' asked Fanny Wragg, pressing a lift button. 'Oh, before I forget, duckie. You've had a phone call from Mr Dracula. He wants you to ring back.'

'I'm not at all surprised,' said Isobel.

'The number's on your desk.'

'I really can't have had a call from Mr Dracula, Fanny. He lives under a tombstone. It must be my solicitor.'

'He didn't say where he was from.'

'Drago.'

'Drago?' Fanny stepped into the lift. 'Sorry, duckie, Jacko Marshall and Vernon Strutt-Walker were having a battle royal at the time. You know how it is.'

Isobel pushed on through the fire doors into Radio Brum's production offices.

'The beautiful Isobel bringing light and culture,' Jacko Marshall sang and all his teeth showed. He looked nervous, shiny and furious. 'I hear we had our little problems last night. Not to worry, girlie. We've all had our probs.' He looked in the direction of Vernon. 'Though little pricks only have piss puny probs.'

'It's one of those days,' said Velma Blood, the production office secretary. 'You know. *Those* days. The programme organizer wants to see you.'

'Thanks, Velma.' Post mortems, she thought gloomily.

She picked up the receiver and dialled Pipkin

and Drago's number. It was almost three weeks since Paddington's arrival. At first he'd seemed an obscene intrusion, but gradually the demands of her ordinary life had taken over again. In the past day or two, she'd even walked through the study, on the way to the bathroom, without noticing the bear.

'Mrs Maccabee? I'm afraid I have some news that you may find rather disturbing. Can you tell me again when you first noticed your daughter's bear?'

'The night before I saw you, Mr Drago.'

'I'm sorry to break it to you like this. Your ex-husband was killed in a car crash six weeks ago.'

'Six weeks?'

'I had a letter from the Maccabees' solicitor this morning. The family had sent our letter on to them.'

Isobel wasn't sure she'd understood him correctly. 'My husband is dead?'

'Your ex-husband. Yes. I will write. But I thought it would be wise to get in touch by phone first to ask how matters stood. Have you had any further trouble?'

'No. Nothing. Exactly what happened to Charlie? You say he's dead?'

'He was driving to Preston when he was involved in a car crash. That's all the information I have.'

'And that was six weeks ago.'

'Yes.'

She was silent.

'I'm afraid this is now a matter for the police, Mrs Maccabee. I'd advise you to get in touch with them.'

'I really don't understand. It's so senseless.' She was thinking of Charlie, not the bear.

'I want you to know we're here if you need us, Mrs Maccabee. Don't hesitate to get in touch if there's anything we can do for you.'

'Thank you, Mr Drago.'

'I'm sorry to be the bearer of unfortunate news.'

When she'd put the phone down Velma shouted across to her: 'Hilary rang again. Can you see him now?'

'OK.'

There were unwritten rules on the station. When Hilary Winstan's door was closed, no-one could knock and walk in. Only when it was ajar was this possible.

The door was ajar now. The programme organizer looked up from the papers he was reading and told her to close it and come and sit down.

She did so.

'Give me a second.'

Hilary always looked as if at some stage in his life he'd had a catastrophic accident which had drained the blood out of his veins. There was nothing wrong with the long, nicely featured face, nor the tall lean body, that eight pints of red blood couldn't have cured. As it was, most of those who worked for him experienced his presence as a chill; his marbled eyes did nothing to dispel the cold.

He laid his reading matter aside. 'Tell me about it.'

Very succinctly and not making the mistake of blaming man, beast or even the gods, Isobel summarized what had happened the night before.

'There are occasions when gremlins get in the works and we lose all our brownie points,' he said. Isobel knew him too well to suppose this was a reprieve and waited to hear what came next. 'And your feelings about your Shires Opera piece?' This pre-recorded seven minute tape was one of the few things in the programme which had gone without a hitch.

It was not the time to be bold, but nevertheless Isobel was bold. 'I was pleased with it.'

'Were you?'

'Oh, yes.'

'Didn't you do a piece on the Shires Opera about three months ago?'

'Yes. The last time they were in the city. They're a very good company.'

'Would you say the piece that went out last night was different in any real way from the piece you did earlier? Apart from the music of course. I feel that PR person they've got – Tina, Tina?'

'Tina Trowbridge.'

'Mzz-z-z Trowbridge, I feel, would do well to take out a patent on the phrase "tremendously thrilling". The baritone still has to achieve the lotus position for half an hour before he can venture on to the stage. And that contralto hasn't lost her appalling penchant for the words "you know". One could be forgiven for thinking one had heard it all before.'

Isobel, who had thrown the piece together at the last minute, said: 'I'm afraid there's not a lot that's new about opera.'

'All reportage should be news,' said Hilary Winstan. 'If it's not news, not new, we don't report it. Listen to that piece again, will you? And if you've still got the tape of the earlier package, listen to that.'

'All right. I will.'

'How long have you been presenting the programme now?'

'Just over a year.'

He gave her the silence in which she might contemplate his unspoken question: 'Are you getting stale?'

She refused to contemplate it. She thought instead she'd like to make sweet breads of his balls. Or could she only do that with the fellow's pancreas?

'I feel the time has come for you to have another think about your conception of the programme. Certain questions might present themselves. When you've decided just what these questions are, perhaps we might talk things through.'

'Fine. That's fine by me.'

'I can't think why no-one thought to unplug that hoover. It shows an extraordinary lack of presence of mind.' He took a Polo mint from the top of the tube and offered the tube to her.

She shook her head. 'Thanks. No.'

Interviews with the programme organizer were as ritualistic as church services. Isobel had made the correct response in turning down the mint. This was the moment when he rendered himself speechless, allowing him not to voice his forgiveness as she made her *mea culpa*. Lord, I have sinned, Lord, I am less than the mucus in your nostril, Lord, I am but dirt under your foot. But Lord, you behold a penitent who will rise up and perform wonders to the glory of your name. She knew the form and twice in her three years at Radio Brum she'd made her act of contrition as he sucked on his mint.

This time he could go to hell.

He took on a very thoughtful look and she knew well enough what he was ruminating about. It boded no good for her future. Breaking the rules at Radio Brum, as in all walks of life, carried suicidally high penalties.

Later, out in the corridor, she realized that her days of presenting the arts programme were numbered. Deep in herself she was aware of a black fury directed at Hilary Winstan, whom she saw as the source of all woe. But that's nonsense, she realized. It's Charlie I'm really furious with. Why did that bastard have to go and die?

Her blood was making a terrible wailing sound.

Yet she hated the man.

Though once she'd loved him.

He was the only man who'd lit up her life.

She tried to walk through Vernon who was coming down the corridor in the opposite direction. 'Watch out!' he yelled. 'That really hurt!'

'Sorry.'

He looked at the programme organizer's door which, as instructed, she'd left slightly ajar, and then he looked at her. 'Rough time, treasure? Well, there's no need to take it out on me. Anyway, where are you off to in such a hurry?'

'The newsroom.'

'My, my. We are a glutton for punishment, aren't we?'

'You're frightfully pale. Did I really hurt you?'

'I'll survive. It's even possible you might survive.' He grinned as he carried on past her. He always appeared to walk on tiptoe, his head and shoulders too far in front of him, his rear thrust out to balance his body. The result made his bottom gyrate furiously.

She stared after him for a moment and then turned and continued down the corridor. She climbed the stairs to the newsroom. This was the only department at Radio Brum which was on the second floor and its position, cut off and above the rest of the station, was apt. The journalists, most of them young men, thought themselves superior to the rest of the staff. All crossing their threshold realized they were in hostile territory, even journalists like Isobel for she had deserted her trade and allowed herself to degenerate into a producer and presenter of arts and other 'soft' items. She was no longer a member of the élite corps of 'hard' news reporters.

When she went into the large room, no-one looked up to greet her though not all the journalists were working. She ventured no greeting herself for she

48

knew, from past experience, it would be completely ignored.

She approached Sunita Jones, the newsroom secretary, a nubile nineteen-year-old who, it was said, ruled the journalists with a rod of iron. Her blond hair was crew cut and she wore the kind of charcoal grey pin-striped suit which is featured in the Femail pages of the *Daily Mail*. Behind her big baby-blue eyes was a computer which retained and classified all the news which poured down the lines. She knew that the Agriculture Minister was John MacGregor, that Tiny Rowland was chief executive of the mining conglomerate Lonrho, she knew the difference between a bishop and a suffragan bishop and how to spell the words which the journalists found difficulties with. Pharmacist, rhododendron, bureau, she knew them all. Her executive briefcase was a toy purple affair but in it, apart from her make-up, filofax and Mills and Boon, was a calculator with which she did untold wonders with the newsroom budget. It was said that if she didn't rise to become the organization's DG, she'd certainly one day become the DG's secretary.

'Can I look at your telephone directories?' Isobel asked this phenomenon. 'I need to get in touch with the Manchester paper I once worked on.'

'Sure thing—' and Sunita unwound her long legs from the stool and strolled over to the rows of directories.

Isobel, finding herself looking out on the garden

which featured in the television show *How Does Your Garden Grow*, noticed that it had begun to snow and began to worry about her journey home.

'What's the forecast?'

'Windy. Sleet and snow showers becoming more frequent. Very cold.'

'Wonderful,' said Isobel gloomily, and got the telephone number she wanted from the directory Sunita gave her.

No-one spoke as she left the newsroom. One of the good things about the hiatus which existed between the journalists and the rest of the station was that the reporters only listened to their own output. They wouldn't yet know about her fiasco last night. They were always the last to hear the station's news.

'Didn't you cut your teeth at the *Blackpool Newsletter*?' she asked Bernie Goldman. It was after lunch before she'd been able to get him at the *Manchester Express*.

'Got it in one,' said her old friend.

'Listen Bernie, can you give me a contact? I want some information.'

'Bit out of your territory, isn't it?'

'I'm not doing a story. I want it for personal reasons.'

'Leslie Dakin's your man. Just mention my name and he'll give you all you want.'

'You're a love.'

'Be good,' said Bernie as he put the phone down.

Leslie Dakin was at a planning enquiry. 'But

they don't kill themselves, luv. Those planning chaps wrap up each day at four and go home. I'll get Les to give you a ring when he turns up.'

'Thanks.'

Isobel, having done as much as she could, got back down to work. It was with some feelings of pleasure that she took Godsie out of her Uher and deposited her in the plastic dustbin used for discarded tape. May you rot in hell, she thought, though she knew Godsie wouldn't do that. She'd be erased and become a spokesman from the Ministry warning of the danger of listeria in soft cheeses or Kaffe Fassett talking about his knitting.

She took an unedited tape about Birmingham's pavement artists out of her drawer, found a machine, and began working on it. She was typing out a cue to the piece when her phone rang. It was Leslie Dakin. After introducing herself and mentioning Bernie, she asked: 'I wondered if you could help me? A man called Charlie Maccabee. Does the name ring any bells?'

'Maccabee. Sandra Tiptree's husband. Sure. That was front page news in these parts. The guy was killed in a car accident. The Tiptrees are the nearest thing we have to celebrities. They say that Sandy's old man is worth a million. A town councillor with his fingers in many a pie. Commodity futures. Share options. Property deals. You name it, he's a big wheel. Sandy's his only daughter. What's your interest?'

'It's entirely personal. Charlie was my husband until Sandra came on the scene. I only heard of

51

his death this morning. I hope you don't think I'm being ghoulish, but for a long time Charlie was a part of my life and I'd like to know about his death.'

'I'm sorry. Yes, of course. Anything you want to know, luv. As it happens I covered the Maccabee inquest.'

'I'd like to know as much as you can tell me. I take it that Sandra wasn't killed? My solicitor only mentioned Charlie.'

'Charlie was alone in the car. He was just leaving Blackpool on the Preston road when he took a bend much too quickly, came off the road and hit a tree. The driving wheel broke off and the stem went through his chest. The pathologist said death would have been instantaneous. He must have been doing over a ton. He'd been drinking heavily.'

'I see.'

'More to it all than at first met the eye. This is strictly off the record, but the traffic control sergeant told me that Charlie's boot was loaded with his gear and he was carrying wads of notes. It appeared Charlie had cashed in some joint accounts and was in the process of leaving the matrimonial home when he was killed. That information didn't come out at the inquest.'

'Are you sure?'

'Never had cause to doubt my sources. The car itself was in good nick. The fault was in the driver.'

'He was going off with another woman?'

'That's the assumption.'

'So he walked out on Sandra too.'

'It was pretty tough on her actually. At the time Sandy was in hospital recovering from a miscarriage.'

'The bastard.'

'She was nuts on the guy of course. Some of you ladies certainly have a talent for picking a wrong 'un.'

'Is . . . does . . . he leaves one child though, doesn't he? He wrote to tell me two years ago that Sandra was having a baby.'

'No. There're no children. I understand their first child was stillborn.'

She found herself unable to say she was sorry; she ought to feel pity for the woman, but she was pitiless. 'Thank you very much for your help. I really appreciate it.'

'That's all right. Any time.'

Isobel put the receiver down. For the first time since she'd heard of Charlie's death she was near to tears. She didn't feel grief for him. She grieved for herself, for a woman who'd been foolish enough to marry such a man.

'Are you going up to the canteen tonight?' Fanny Wragg had appeared at the side of her desk.

'No. Sorry. It's such a foul night I'm not going to hang around.' Isobel pulled herself together.

Vernon burst through the doors. 'I forgot my bonnet—' he said and snatched up a black leather cap from the top of a filing cabinet. 'Nightie-byes.'

'Do you know I've suddenly realized why

Vernon looks so God awful pale today,' said Isobel. 'He's had his hair dyed, hasn't he? He's gone blond.'

'Have you only just noticed?' Fanny laughed at her. 'He was twitted something awful by Jacko Marshall this morning. That was why they had a row. If you ask me Isobel, you're not quite with it these days.'

FOUR

It was Saturday afternoon when Isobel set off along the towpath for Bruno Seuret's house at Wychnor. After two days of indecision she'd rung him that morning. She hadn't been able to stand the frustration of not making up her mind any longer.

'You perhaps won't remember me, but I'm Isobel Maccabee. My ex-husband Charlie was at one time a member of your department.'

'Oh, but I recall you very well,' was his disconcerting reply.

'You do?' She hadn't been able to picture him at all clearly until he'd enunciated the Gallic 'r', rolling it off some high ridge on the roof of his mouth. His voice formed into the memory of a muscular man of medium height with an unruly ruff of crinkly black hair and chestnut coloured eyes. She realized the French word *marron* described his eyes better, for there was much more of a snap to it.

'I was wondering if I could come and see you, Mr Seuret. It's about a personal matter. I think you may be able to help me resolve something.'

'I'm intrigued, Mrs Maccabee. I shall be

delighted to help. But I'm selling the Lodge and I've three separate lots of people coming round today. However I will be free after – let's say just after three to be on the safe side.'

'Are you sure you can manage it?'

'Quite sure, Mrs Maccabee.'

Wychnor lay a mile to the north of Alrewas in rolling Staffordshire countryside; an empty church, schoolrooms which had been converted into housing, Burhay Lodge, scattered farms and, some distance from the church, a manor house which overlooked the Trent valley.

There had been a sharp frost overnight. A white rime still furred the landscape though the sun had broken through the haze by the time Isobel set off from Samson Cottage. She was wrapped against the cold in a fleecy anorak and track suit, a white knitted cowl over her head and wool-lined rubber boots on her feet.

The canal looped through the village, passing thatched cottages, new bungalows and the squat tower of the twelfth-century church. The waterway had been built with money raised by Georgian potters and salt producers to link the Trent with the Mersey. From time immemorial, the village had seen many travellers. The church itself had been sited on the crossing of the Salters' Way with another ancient track.

Even though ice was forming at the edges of the canal, one or two fishermen had found themselves a peg and were settled among their equipment. The village was bound on both sides by locks;

beyond the northern one was the Quarter Miler, a single-file iron bridge spanning the converging waters of the canal, the mill stream and the River Trent. Further along the towpath crossed shorter bridges which allowed flood waters to escape into the reedy water meadows on the west bank. From this direction she could hear distant gun shot; the land of large sporting estates lay all round. The noise of the approaching weir began to fill her ears.

She tried not to think about her impending meeting with the Frenchman.

She'd spent the last two days brooding about the bear. There had been no further incident and reason told her to leave well alone.

And yet.

And yet . . .

She was never sure about the sensibleness of following her intuition; in her experience feelings were all too fallible. But it was because of some instinctive apprehension of danger that she was going to see Bruno Seuret.

Of course it was ridiculous. She knew perfectly well she was in no danger. But she told herself there could be no harm in doing a little investigating.

As she reached the weir she saw gulls – fifty miles from their seaside territories – playing at the edge of the wide shallow waterfall which marked the point where canal and river parted. They turned their tails to the drop and with a whoosh sailed over the top into the river several feet below. They flew back and the game, for to Isobel it seemed a game, began all over again. The swans, their long necks wet and dirty from constant dipping in water, stationed themselves some distance from these antics. They made a supercilious looking audience.

In the spring and summer the banks were alive with wild flowers, campion, feverfew, wood violets, dog roses and clover; now the only remains of that profusion were the giant skeletons of Queen Ann's lace and mare's tail, hoary bones which keened in sniping wind. There was a stile just before the bridge at Wychnor, now used for cattle, though an earlier one had vibrated to the marching feet of Roman legions. She climbed over into pastureland and trudged uphill to St Leonard's Church. The square tower, built of brick, rose up from flaking red sandstone walls. Though the building was now infrequently used, the graveyard was kept neat and tidy. Isobel always thought of it as a *Marie Celeste* church for it presided over a mostly empty landscape. She stared at the building, sitting squat and grim on a promontory which overlooked the canal and, a mile to the east, the A38, a road laid in the wake of the Roman highway Rykneld Street.

Reaching the edge of the meadow, she unlatched the gate and stepped into the lane. A gull swooped in circles round one side of the church tower, giving the building a leery lop-sided halo. The noise of gun shot was louder; pheasant shooting probably, she thought, though rabbits had to look lively in these parts.

Burhay Lodge lay off a lane which ran by the

side of the schoolhouse. The building looked like a Victorian doll's house, tall and gaunt, with a door in the middle. There were three sash windows on the first floor and one either side of the door. Trees in the orchard next to the stable block were white and leafless against a chilling haze.

As Isobel walked up the narrow brick pathway, the front door opened. Bruno Seuret, in a navy blue crew-necked sweater and jeans, stood at the top of two worn stone steps. He was not quite as she remembered him: something of the Anglo-Saxon cartoon of a Frenchman had crept into her picture of him. She'd imbued him with an air of *savoir faire* he didn't have; in fact there was a shy puckishness about him.

'Please come in. I saw you coming up the lane.'

'Thank you.' Now she was here she felt stiff and rather embarrassed. 'Do you think you might have sold your house?'

'I think I might have.'

She realized, for the first time, that when he mentioned the property he said 'I' and not 'we'. When she went into the cadaverous hall which led directly to the back door, she noticed the lack of plants or flowers. Her housewife's eye noted more; though someone had made an attempt at dusting, there was nevertheless dust on the tripod legs of the round table and on the cross rails of two chairs either side of it. A cobweb trailed from the ceiling to the heavy brass light fitting.

'Let me take your anorak. Would you like some coffee?'

'That would be lovely.'

He showed her into a lounge which was too small for its height, but there was a cheerful glow from the blaze in the great mauve marble fireplace. 'I won't be a minute,' he said and left her to warm her hands.

'Are you and Caro leaving the district?' she asked him as he brought a tray of coffee in.

'Didn't you know?' He looked at her in surprise. 'We split up over a year ago. Now we're going through the gruesome post-funeral arrangements. Splitting our assets.'

'You're divorced?'

'Not quite. It's going through.'

'I'm sorry. I'd no idea. Have you somewhere to live?'

'I'm going back to France. My father died in August and my mother can't run the business single handedly.'

'Oh dear, I didn't know. Have I put my foot in it?'

'Not at all. Now how can I help you? Your telephone call aroused a good deal of no doubt unseemly curiosity.'

'Can you cast your mind back to my daughter's death? I had a nervous breakdown and just before I came out of hospital, you and Caro went to the cottage and cleared out all Anne-Marie's things.'

'That's right. Charlie simply couldn't face doing it himself. He said you'd told him you couldn't come home until it was done.'

'That's quite untrue.' Isobel was astonished.

60

'Really. It must have been Charlie who couldn't stand living with all her things around him . . . Charlie's dead. He died in a car crash.'

'Good God.'

Surely it's only the good who die young, she thought. Can Charlie really be dead?

'When did it happen?'

'Six weeks ago though I only heard about it on Wednesday. It's so very – strange. I lived with him all those years and I bore him a child. And yet no-one thinks to tell me he's dead. It's as if our marriage had never existed. As though that part of my life had no meaning at all. Of course he was a bastard. But I did love him once. He was part of me for a long time. We were a family. It seems so cynical somehow to believe I would quite literally not care if the bastard were alive or dead.'

'Poor old Charlie.'

'It's . . . well, an awful mess. I want to grieve for him. But how can any sane woman grieve for a shit like that?'

'What about Sandy?'

Sandra will be all right, she wanted to say. That woman's as strong as a horse. Plenty of muscle in her hind quarters and a good deep chest. But Sandra's babies had died, hadn't they? she thought with a start. She said: 'She wasn't with him. She was in hospital having a miscarriage.'

'Oh Lord.'

'Charlie was in the process of running off with another woman when he died. With the proceeds of their joint accounts as I understand it.'

He was silent.

'The irony is that after all his sexual adventures he left no children. At least none that I know of.'

'I'm sorry. You've left me . . . he was running off while Sandy—'

'Yes.'

'Perhaps it's as well he's dead.'

She looked at him. She found herself saying: 'Yes.' Not only did she say it, but she realized she believed it. She felt relieved, as if she'd at last come to a decision about her ex-husband. 'Yes,' she said again.

'Would you like some more coffee?'

'Please.'

'He was a very good teacher, of course. The funny thing was that the boys as well as the girls responded to all that sex appeal. Kids like people who are full of life. Full of the old Adam.'

'Anne-Marie adored him.'

'Anne-Marie. You wanted to know what happened to her things?'

'Yes. I assume they went to the Oxfam Shop or the Hospice Shop?'

He rubbed his jaw between thumb and forefinger. Now he wasn't looking at her she had a moment in which to study him without the danger of their eyes meeting. She'd felt all along – awkward, yes that was the word – in his presence. Does he find me attractive? she wondered. But then she realized that being admired by men had never been a source of embarrassment to her in the past. It's me, she thought. I find *him* attractive.

She was both astonished and rather pleased with herself. She had, since Charlie, only been aware of an indifference towards men.

'Your daughter's belongings went into the loft above the stables,' he remembered. 'That's where all our own attic kind of stuff went. Later I remember helping Caro to load at least one lot in the car. She'd sorted the stuff into boxes and when she was in Lichfield she'd drop one or two boxes off at the charity shops. That's what happened. Caroline was seeing to it. Why do you ask? Is it important?'

'I'm not sure.' She then told him of finding the bear. 'But as Charlie died before it happened, I know now it wasn't him. Nothing has happened since. Perhaps it's silly to take it seriously.'

'But you *are* taking it seriously. Otherwise you wouldn't be here.'

She sighed. 'Yes.'

'I don't want to alarm you. But I'd call the police.'

'That's what my solicitor advised when we found out it couldn't have been Charlie.'

'And yet you hesitate?'

'Of course. I feel as if I'm in a very difficult position. A woman who has been in a psychiatric hospital once is . . . well . . . would they believe me?'

'You think they'd suppose you were making the whole thing up?'

'Put yourself in their shoes. Isn't that the likeliest possibility? Especially now Charlie's out of the picture. I mean, why should anyone do such a thing?'

'But someone did.'

'Yes.'

'Then I don't see what alternative you have.'

She was silent.

'I really think you should call in the police.' He paused, choosing his words with care. 'I don't want to alarm you, but it is a very sick thing to do .'

'Something else could happen?' Her body hairs began to rise.

'I don't know.'

She looked towards the window; nothing stirred in the white, frigid world beyond. And then, just as she was about to look away, there was a movement below the yew hedge. A pheasant dived between branches. In the distance was the crack crack crack of shot.

Following her glance, Bruno said: 'Open season.'

'We see very few near the village. I imagine they're not too fond of man.'

'As soon as I've time, I'll take a look in the stable loft. See if any of Anne-Marie's things are still here. I'll let you know.'

'Thank you. That's very kind of you.' She rose. 'I'd better be off while the light still holds. Anyway, I expect you're up to your eyes in it. When are you leaving for France?'

'Not until the end of the summer term. The head made me promise that. If I sell the place before then – I'll live in digs.'

'I'm sorry that . . . well, it didn't work out between you and Caro.'

'So am I.' For a moment he looked so weary that

he physically seemed to diminish and then the puckishness was back. It defends him, she thought, like the aura of a good fairy; an invisible shield against harm.

'I'll be in touch,' he said as they parted at the front door and then, when she'd reached the bottom of the stone steps: 'You know, I always had the greatest admiration for you.'

She turned to look at him, astonished.

'The way you picked yourself up off the ground after Charlie left. The way you got on with your life.'

She became hot with embarrassment. 'I had to keep the wolf from the door.' She hurried off down the path, turning and waving as she shut the gate after her.

Though it wasn't much more than four o'clock, the haze was deepening all around her. The gun fire had stopped, but she could hear her feet crunching on the frosty ground and the quiet piping of a wind which heralded the night. When she reached the abandoned church, she paused for a moment; its sides seemed to move, to heave almost as the darkening vapour swirled.

She heard the Frenchman's voice: 'I don't want to alarm you, but it's a very sick thing to do.'

She quickly opened the gate into the meadow and plunged down the hill to the canal. To the east she could see the headlights of traffic hurtling along the A38, but though the dual carriageway was only a mile away, it seemed in a different world. Here, as she climbed the stile, an owl screeched. Here there was a soft shuffling sound in the reeds to her left. A twig snapped.

Her heart contracted.

A rabbit, she thought. A water rat.

She began to whistle to herself as she hurried along the towpath; whistling to keep her spirits up, to ward off the demons of approaching night.

She crossed the first few iron foot bridges and, as she rounded a bend, she saw in the distance a hooded figure. The wand he held against the dying light began magically to elongate. It rose twelve feet into the air. A fisherman packing up for the day, she thought. I must take hold of myself.

Why am I so frightened?

She saw two perfectly round toy eyes with black polished centres and rims of amber. Instinctively her shoulders hunched, protecting the soft vulnerability of her neck.

The lights of the village gleamed in the distance. She began to discern the tower of Alrewas church and, further to her right, the five-storey Georgian mill built on the site of the village's medieval grain mill. She was almost home. As she crossed the Quarter Miler she began to relax a little.

She turned, as she often did when she reached this point on the towpath, to look again at the mill. It had been built to take advantage of the canal, cotton coming through Liverpool from America to be spun here in the village before being shipped off to Germany and Russia. After a fire, the mill had been partly rebuilt in Victorian times; worsted had been spun, then flour milled. Later cattle food was manufactured. The mill, trim and still in use, rose in darkening vapours like a great liner. She looked up sharply as a gull cried overhead.

It was quite dark when she reached the narrow alley which led to her cottage. The street lamp, bracketed to the gable end of the Victorian terraced house, showed brick sweating with cold and damp.

As she opened her front door she listened for the tick of the grandfather clock. The three quarter hour began to strike; four forty five and already night. She'd left the central heating on and the cottage was warm, but when she'd taken her anorak off she couldn't help shivering. She lit the fire in the inglenook. She was an expert with log fires. Plenty of dry tinder, rolls of paper and coal on the top of the wood to draw the flames through. The blaze roared. When she'd thawed she felt better, hungry. She put her tea on a tray and settled down by the fire with the paper. Later she watched television.

It wasn't until she was getting ready for bed that she went through the study on the way to the bathroom. She'd gone past the rocking-chair when she paused, perplexed. She turned back. Paddington Bear was gone.

At first she was very calm. She thought she must have put the bear elsewhere when she'd cleaned out the cottage that morning.

First she looked in the study itself, then she went down to the kitchen to see if she'd mixed him up with the brushes and dusters she'd taken downstairs. She looked in the living-room, she looked in

67

the studio. By the time she started looking in the cupboards her hands were trembling.

She made a conscious effort to control her increasing panic. She inspected all the doors and windows in the cottage. There was no sign of a forced entry. She checked her keys. They were all there. No thief had entered unless he'd materialized through brick and timber walls.

She made a more thorough search of the cottage.

Paddington Bear was gone.

She began to wonder if she were taking leave of her senses.

FIVE

It was three o'clock in the morning. Isobel was wide awake; at one stage she'd been so distressed that she'd been unable to keep still. She'd found herself thinking aloud: 'That's my daughter's bear. It belongs to me. Who could have done such a thing? Who could have taken it from me?' She'd paced the bedroom and then the lounge.

She'd been outraged when she'd found the bear in the rocking-chair. Its presence had both distressed and frightened her.

Now she felt its absence as a terrible loss.

Twice she'd gone back to the rocking-chair. She'd willed those wooden arms to produce her child's bear.

The chair remained bereft.

Now she was sitting on the floor in the living-room, knees curled up and feet tucked into the bottom of her navy blue, towelling dressing-gown. She was unable to stop twisting her wedding ring. She was rubbing the skin raw.

Suddenly she kicked her feet free of the dressing-gown and went into the kitchen. She'd not drawn the curtains and the light from the street lamp spilled through the lattice window on to the stainless steel sink. A small Victorian sash window in the gable end of the cottage remained in darkness; fumbling about on the working top under it she found the gin bottle. She took the gin and a glass through to the living-room. She carefully poured two measures. She'd to watch how much she drank for her body couldn't tolerate too much alcohol. Her heart was thrown out of rhythm.

When she'd sipped most of the drink, she found she'd summoned up enough courage to ask herself if she'd imagined the bear. Had it really been there?

Of course it had. What a perfectly ridiculous question. Fanny had been with her when she discovered it. Fanny had seen it too.

'Do you hear voices?' Dr Rainbow had asked her.

But he never asked me if I saw things, she told herself now. He never asked me if I hallucinated in that way. Fanny saw the bear too, didn't she?

But what if she'd imagined that Fanny had seen the bear?

Was her mind playing tricks on her again?

'I'm quite all right,' she said aloud. 'I've never hallucinated. How can anyone go mad in two completely different ways? Surely I'd go mad in the same way as before?'

The bear was there.

Now it was gone.

'Do you hear voices?' Dr Rainbow had asked.

Her mind began to spin. Could I be going crazy? She began to remember the day, almost five years ago, when she'd gone down to the clinic in Birmingham to see him.

She'd got off the bus at the police training centre. In the distance, through snowy trees, she could see the top of the broadcasting centre where she was later to work. 'Turn left at the county cricket ground,' Charlie had told her, reading from the Birmingham A to Z. 'Just across the road from the police training place.' She'd known he wouldn't come with her. Even then she was going it alone.

It had been a difficult journey. She'd only been out of the psychiatric hospital three weeks. She'd got off the train before she'd reached the city, convinced she was going to die. She hadn't died; she'd stood in a station lavatory, her heart pounding so hard it shook her body. When the worst was over, she'd waited for the next train.

It was the consultant at the hospital who'd arranged for her to go and see Dr Rainbow and ever since the appointment had come in the post, she'd been getting herself ready for the journey. Travelling was difficult since she'd cracked up, for the world had fallen apart too and she seemed forever clinging to air as pavements gave way. Occasionally walls, gates, lampposts and hedges receded from her and she thought she was dying. She tried not to yell for help because people would think her crazy.

She'd died a lot of times since she'd cracked up. Each time her body knew it was the last time.

Now a foot cautiously tested pavement. Snow

was melting about edges of concrete and later the skin of water would turn to ice. She'd put on her jeans because she felt she couldn't wear Wellingtons with a skirt. But would Dr Rainbow think she was serious – and seriously ill – if she turned up in jeans? Jeans were so casual. Yet she'd heaped on sweaters in the hope of disguising her sick thinness. Her obsessional need for concealment was always conflicting with a need to reveal herself. For days on end she'd simply jam, paralysed by indecision.

'I've got to be there for three o'clock. He's seeing me at three,' she'd told Charlie. Like a child repeating a lesson over and over, fearful she'd forget.

But would Dr Rainbow see her?

She'd the greatest difficulty at times in seeing herself; she seemed to slip in and out of life, only fitfully here. Present and correct. Often she was absent, as immaterial as a ghost, no more than a puff of cold air. In dreams she turned into floorboards, a coat hanger and even a tin of tomato soup. As she wasn't any body, she could be any thing. Of course, she wasn't going to tell Dr Rainbow about this, because he'd think she was mad. She thought she was mad and that was bad enough. On the other hand, she knew she needed help and if a psychiatrist decided she was perfectly normal – because she told him so – he wouldn't bother with her.

It was a bit of a problem.

In the past the simple question: 'How are you?' had produced so much conflict in her that the tension had set up uncontrollable tremors.

Her mind suddenly went on and off like a light bulb. She jerked in horror and then she realized she was passing palings; the wooden struts were opening and closing off sunlight. The most innocent of events threatened her because her interpretation of the world was full of dread. Now she could hear her heart in flight, leaping and stumbling. Her palms began to sweat.

She tried to turn her attention outwards, towards the county cricket ground. A blue and white striped betting shop hovered in the cold, its flags pasted to the sky; circling stairs to the stands were empty. Those stands could buckle and curl, the twenty-foot high wire netting unwind and tie itself to the tail of the wind. Yes. The world could push off at any moment. Sticking her hands into her anorak pockets, she clung to the clothes she was wearing.

She began to look for Ferrybridge Road. I'm going to get there, she realized. Though she'd been determined to reach the clinic, she couldn't help fearing that it would simply be beyond her.

Was that it? She was now facing a neo-Georgian building which crested a hill. Slowly she plodded up the hill towards it; cloud poked out the sun and it was chilly.

The sign said the building was an old people's home. The clinic was further still. There was a slight stirring round her face and she realized it had begun to snow again. She turned up the collar of her anorak.

The snow thickened as she followed a high wall downhill. She was aware that her toes were going numb. She wasn't sure whether it was because she sensed this was the wall of the clinic and she'd literally got cold feet or if the sub-zero temperature was to blame. She had thought of the journey, not of arrival. She came to gateposts. There were no gates. The sign said Underheath Clinic. She knew she wasn't going to turn away and yet suddenly being there knocked the breath out of her.

What am I doing here?

Going to see Dr Rainbow.

Who is he?

She couldn't answer that. She couldn't conceive of Dr Rainbow. He was a future which was unthinkable.

As she followed a turn in the drive she saw a Victorian mansion. It was a jumble of William and Mary gabling, Greek columns, steel boiler-house chimney, church stained glass and Elizabethan casements. Inside were two women who sat in a glass-fronted reception area. They directed her left, through double doors.

At first she thought she'd entered a ballroom in which people were at the moment amusing themselves by playing badminton. In the distance, by the net, was a hugh black marble fireplace with a mirrored overmantel. Then she noticed that the eastern wall was filled with long stained-glass windows and that the wooden roof, which vaulted over two floors, was carved with geometric tracery like that in churches. She decided that at one time the room must have been used for religious services. This, though, was refuted by the west wall which opened on to an enormous conservatory.

Isobel crossed the parquet floor and sat on one of the chairs grouped round coffee tables. The tables appeared to have been produced in occupational therapy. They hung together with such painful awkwardness that she thought it would be a kindness – and relieve everybody's anxiety – if they were taken apart.

Clutching her shoulder bag, she looked again at the extraordinary hall she'd entered. A railed gallery went round two sides of the ballroom-church-badminton court, giving access to what had perhaps once been bedrooms. There were many rooms off both floors and, now and then, people emerged or disappeared.

She found, to her surprise, she had no difficulty distinguishing staff from patients, even though no-one wore uniform. The patients all had the look of strain inherent in the laminate and wood of the coffee tables; staying in one piece seemed unlikely in view of misbegotten joints and unsupported superstructure. Their instability made Isobel so nervous she looked about for more comfortable figures.

The psychiatrists, psychologists, psychiatric social workers and nurses looked solid. They walked in the fullness of their stretch. They looked wise. They looked good. They looked busy and important and full of themselves. They commanded the light of the many eyes which watched them – anxious eyes ferreting out a reassuring bit of suiting, a comfy crêpe sole, even the severity of an alternative boiler suit. Their faces waxed in the light of these many eyes. And yet in a strange way these busy and important people made their patients feel important too. Important enough to be cases which warranted attention, interpretation, discussion at case conferences, of being wrapped in a folder and put in the care of a filing clerk.

Turning her attention to the badminton players, who were undoubtedly patients, she thought that people in the throes of mental anguish shouldn't be playing games, especially when their misbegotten joints were taken into account. She then thought that doctors and nurses should wear uniforms and wondered why there was a conservatory stuck on to what purported to be a church nave. And what was a martyrdom of stained glass doing in a ballroom?

She decided that though Dr Rainbow may see her, she wouldn't be seeing him. Enough was enough. She cut out most of her surroundings by lowering her eyes and began to feel a bit safer. She didn't, however, lose sight of the big clock which marked the end of the hall and the beginning of the conservatory. It was five minutes past three. He was late.

How would she know him among all these people?

How would he recognize her?

He didn't, but she recognized him straight away. He was going round the hall asking people if they were her. He wasn't having much luck, she observed. She thought she'd have to try and know who she was, because she didn't think he was going to be much good at it.

She observed him further. He was older than she was by about ten years and wore glasses and was so tall he stooped from a lifetime of looking down on the world. He was slow and patient and walked with a heavy tread, but she detected something gleeful in him. She thought that he probably liked saving souls. Anguish was his *métier*; it was all food and drink to him.

She saw that his conscientious quest was propelling him nearer to her, but she was nevertheless sure he'd prove to be lazy. If she wished him to save her soul, she'd have to make him. He'd wriggle out of such hard work if he could. She began to feel quite indignant. What did he think the Welfare State paid him for?

Having surveyed Dr Rainbow, she modestly lowered her eyes.

'Mrs Maccabee?'

'Yes.'

Very warily, she followed him. Her spirit was so loose it no longer seemed confined to her body. It became her third eye, sometimes darting in front to take an anxious look at him, peering down his ear, lifting up an eyelid, testing the consistency of his skin – was he tough enough for the job she might entrust him with? – giving him a poke in the neck to see what happened.

He opened a door and led her a few steps down a murky corridor and then paused to extract a large bunch of keys from his pocket. He unlocked a door and she followed him into the unevenly shaped room, perhaps made by partitioning a larger one. She was aware of polystyrene tiles on the ceiling and a small string and nail assemblage on the wall, but afterwards could never remember just how terrible the curtains and carpets were. In this she was helped by the deep shadow which covered much of the room. There was a settee in the corner which should have gone up with Guy Fawkes on 5 November. Or was it a couch? She certainly wasn't going to examine it or its name in detail.

He claimed the chair nearest the door and that alarmed her. He didn't sit behind his desk, but in front of it. This offended her sense of propriety. He sat too close to her. This made her joints burn with agitation. She'd like to have climbed up the wall, but didn't want him to suppose she was at all disturbed.

He appeared to be busying himself with paper. He chose to write with a biro, but then a man who had polystyrene tiles on his consulting room ceiling was no doubt capable of anything. He wrote awkwardly, she noticed, as though some small mechanism in him were partially jammed. This cheered her a little. 'Your papers have come through from the hospital,' he said.

She, too, was important enough to be a subject. A case.

She couldn't remember having been much in evidence at the hospital. She'd slept on a DHSS bed, ate DHSS food, taken DHSS drugs, pretended to be in hospital when in reality she was nowhere to be found. She wondered how they could have written about someone who was missing. Who'd write about people who aren't there?

As she watched the psychiatrist, she was aware of him covertly watching her too, though he was writing. She didn't meet his gaze, but she noted that he wouldn't be above flirting with her. That he could find her attractive baffled her. Did he know he was paying court to a lady who might turn into a floorboard or a carton of yoghurt at any minute? Not to mention a tin of tomato soup or a puff of cold air? Really. His wife ought to take him in hand. She'd no business letting him out. A small smile played round her lips.

It seemed to her that whatever was going on between them had nothing to do with what he was writing down on that paper, but she continued to answer his questions.

She noticed his handwriting sloped to the right though some uprights fell flat on their backs. This didn't, she found, inspire confidence. In fact she wasn't at all sure she wasn't going to jump up and race through the door.

Her anxiety mounted so high that once more her spirit came loose.

She used her lightness of being to slide behind his back and take a sneaky look at what it was made of. He remained steady under a scrutiny which impudently viewed all it should not, which shoved, pushed, prodded, jumped on, tweaked.

Gradually, Isobel was aware of a hand forming in her mind. She reached out her hand and felt him grasp it firmly. She became aware of his muscle tensing with strain as he took the full weight of her.

In reality they remained some feet away from each other. She went on answering his questions, he went on writing.

'I became ill six months ago,' she told him. 'I went shopping in the lunch hour at work. I went into a department store and I had what I thought of as a heart attack. My heart went off at an incredible rate. It went crazy. I thought I was dying and I waited to die. But I didn't die. After that first time, it kept happening. I kept having these heart attacks and I kept waiting to die, but I didn't die. They said at the hospital that they were panic attacks. Acute panic. Well, of course I panicked. It's not so unreasonable, is it? To panic if you are dying. I died so often I couldn't believe I was alive any more. When you die as often as I did you expect to be dead. At the hospital they said I had agitated endogenous depression and gave me pills. I didn't feel depressed. I don't feel anything at all. I never cry. At the beginning I felt physically ill. Terribly ill. I lost a lot of weight. I couldn't eat. I was too ill to eat. I lost three stone. I don't understand dying and not being dead. I died too many times. I thought I must be dead. Perhaps that's why they put me in a psychiatric hospital.' Isobel stopped, but because he didn't say anything she thought he must be expecting to hear more. She continued: 'Just before they admitted me I looked in a mirror at the shoe shop I was in and I didn't recognize myself. Didn't know the woman I was looking at. I had no idea it was me. I thought the woman looked interesting, but I didn't know I was looking at myself in the mirror. It was a stranger. And then I saw the woman was wearing my skirt and had my safety pin in the waistband to keep it up and then I realized I was looking at me. I made a leather belt in hospital.'

'You looked in the mirror and didn't recognize yourself? I've never heard of that before.'

'Haven't you?' That didn't alarm Isobel for now he was holding her hand she felt safe. In reality he was laying aside the sheets of paper he'd been writing on.

He said: 'I've had hundreds upon hundreds of patients and I've never heard of that. Not in over twenty years' work.'

'Do you mean there are normal ways of being crazy?'

'Normal ways. Yes. More or less.'

'They thought I was a bit odd at the psychiatric hospital too,' said Isobel.

'How are you now?'

'All right,' she said, thinking perhaps she'd revealed too much already. A psychiatrist apparently expected a patient to be crazy in the right kind of way. As it appeared she wasn't, would he think her too mad to treat? She wished someone had told her the rules of the game. This was awful.

But he didn't appear to be put off. 'Why did all this happen?' he asked. 'Why did you go in a store and have what you thought was a heart attack? Why did you become ill?'

'I don't know.'

'Were you distressed? Unhappy?'

'No,' she said. 'I was as right as rain. That day I'd had my lunch. I felt quite all right. Normal. And then my heart went crazy. It was a bolt from the blue. I don't know why it happened.'

'But your daughter had died, hadn't she?'

She looked at Dr Rainbow.

'What was your daughter called?'

She realized there was no help for her. She couldn't even say Anne-Marie's name. Slowly, gently, she untangled her hand from his.

'I'm a psychotherapist,' he said.

'I feel ill. Physically ill. I don't feel depressed,' she said.

'You are on anti-depressants now.'

'Yes. But it seems so strange. Taking pills for depression when you don't feel depressed.'

He doubled the dose, writing her out a new prescription in his awkward hand. As she put it in her shoulder bag, he said: 'I think I can help you.' The room was quite dark now and he made no move to put on the light.

But she'd thought then that no-one could help and she hadn't gone back, though she'd written him a polite note.

'If you change your mind,' he wrote back, 'please get in touch.'

And knowing that she could, that this avenue was not closed to her, had been a source of some comfort to her as very slowly she'd re-oriented herself and come back into the world.

Looking back through the years, she saw she was not now as she had been then, she was as much in her right mind as she'd ever be; as sane as the next.

Having been mad, she realized, was not without advantage. It taught you what sanity was.

She knew with absolute certainty that the Paddington Bear was real. She could ask Fanny if she wanted to, but she knew Fanny had seen the bear too.

Someone had entered the cottage and put the bear in the rocking-chair.

Then they'd taken the bear away.

Someone who wished her terrible harm.

She shuddered.

Why?

When she discovered who it was – and she saw she must do this – she would also know why.

Very slowly, very carefully, for her finger was throbbing, she twisted off Charlie Maccabee's wedding ring.

It's a funny place to start, she thought, but I'll start with chucking his ring away.

SIX

Isobel frowned as she concentrated on toasting crumpets; too near the flames and smoke spiralled from the pale doughy rims. Drue Lycett-Green was watching her. The old lady was sitting on a high-backed armchair, softly lit by one of the three rosy lamps scattered about her drawing-room. Though it was almost dark, the puce damask curtains hadn't yet been pulled. Small greyish rims of snow were thickening along the glazing bars of the deep sash windows. As the wind veered, snatches of church bells mingled with the crackling pine logs; the village bell ringers practised most Sunday afternoons.

Mickleholme Villa was one of the largest houses on Main Street, a three-storey Victorian pile. The blue black Welsh slates fell off the roof, unexplained damp patches appeared through wallpaper, downspouts split and toadstools suddenly erupted under the kitchen sink, but Drue wouldn't be moved. 'One is perfectly used to living in discomfort,' she said. 'It's what one was brought up to after all.' And Isobel was left to suppose that comfort wasn't a state of being a lady aspired to.

That the house became daily more unsuitable

for Drue to live in was obvious to everyone in the village. Since her second heart attack the old lady found it difficult to keep warm. 'Something seems a little amiss with my internal heating arrangements,' Drue admitted herself, only to immediately doubt the evidence of her senses. 'Or does one imagine it? One gets to the state where so much of one's body functions below par one picks a quarrel with everything. The flesh, my dear, is so unreliable. One does rather resent it perishing while one is still in it.'

The old lady looked Byzantine in her turban of blue silk, worn to disguise her thinning hair. She was bundled in assorted layers of cashmere sweaters and elastic-waisted trousers. Her puffed ankles bulged over her slippers like untrimmed pastry. Diamonds hung from her ears and more fine stones adorned her fingers; none shone as brightly as her very bleak grey eyes.

A companionable silence existed between them as Isobel buttered the crumpets and piled them one by one on one of Drue's china plates. She pulled a side table nearer the old lady's chair. As she did so, Drue tapped the back of her hand. 'You must pour. The pot's getting too heavy for me now.' So Isobel presided over the Georgian silver tea set. Drue loved her luxuries; her silver, her gems, her china, her oriental rugs and Biedermeier glass. It was said in the village that she played the Stock Market and had the devil's own luck.

'After the crumpets we'll have some of Mrs Bennett's Saffron cake,' Drue said as Isobel handed her her tea. 'And then I shall have my smoke and bugger the doctor.'

Isobel grinned and watched the old lady tuck in before helping herself. Later she got one of Drue's cigarillos and fitted it into a long black holder and lit it for her. Drue managed to smoke half of it before admitting defeat. 'I suppose one ought to bow out when one's too far gone for smokes. But one so loses the grace to do the right thing,' she said. 'One hangs on like grim death, my dear. Grim death. Hardly apposite.' She chuckled. 'It's surprising how when one's body goes to pieces, one supposes the rest of the world to have gone to pieces too. As if they were one and the same thing. But however imperfect this imperfect world, one does so infinitely prefer it to the next. God could wait forever for my money. He's altogether too previous. Give me Mrs Thatcher or even, though one hesitates to say it, the little man from Wales. Now. Are you going to tell me what's the matter or are we going to go on pretending?'

'Is it so obvious?'

'You did tell me you had to go to the solicitors,' Drue reminded her. 'Ever since then you've looked like a cat with maggots in its fur. I've tried to be tactful and not pry – but really . . . I'm getting to the state where I'm waking at three in the morning and wondering what's wrong with you. You're making me forget my own aches and pains. That's altogether too much. One gets so uncomfortable when one has to forgo the comforts of being wrapped up in one's self. I suppose it's to do with that jolly awful Johnny you were idiot enough to marry?'

'He's dead.'

'H-hummp,' Drue said and then: 'That is unexpected news. And quite out of character if I may say so. I should have thought he was a man who took jolly good care of number one. Still it's not altogether displeasing at my age to hear of a death among the young. Reprehensible, no doubt, but there it is. He always looked as fit as a flea. How on earth did he manage to die?'

'He crashed his car.'

'Tell me the rest.'

Isobel told her everything.

Drue, examining what she'd heard, said eventually: 'It's a woman of course. What an extraordinary affair. The sort of thing one would never read about if all one took was the *Financial Times*.'

Isobel found she was laughing. 'Really, Drue. It's more than a matter of bad taste. It's quite awful.'

'Yes. I know that, my dear. But one can't help noting the quality of mind. Or lack of it.'

'So your money's on a vulgar woman?'

They both laughed.

'Seriously—' said Isobel.

'Seriously,' said Drue, 'it's a very womanly thing to do, don't you think? Men, my dear, are so much more to the point. Iron bar. That sort of thing. Women are poisoners. And this is a kind of poisoning, isn't it? It's to do with love, of course.'

'Love! I haven't seen a man since Charlie left.'

'Have you thought of this woman he went off with? A games mistress, wasn't she?'

'Sandra. But why? That makes no sense at all. After all, she walked off with my husband. I was the injured party.'

'You can't expect one to work out the fine detail,' the old lady said irritably. 'All I'm saying is my money would be on her. Who else is likely to have any of Anne-Marie's toys?'

'That's what I'm trying to find out.'

'Of course there could be a joker in the pack. A sick mind in the village. Why haven't you contacted the police?'

'I really would rather not.'

'One would always hesitate, my dear. I do see that. It's those shoes they issue them with. But you'll have to tell them in the end. It's safer surely to do it now.'

'So you don't think this – this harassment – will stop?'

'Do you?'

'I don't know.' She decided: 'If it does go on – if one more thing happens – I'll tell the police.'

'Perhaps I've given you the impression I take it lightly. I mean . . . well, I was somewhat taken aback. But the more one thinks about it . . . I know evil is out of fashion. But one is aware of how evil this is. A psychiatrist would no doubt have other names for it. I really don't like the sound of it at all.'

Isobel got up and drew the curtains. As she was putting the dirty crockery back on the tea trolley, Drue said: 'Get me the Tarot.'

'Not on your life.'

'I could read them.'

'Certainly not.'

'Don't you believe in the cards?'

'I believe in you. And don't you go reading them behind my back.' She turned at the door, leaving the trolley of dirty pots for a moment. 'After all, you wouldn't read of Tarot divining in the *Financial Times*.'

'On the Hong Kong exchange they roasted a pig on the trading floor during the crash of '87. They hoped to propitiate the gods. I feel, speaking for myself, that money is never vulgar. Only the lack of it.'

Isobel laughed. 'All the same, I'd rather you didn't read my Tarot.'

'Shoo, shoo,' the old woman said. 'And please put the pots away when they're washed. One really *must* propitiate Mrs Bennett.'

In Mickleholme Villa's large, gloomy and improbably duck egg blue kitchen, Isobel reviewed what Drue had said.

But why Sandra?

Why anybody?

After washing and drying the pots, she arranged the tea towel in a manner Mrs Bennett was known to approve of. Joan Bennett had first begun working at Mickleholme as a cleaner and then she'd become an occasional cook. Since Drue's last heart attack, she'd added some nursing to her duties. Both of them were attuned to the nuances of fashion in domestic employer-employee relationships. Joan called her employer Drue and Drue called her employee Mrs Bennett. The social distance between them voiced to their mutual satisfaction, they waged war from behind the lines they'd drawn.

Isobel put the pots away, stored the butter in the fridge and collected her anorak from the hook behind the kitchen door. Surveying the room again, she saw nothing which would offend Mrs Bennett when she came in on Monday morning. She went to say goodbye to the old lady.

'I'll see you to the front door.' Drue hauled herself up to her feet, unhooking her stick from the arm of the chair.

'There's no need.'

'I must have my exercise. Keep going, my dear. That's the ticket. Never say die.'

'Don't stand by the door. You'll get pneumonia.'

'I've had it twice,' Isobel was informed. 'Very undignified. One keeps on coughing up phlegm.'

'Do turn back now, Drue. I'll open and shut the door as quickly as I can.'

'Fuss. Fuss.' And as Isobel stooped to kiss her cheek, the old lady thrust her index finger towards her anorak. 'My money's on you. Look what you've come through already. You should be pretty well fire proof. It's all so extraordinary. But then these days people wear safety pins through their noses. Women my age bare their empty bags on the beach. One can't think what Jane Austen would have made of it all. Watch the step.'

'I will. I will—' Isobel, head lowered against

gusts of sleet, dashed down the path and across Main Street.

She found herself hesitating before turning the key in the cottage door. No, no, she thought. No-one is ever going to make me scared of crossing my own threshold.

What if Paddington Bear has come back?

No.

She wouldn't race to look.

She put a match to the fire she'd laid earlier, took off her anorak and picked up an unread section of the Sunday paper. She still had some work to do, preparing for an interview tomorrow, but she decided that could wait.

Later, of course, she did go to look. Halfway up the stairs she became convinced she'd find the bear. She just knew she would. All safe and sound with his silly boots on. Quite unharmed.

The rocking-chair was empty.

In her mind she saw her daughter trailing the bear by a hand so he bumped and thumped along the floor. 'Mummy, Mummy, where are you? Paddington wants a sweetie. Mummy, where are you?'

She realized she could no longer remember the exact sound of her daughter's voice.

That was unforgivable.

Her own daughter's voice.

In her panic she turned round on herself, looking for that sound.

She shook herself.

There was work to do.

She went back downstairs, pulled out a book from a plastic bag and settled herself by the fire. *Rosie's Glittering Prizes* was the autobiography of a showgirl who had become famous for giving television quiz game winners the wrong prizes. Much of the book was about her affair with the even more famous quiz master and was sprinkled with what economists now called 'big ticket items'. There was a £90,000 Porsche, a £250,000 love nest and 'Dinkie bought me a £10,000 sapphire to go with my eyes'. Dinkie apparently liked bonking in the shower and three minute eggs. Once he dressed her, beginning at the bottom by painting her toe nails. It was, they both found, a profoundly moving experience. Unfortunately the exigencies of Dinkie's hard-pressed life prevented a repeat performance. When not in the studio, he'd hardly time to breathe between speaking engagements at Inner Circle functions, opening car showrooms and going home to his wife. There were also lots of pictures of celebrities whom Dinkie knew, though Rosie did not, for their affair was a closely guarded secret. But now Rosie felt the need to tell all for, when all was said and done, honesty was the best policy.

All it needs now is for Dinkie to sue her and she's got a bestseller on her hands, Isobel reflected and she jotted down some questions she'd ask Rosie when she interviewed her tomorrow. On average Isobel did one interview a week of a similar sort. They were broadcast in Jacko Marshall's evening rush-hour programme, sandwiched between traffic reports and playing listed records.

She sighed and stretched, settling further back in the armchair. She was aware of her writing block slipping off her knee, but felt too drowsy to catch it.

Suddenly she knew her daughter was very near to her. So near she ought to be able to see her, but she couldn't. And then she realized that was because there was a gauze across her eyes. She was recovering from a head wound and she was bandaged.

Someone held her hand and was leading her to Anne-Marie. 'Is is you, Drue? Where is she? Where's Annie?' She was liberated by joy. They'd take the bandages away and she'd see her child.

But quite inextricably it began to grow darker. She became afraid that soon it would be too dark for her to see Annie. Her daughter would be lost to her forever.

'Take the bandage off, Drue! Take it off now.'

'It's not time,' Drue said. 'We've to be jolly careful. You're not well enough.'

Isobel's fingers groped to her cheek. She ripped the bandage away. As she did the ship she was in sank. She found herself being carried over a waterfall and she worried that her anorak would get wet. But it was quite dry when she was washed up in an underground bunker. The bunker, she began to realize, had been turned into a broadcasting studio. Fanny Wragg was covering a war conference being held by a lot of very angry Turks. One by one these men got up and said dangerous things. One said: 'Drue is an enemy spy.'

And then a great crack appeared in the studio

floor and Isobel tumbled down a hole. The hole began to get smaller and she realized it was a funny shape. It was long and thin and yet it widened out at the top so that there was room for her shoulders.

Someone seemed to be in this confined space with her.

Rosie said: 'It's a love nest. Dinkie gave it me. It's worth a million.'

Isobel became very frightened.

It's a coffin.

In her panic she lashed out.

A child began to wail and wail.

She woke with a start to the sound of the front door bell. Tears were trickling down her face. She brushed them away and as she did so she began to feel very angry. Nonsensically she was thinking: 'How dare anyone ring my bell?'

She was disconcerted to find Bruno Seuret on her doorstep. He looked furry. He was wearing a sheepskin jacket and the collar was pulled up round his ears. 'I hope you don't mind my calling so late,' he said.

'Please, come in—' She stood aside. Following him, she saw he made her living room small. 'Let me have your coat. Would you like some coffee?'

'Please.'

'I won't be a minute.'

Hanging his coat behind the kitchen door, she turned to make the coffee. She heard him behind her. And then she was aware of him opening the door into her studio.

Just like Fanny, she thought. Without a

by-your-leave. She was full of indignation. But why were the discs of her spine crunching together? Not indignation, not fear, though there was some fear in it. Oh, she knew this back-bone crunching of old. Charlie had had this effect on her. Sometimes it was when she'd caught an unexpected glimpse of the bastard, sometimes when she'd pictured him in her mind. It had even happened after he'd left her. Charlie had certainly sent all manner of shivers down her spine.

She took the coffee tray into the studio and cleared a space on the bench.

'You've a wonderful eye for form and colour,' he said. He was holding a canvas by the French window. 'I think they're very good. I hope you don't mind my saying so. I really had no idea at all. Charlie never said anything you know. Not a word. These are poppies, aren't they? I never knew there was such a thing as yellow poppies.'

'They come in all colours. From scarlet to white and even blue. The yellow ones seed themselves into the garden year after year. Those are flag irises which grow at the side of the canal. And that's flax.'

'I wonder why Charlie never said anything.'

'I didn't start painting until after he'd left me. I did win a scholarship to art school when I was a kid, but I took a job on the local paper instead. I fancied being a journalist. I began painting with a box of kid's water colours. I felt I had to do something. I made a leather belt while I was in hospital, but really I'm no good at craft work. Cack handed.'

'What's that?'

'Clumsy with my hands. I actually began painting when I landed this part-time job with Radio Brum. My main trouble at that time was lack of concentration. I kept losing the thread. Painting was an exercise in improving my concentration. I found I really liked doing it after a while. And then when I was better, it was a wonderful form of relaxation. Painting is just the opposite to my job in broadcasting. It's solitary. No people. No noise. No nothing.'

'And always plants?'

'Plants aren't people. I think that's why I chose them in the beginning. They weren't going to upset me. And I was always interested in botany at school. I like plants. When I went over to oil paints I had a fight – me and the paint – for a year. We still have tremendous wrestling matches. More than once the turps has been let down with tears. Sheer frustration. But I will keep hammering away. I'm a terribly pig-headed woman.'

'Determined. Not pig-headed.'

'Whatever. I will keep hanging in there having a go. Sugar?'

'No, thanks. I've gone through the things in the loft over the stable.' He put down the canvas and took the cup. 'There's a box of Anne-Marie's stuff.'

'Oh dear.'

'Lego. Some soft toys. One or two Dick and Dora books.'

'Caro didn't take everything to the charity shop?'

'No. She obviously overlooked this box.'

'The Paddington Bear could have been among them I suppose.'

'The stable block is never locked up. And I'm away all day. But who would know your daughter's things were there? I didn't.'

'Sometimes it feels so frightening,' she said. 'I'm not me at all, am I? I'm some monstrous object a sick mind has made up. I'm just something to hate.'

She looked at him. 'It could be anyone, couldn't it?'

He said nothing.

'It could even be someone I don't even know,' she said. 'Someone who has just kidnapped me and woven me into their own black fantasies. I've even doubted my own sanity. I don't even have faith in myself.'

SEVEN

Even as she drove down the slipway on to the motorway at Stafford, Isobel was telling herself how foolish she was being. Throughout the week the conviction had grown that her tormentor was Charlie's widow. 'It's a very womanly thing to do, don't you think? Men, my dear, are much more to the point. Iron bar.' That's what the old lady had said. She'd also said: 'It's to do with love.'

How can it be? Isobel asked herself again.

What reason could Sandra possibly have for persecuting me?

I'm mistaken.

And yet she nosed her car on to the motorway.

She told herself she had to start somewhere; if she could eliminate Charlie's widow she could at least look elsewhere.

All week she'd found herself waiting. Waiting for what? Something to happen. For the bear to reappear?

That was another reason why she was going to Blackpool today. At least she wasn't waiting; she was doing something.

It had taken her some time to get ready. She'd dressed herself in a smart three-piece tailored suit.

Under that she wore new black silk lingerie and delicately patterned black stockings. On her small feet were suede high-heeled shoes with bows on their backs.

She'd made herself up carefully, scented herself, discarded her everyday watch in favour of her gold one. There was a shield-shaped brooch at her throat.

Isobel was not about to face the second Mrs Maccabee without all her war paint on.

Without being dressed to kill.

Certainly not.

Now she looked at her left hand on the steering wheel and, ringless, still wore Charlie's ring in her flesh, a deep shiny circle of pearl-coloured skin.

Flesh of my flesh, she thought grimly.

The first thing his whore will notice is his ring on my ringless finger.

What will I say to her? What will I do?

Isobel checked her war paint in the driving mirror.

She's making a mockery of my grief. She's laughing at my dead child.

Suddenly she was shaking with anger.

I'll kill the bitch.

Her anger began to frighten her; it was so much bigger than she was. And getting bigger. It was as if a fuse had been lit inside her and an explosion was slowly detonating. A big bang. Quite enough flying matter to create a universe.

Or destroy one.

She was, and she knew it, itching to get her hands on Charlie's whore.

Was this the real reason she was going to Blackpool?

The surprising thing was that it wasn't the bringing of Paddington Bear which had detonated this explosion inside her, but his taking away.

It was finding those rocking-chair arms bereft.

But I don't want the bear, she thought, utterly bewildered. What do I want with those dreadful toy eyes and that pursed-up, horrid little mouth?

Her foot hit the accelerator harder. She was now in the outside lane.

And then, very deliberately, she took hold of herself. She made herself ease back on the pedal. She made herself drop back into the second lane. By breathing deeply she tried to lower her furious heart rate.

Sandra need have nothing to do with it, she told herself. Hasn't she just lost a baby herself? Hasn't she had two miscarriages?

What's misbegotten will miscarry.

No.

She could find no pity for Charlie's widow.

In the hope of distracting herself, she switched on the radio. The inflections in the broadcaster's voice annoyed her; hard down on every fourth or fifth word. Keep 'em awake; keep 'em listening. She turned the dial, trying to get some music. Then she switched off.

She was trying to remember Sandra clearly. Not horsey in the traditional sense of tally-ho and buck teeth and yet there was something horse-like about her. Those trim but powerful buttocks, Isobel thought. A good ride. All that shaggy mane and depth of chest. A strong woman. Who would have thought a mare like that would miscarry? She looked built to be a mother of a nation.

Wicked old mother nature, pulling a fast one. Laughing up her sleeve.

Isobel found herself dwelling on Sandra's musculature.

Was I really thinking of having a fight with that woman?

She could break every bone in my body.

God damn and blast Charlie. May he burn in hell.

Perhaps he is.

She looked again at the ring on the ringless finger.

How could you leave me for a clod-hopping horse-brained games mistress? she mourned. Who got taken for a ride? Oh, Charlie. I was really one with you. Flesh of my flesh. You bastard.

It began to drizzle. She turned on the wipers. The snow had been washed away earlier in the week, revealing once more an Anglo-Saxon world covered in lichen. Tree trunks, concrete, tarmac, bricks, all mouldering softly under a sheen of green beneath a moist English sky.

She thought of switching the radio to her own station's wavelength, but remembered it was getting towards Saturday lunchtime and soon the football would begin.

I'll try not to think, she told herself. Or think pleasant thoughts. Bruno Seuret. Oh, bugger him.

I need a man like a hole in the head. Look what happened the last time. Don't psychologists say that a woman who picks one bastard always picks another? What did the *Marriages Made in Hell* chap say on Jacko's programme last night? 'Some women don't seem able to get enough punishment. They're always on the look out for more.' Smart Alec, she thought. Trying to make his name so he'll get a chair at some tin pot little university. All human nature in a match box.

Smarmy-arsed little prick.

And she felt her anger rising again.

Against a man she'd never met talking about a book she'd never read.

I'd pick a fight with a blade of grass at the moment, she thought, and was dismayed.

If I don't tear someone else to pieces I'll tear myself apart.

Who took my bear?

Rock-a-bye

Rock-a-bye

Rock-a-die baby . . .

And yet by the time she reached Blackpool her anger – that big bang, that destruction huge enough to create a universe – was in hiding. Trying to stiffen her resolve, she sought her anger out; she found she couldn't call on it at command.

It appeared she might have to face Charlie's widow with her knees shaking, like a frightened kid.

How foolish she felt driving down the front at Blackpool.

What on earth was she going to say to Sandra Tiptree?

She thought of one or two sentences. Each seemed more ludicrous than the last.

'Good afternoon. Do you remember me? I'm Charlie's first wife.'

It was grotesque.

I don't want to see the woman. I don't want to see that whore. What happens if she starts to snivel?

Would I cry too?

Dear God. We might end up wailing together for that unspeakable bastard. Charlie's sobbing leftovers.

Why did I come up here? What good can it possibly do?

There was her fear too.

Sandra might not cry. Sandra might be angry. Very angry.

Or was she frightened of losing control of herself? Her own temper?

I must go back, she thought.

But no. It appeared she must not. For she kept driving on.

When she reached Squire's Gate she turned inland. Sand was piled up against curbs and walls, salt dulled the windows of shops, paper blew. Even though her windows were closed she could hear the screech of gulls.

She twice had to ask the way to Heritage Court. It turned out to be a cul-de-sac. Six large bungalows, each with a door in the middle flanked by box bays, were well set back in open plan gardens. They were built of reclaimed brick and there was a lot of Tudor lattice and gabling.

Isobel parked her car outside number six. First she looked at the second Mrs Maccabee's ruched and frilled blinds and then at a stone donkey in the middle of the lawn; it carried paniers planted with winter flowering heathers.

She turned and looked at herself in the car mirror, combed her hair and touched up her lipstick. She dabbed more scent on to her wrists.

As she walked up the driveway, she still hadn't decided what she'd say when Sandra Tiptree opened the door. She would never, she knew, be able to call the woman Mrs Maccabee – after all, that was Isobel's name – and yet she certainly didn't want to call her by her first name.

As she rang the door chimes she rehearsed: 'Did you break into my house and put Anne-Marie's bear on the rocking-chair?' Would she really confront this woman? Say that?

And if she did what good would it do? Sandra would simply deny it.

Even though she was aware her situation was untenable, she rang the bell again.

'You took my Paddington Bear.'

It will end up in an undignified scuffle. Something squalid and ridiculous. 'You'll feel ashamed of yourself.' The admonishing voice in her head was her mother's. 'You'll regret it, madam.'

'Not if I hit the bitch on the nose,' she told her mother.

She rang the chimes again.

A sharp wind pinched her cheeks. She rubbed her hands together and then used one to hammer with the knocker.

It had simply never occurred to her that Sandra Tiptree wouldn't be in. She'd been so swept up in the turmoil of her thoughts that such a practical possibility had never presented itself.

Of course she's here, she told herself now, on no evidence other than she'd driven over a hundred miles to have it out with the whore.

I'll wrinkle her out.

She went round by the double garage to the rear of the bungalow. The back garden was fenced in by high interwoven panels of larch. There was a patio, a small lawn which rose steeply from the paving and dotted beds of shrubs. None of this formed a whole; each bed of shrubs appeared to be in the wrong garden.

Though the windows were latticed at the front, the French windows at the back of the building were Georgian paned. Isobel peered in. The long wide corridor of a lounge was empty in the kind of way which suggested it was a room in an estate show house. No pile of magazines and newspapers, no glasses case, no empty tea cup, no shoes kicked under a chair.

She moved to the side of the house. Behind the garage was a side entrance and – bereft of lead or Georgian pane – a large kitchen window. She rose on tiptoe, shaded her eyes, her nose almost touching the glass. This room, too, was pin neat. A dish cloth, hardened almost to cardboard, was stretched over the brown fibreglass sink. Looking up, she saw the top window was slightly open. Suddenly it occurred to her that it would be easy to break into the bungalow.

She could look round and see for herself if any of Anne-Marie's toys were here.

Isobel was an honest citizen. Once or twice in childhood she'd scrumped apples, but this was the limit of her criminal activities. If a shopkeeper gave her too much change, she handed it back. If she found something she returned it. She was even truthful when making out her expenses sheet at Radio Brum. She'd wondered at times if she'd balanced this urge to be good – when perhaps she longed to be bad – by wedding herself to the entirely dishonourable Charlie. That bastard had certainly been bad enough for both of them.

However that might be, Isobel, who never broke the law, now decided on illegal entry.

The decision both excited and frightened her, but mainly she was astonished at the ease with which she'd arrived at it. Plainly doing what you shouldn't was not that difficult after all.

But she was entirely unsuitably dressed. She took off her jacket and hung it neatly over the umbrella-shaped clothes-line concreted into paving by the back door. She rolled up her sleeves and lifted the dustbin, empty she discovered, and set it under the kitchen window. She took off her shoes and wondered what to do about her tight skirt. Remembering her schooldays, she pulled it up and tucked it in round the bottom of her knickers.

Using a couple of bricks as a step up, she climbed on top of the bin. She threaded her finger through the top window, opened it wide and then extended her arm down and unlatched the bottom one. It was only then she realized that this window was going to swing out into her body.

She clambered down, pulled the window back and then climbed back on to the dustbin. Re-tucking her skirt, she swung backwards through the opening. The kitchen sink was just below her. Cautiously she extended her legs over the taps. One knee on the draining board, she lowered the other foot towards the ceramic floor. Grasping a tap, she manoeuvred her hips flat against the sink. Both feet touched the floor tiles.

Shaking out her skirt and breathing deeply, hot and yet with a sense of triumph, she looked round at the second Mrs Maccabee's kitchen. It was a lot cleaner than the first Mrs Maccabee's. This, the first Mrs Maccabee decided, was a character fault; the poor cow was obsessive.

But would a really obsessive personality have forgotten to properly close her windows? Isobel, even when confronted with Charlie's whore, was plagued by fairmindedness.

That bitch is a better housekeeper than me.

She unlocked the back door, retrieved her jacket and coat and went to explore.

The lounge had an inglenook and lots of dark Ercol furniture. There was a separate dining-room filled with mock regency pieces and a large utility room with bone-dry clothes on a wire clothes-rack. Among the items were two well-washed pairs of men's briefs and an odd couple of men's socks.

Though electronic clocks silently moved on, the feeling that the house had been abandoned grew in Isobel. The deep freeze, juddering to life, didn't dispel that feeling.

She went into the hall. Moved by the desire to see her own housewifely skills in a better light, she cleared the untidy heap of free newspapers and post from the door mat and stacked it on a table, sorting it into even-sized piles as she did so. She disturbed the air sufficiently for a disintegrating leaf to fall off a dead plant.

Walking further down the hall, she first found the master bedroom. Photographs of Charlie, Charlie with Sandra, Charlie, Sandra and in-laws, and Charlie at the centre of a triumphant cricket team, crowded a cream and gilt chest of drawers. She picked one of them up. She'd forgotten that Sandra was slightly taller than Charlie and had chubby cheeks which gave her an innocent, almost childish look. Charlie, who'd always been devilishly handsome, had begun to look distinguished as well. Powerful, thought Isobel, perhaps just powerfully pleased with himself. She looked at the cream and gilt bed with its candy pink, quilted satin cover. No doubt the scene of many a good innings.

May he rot.

She opened the wardrobes. They were half empty. In a drawer by the bedside was a jewel case, but some feeling for propriety wouldn't allow her to open that. After all, Anne-Marie's toys couldn't be in there.

In the *en suite* bathroom Charlie had left only two unused razors.

The second bedroom was fitted with bookshelves and many of the books were in French. Charlie's domain. Though Isobel knew him as an untidy man, a flinger of socks into odd corners, a dropper of sheets of newspaper and orange peel, here all was preternaturally neat. There was very little trace of the man she'd known, let alone Anne-Marie and the wreckage of his past life.

She froze on the threshold of the third bedroom. It was decorated in pink and blue. There was a cot, a chest of drawers, a basket full of baby soap, cotton wool, talc, cream and safety pins. Two piles of nappies were in another basket. Small fluffy toys stood in a row on the window ledge. There was a baby bath and stand, a very smart coach-built pram, the hood up; from it dangled a family of lemon chicks. Both cot and pram, she noted, had been made up. The covers were folded back in a triangular fashion, ready to receive a baby.

None of the toys had been Anne-Marie's.

Isobel, unable to put a foot in the room and yet unable to step back, was haunted by the silence.

All Charlie's babies, she thought.

Dead issue.

Too shocked to move, she stood there growing colder. She felt sensation die away in her fingers and toes.

'Mummy,' wailed Anne-Marie, a tug of voice from the sepulchral heart of this room. 'Mummy, where are you?'

But Isobel couldn't go in.

Later she shut the door and went away.

EIGHT

Isobel glanced at the production office clock again. Ten minutes to ten. She continued to riffle through *Matchstick Maidens*, Professor Sarum Stanley's book on painter L.S. Lowry's hidden women – those works which, after his death, had been taken to the National Westminster Bank in Manchester and sealed in a vault. She should have read the book the night before so she'd be ready to interview the author who was due at Radio Brum in a few minutes.

'Lowry—' she furiously wrote now '– born 1887 in Salford, died 1976 Glossop—'

'There's a call on my line for you, sweetie!' shouted Vernon Strutt-Walker. His hair was getting lighter and lighter. His alabaster skin, which appeared unremarkable when contrasted with brown locks, had taken on a frightful luminosity. 'Designer slug,' Jacko Marshall called the whole effect, but only when he was sure Vernon could overhear him. 'Sweetie!'

'Carol Ann—' Isobel was writing. Now where did Lowry meet that kid? 'All right! All right!' She put on a kicked-off high-heel shoe as she hopped across the production office.

'Have I caught you at a bad time?' It was Bruno Seuret.

'Up to my eyes. May I ring you back?'

'No need. Just to ask you if I can take you out for a meal on Friday night? Pick you up around seven?'

'You're sure?'

'Of course I'm sure.'

'All right. Fine. Lovely. Look forward to it.'

'See you Friday.'

'Who is that gorgeous *homme*?'

'How do you know he's gorgeous?'

'The voice, sweetie. Whatever you do with him don't bring him on the station. Hilary might give him your job. Worse still, he might give him mine.'

'Who has been calling the Town Hall Press Office!' shouted Velma Blood, the production office secretary.

'My darling, we wouldn't presume,' Vernon said. 'And you can tell switchboard Isobel's got a phone of her own. There's a good little girlie.'

'Will you all be quiet!' roared Jacko Marshall, waggling his recciver furiously. 'I can't hear!'

Isobel, back at her desk, began writing again. 'Carol Ann sent Lowry a letter in 1957 and later he caught a bus to Heywood and went to see her—'

This time her phone rang. 'Your guest's down at reception.'

'Oh, shit. Tell him I'll be there in a minute.'

'Isobel, how long's your panto package?' roared Jacko.

'Five.'

'Where the hell is it?'

'In your box. I put it there last night.'

'I can't find it.'

'Well, it's there.' Isobel hopped up.

'Where?'

'There. I'm not your nanny. Look, for God's sake.'

'Somebody's got to be calling the Town Hall,' Velma Blood said, now cradling the receiver between her shoulder and cheek and typing again.

Isobel pushed through the door into the corridor and, when she reached the bottom of the stairs, swerved to avoid a newsroom journalist. Held up in front of his eyes was a piece of copy paper and he was moaning to himself '. . . those clergymen who have publicly declared their opposition to women priests denied causing a split in the Church of England—' his booted feet tapping out the rhythm of his words as he hurried down to Radio Brum's studios.

The programme organizer's door was wide open and as Isobel passed Hilary Winstan called to her: 'A word!'

Hilary rose from behind his desk as she went in. She could smell his aftershave; she also scented danger. 'Do you remember our little chat a week or three back about *Brum Arts?*'

She remembered, but it hadn't been something she'd been able to come to grips with; he'd asked her, she thought, to look for that which was missing. A magic ingredient. Up to now she'd not been able to find that which, apparently, wasn't there. Even thinking that she'd have to think about it had given her headaches. But she nodded.

'I thought I might have heard back from you by now.'

'I haven't quite reeled in the threads yet—'

What exactly had he said at the time? Certain questions might present themselves.

Well, they hadn't.

She looked at him, trying to read his face. What questions?

She then thought of all the questions she'd soon be asking Professor Sarum Stanley; more questions she hadn't got. Answers, she was beginning to think, were far easier.

Jingling coins together in his pockets, he said: 'One could feel that means and objects could be getting out of line.'

All of which was Double Dutch and yet as clear as day. My programme's for the chop in the next schedules, she thought. Or I am. We both.

'We're getting a lot of letters in.'

'Are we? That's a surprise. How many?'

'One or two.'

'Ah. Yes. Perhaps I could see them?'

There. She'd shot herself in the foot. Everybody knew that nobody wrote into arts programmes unless they wanted to be on them. Now she'd have to invent some real listeners and make up letters from them.

She wondered if she could appease him with a double dose of the Lord-I-have-sinned routine but she'd no time for that. Professor Stanley was wait-ing. Though she was aware that this was not what the programme organizer wanted to hear she said:

'I'm afraid I've got a studio booking in a few minutes.'

Hilary picked up his polo mints, wiping tinsel wrapping back as if cleaning blood from a knife. 'Run along. Run along. We can have our chat another time. Soon though. Soon.'

She flew out and down the corridor to Radio Brum's reception desk which was on the ground floor.

She'd no difficulty in recognizing the professor and she almost groaned aloud. He was an etiolated figure in a battered leather overcoat. An extremely long multi-coloured scarf – knitted for him by some passionate girl student? – was wrapped about a long neck. Fuzzy grey hair haloed his head and in profile he presented a complete circle, forehead and chin curving away from a beak nose.

Ripples of leather coat and scarf spun like the materials of a magician's cloak as he turned moodily towards her. 'There you are,' he said. 'I presume it's you?'

'I'm sorry I've kept you waiting.'

'Are you? Are you indeed? Well then, dearie, lead on.'

'We've a few minutes before our studio booking,' she told him. 'I'll take you up to the production office. We can clear our lines of communication.'

'Can we? You mean you haven't read my book?'

'Of course not.' She paused. 'I mean, naturally I've read your book.'

'I might as well see the TV people while I'm here. Perhaps you can pass me along later?'

'I'm afraid I can't do that, professor. You'll have to ask your publishers to get in contact with them separately.'

'Hardly efficient.'

'This way.'

'And what do you think of the rent collector's work?' The question curled like a whip lash over her head.

Isobel paused at the top of the stairs. She looked down at him. 'I hope in the little time we have you'll tell our listeners what you think of Lowry. Wouldn't you judge my opinion to be irrelevant?'

Suddenly he chuckled. 'All right, dear. Fair enough.'

Isobel took him down to the production office, got him a paper cup of coffee and then asked: 'Perhaps you can give me a little more on your personal background?' In her experience biographers always preferred to talk about themselves rather than the subject of their books. It was, she'd discovered, a good place to begin.

'Haven't my publishers sent you the bumph?'

'First hand information is preferable. Wouldn't you say?'

'Is it? Is it now?'

Her phone rang. 'Hell—' she muttered and picked up the receiver.

No-one spoke. The line went dead.

'We must press on—' and she dropped the receiver back.

When she'd finished covering a page with notes about him, he began to call her by her proper name for the first time. He also gave her a compliment. 'You write with extraordinary rapidity, Miss Maccabee.'

She found it pleasing not to feel frost-bitten every time he looked at her. She smiled and said: 'Now shall we move on to your work – not only the book, of course, but the *Matchstick Maidens* exhibition coming up at the *Look Here* gallery in Birmingham—'

'Ah. You want to know why so many of Mr Lowry's dolly birds lost their heads?'

'And those grotesque collars he draws on some of them. In your work on him you say those are instruments of torture.'

'So I do. So I do.' He was now quite jocular. 'Perhaps he just found women a pain in the neck.'

Her phone went again. 'Damn.'

'Mummy,' said Anne-Marie. 'Mummy, I'm here.' The phone went dead.

She put the receiver down and stared at it. She scratched her neck.

'Yes. Dolly birds—' she said to Professor Stanley. She picked up the line of questioning as if the phone call had never interrupted it, but before she took him down to the studio, she rang the switchboard. 'I'd a call about five minutes ago. Do you know if it was external? Did you handle it?'

'Sorry. Busiest time of the day.'

'Thanks.'

'Mummy, I'm here.' A remote part of her construed her daughter's words as terrifying and yet she was quite unable to feel her terror.

117

She found herself continuing to act as if she'd never heard Anne-Marie's voice.

'I'm looking for one or two good descriptions of the drawings. I know you won't fall into this trap, professor – but many people do forget that all listeners can do is listen. Of course you won't have any problems,' she told him firmly. 'Not a man like you, thank goodness. All this seems to come naturally to you. Have you done much broadcasting?'

'Well, no. None to speak of. Not at all. I'll have to place myself entirely in your hands.' Believing in the truth of this assessment of his situation, his attitude towards her shifted even further. Isobel, to her surprise, found doors opened for her and was even asked, in a tone which suggested he would value her opinion: 'And what do you think of my little work?'

'It's a very questioning book,' she heard herself saying, questions being very much on her mind that morning.

'Exactly. Exactly. Jolly good. Jolly good.'

She felt he'd given her eight out of ten; she suspected that he himself was the only human being he'd award ten out of ten to, and then only rarely. But she smiled at him and this apparent mutual admiration society found a studio. The glow of goodwill even survived the total destruction of the professor's set lecture on Lowry.

'Not at all a bad piece,' she said when she'd stopped the tape and she meant it. 'Congratulations.'

'One got over the main points, don't you think?' And he showed a lot of very large teeth when he grinned. Aware of being totally in control of his situation again, he added: 'That's it then, dear. Time's up. I must go on. There are those telly people.'

'I can't help you there, I'm afraid. You could try their reception desk. It's on the other side of the foyer to ours. I'll take you down—' and she did so before he could ask for a copy of the interview they'd just taped, or a personal meeting with the manager of the station or a five-figure fee for his broadcasting expertise – or all three.

Later she and Fanny Wragg went up to the canteen for lunch and Fanny asked her: 'Did you know that they're going to completely re-jig the schedules in the New Year? Vernon Strutt-Walker told Sunita in the newsroom that Jacko Marshall would be coming off the late afternoon show.'

Isobel was too wise to ask her if she'd heard anything about *Brum Arts*. But as they dissected Jacko and his show, she found herself wondering if Fanny had rung up and said: 'Mummy, I'm here.'

Or was it the designer slug?

No, she remembered. He'd been in the production office at the time.

Her fingers twitched on the handle of the fork.

Annie's alive.

'They say the news editor is bonking reception.' Fanny had moved on. 'Personally, duckie, I don't believe a word. That female wouldn't bonk anything earning less than twenty thousand a year.'

'They're putting up the Christmas decorations already.' Isobel had only just noticed the first flush

119

of glitter beginning to dangle from the canteen ceiling. 'I'd forgotten all about Christmas.'

She wasn't struck down until mid-afternoon.

She was looking in her contact book for the number of the Birmingham Hippodrome when the page began to blur. Strings snapped and her heart fell out of its cage of ribs. She was left unbeating, heartless.

A silent scream formed in her head. There was no breath to let it out.

Her heart jolted to life again. It pumped out a continuous sweat of horror.

She staggered up from her chair. Pain shot down an arm. Her knees rattled into each other.

I can't believe it, she thought.

It's not happening.

I was all right a minute ago.

I'm having a heart attack.

I'm dying.

Twisting from the waist, desperately gulping for air. Waiting for her last gasp. Seeing the shiny edge of a grey filing cabinet slur away and the velvet bow in Velma Blood's hair lurch into sight. That was replaced by Jacko Marshall's see-sawing bow tie.

Her knees sliding together in an effort to prop up her sagging body.

I'm dying.

One hand flung out, clutching at nothing.

Help.

I'm dying.

Help me.

Not one of these words able to find a way out through her horror.

I can't die here.

In this room.

Bow tie. Filing cabinet. A trivial casual nothing. An organizational end.

Rain, sky, wind, sun.

That's the way to go.

Heart dropping down, down, down and she with it. Spiralling florescent tubes, a thread of station output, the black-coated square steel leg of her desk.

Jacko saying: 'She's drunk? She's drunk.'

'Isobel—'

'She's had a heart attack.'

'Don't talk rubbish.'

'Get the sister, Velma. Get the sister.'

'Isobel—' Her head pulled into a lap of denim and the designer slug looking down at her with eyes not in the least sluggish. They were bright with curiosity. 'Do you hurt? Where does it hurt?'

'My heart—' she managed to whisper at last.

'Nonsense,' said Jacko.

'Shut up,' said Vernon. 'Your heart, sweetie? Is that what you said?'

'Heart. Women don't have hearts. She's as drunk as a skunk.'

'Can't you get her up?'

'Better wait until sister arrives.'

'Move the tape machine, can't you? Give her room to breathe.'

'Has she got a pulse?'

'It's the change. I knew a girl of twenty-five who went on the change.'

'I wonder if the engineers could fix something.'

'Engineers?'

'You know. Electric current. Bang. That's what they do in hospital. It restarts the heart.'

'Oh, do shut up, Fanny,' Vernon said. 'There's a pulse all right. Going like the clappers. Going crazy.'

'Are you sure? Oh, you don't do it like that. You're hopeless.'

'Of course you do. I know how to take a pulse.'

'Switch the lights on,' Isobel told them.

'They're on, Isobel. They're on.'

But she was now unconscious.

NINE

The light was on in the bedroom of Samson Cottage, but the curtains weren't drawn. Isobel was propped up on a pile of white pillows, arms stretched out stiffly in front of her. Fingers whispered as they quivered on the blue candy striped duvet. Her GP, Bryan Sanscrit, was sitting on a cane-seated Victorian papier mâché chair. He'd asked for her story and she'd told him, holding nothing back. After examining her, he'd put his instruments back in his leather bag. He was looking at her; she wasn't looking at him. She felt guilty. She ought to be well and was not.

Her heart pumped out horror at over two hundred beats a minute.

'It's happened to you before, hasn't it? You know what it is. An acute panic attack.'

'That was a long time ago. Four years ago. Five.'

'After your daughter died.'

'Yes.'

'You went into a psychiatric hospital.'

'Yes.' She remembered sitting on a chair in the middle of the room at the hospital, her judges in front of her; the consultant psychiatrist, the registrar, the houseman, the psychiatric social worker and, by the door, the ward sister. 'Agitated endogenous depression. I'm not sure I could cope a second time.'

'How long were you in hospital?'

'Three months.'

'Mummy, I'm here.' That's what Anne-Marie had said.

'They asked me – at the hospital . . . or did Doctor Rainbow ask me later, at the clinic? . . . They wanted to know if I heard voices. I've never heard voices. And I've never hallucinated. A girl from work, Fanny Wragg, also saw the Paddington Bear. At the time my car was being mended and she gave me a lift home.'

He said nothing.

She said: 'I suppose it all sounds highly unlikely. Even I think it's highly unlikely. Why should anyone do this to me? It's much more reasonable to suppose I'm going crazy. I see that. And if I'm not going crazy I soon will be. I can't get that voice on the telephone out of my head.'

'What voice?'

'My daughter's. Anne-Marie.'

'She's dead.'

'Yes. I know.'

'And you no longer have the Paddington Bear.'

'Someone broke in and took it.'

'Exactly when did you hear of your husband's death?'

And suddenly she couldn't remember because it seemed to her he'd been dead a very long time.

Dead to her at any rate. 'I think about three weeks ago. It must be that. Yes.'

'How did you feel about that?'

Did she care the rat had died? No. Yes. Of course not.

'Mixed feelings?'

'I suppose so.'

'How are things going at work?'

'Well. Fine. OK. I've got my own arts programme, you know. And I do stuff for the general output too.'

'Everything's OK there?'

'Certain questions might present themselves,' Hilary Winstan had said – a man who appeared to have so little blood in his veins he might be after hers. How could such a bloodless creature survive otherwise? 'Well, I suppose I'm not at the top of my form. More trying to get by. All this has well – the ground seems to be going from beneath my feet.'

She leaned further back in her pillows. Her night-dress was already sticking to her. She noticed that he observed this even though her eyes were closing slightly. The terror would soon seep into the sheets, into the bed itself. As Charlie had been unable to stand her terror, she'd learned how to operate on two levels. She could appear to be quite normal, answer all questions, remark on the weather, smile; she could do all this while silently screaming her head off. She'd perfected the art of being quite all right while in a state of nameless dread.

He said: 'You think someone broke in and put your daughter's Paddington Bear on the rocking-chair. Then took it away again?'

'I found him gone.' Her eyes opened wide again as she viewed in her mind the bereft arms of the rocking-chair.

'And then someone pretending to be your daughter rang you at work?'

'Yes.'

'And you've no idea who did this.'

'If Charlie were . . . but he's dead. I've no idea. None at all.'

'And you haven't been in touch with the police.'

'I don't think they'd believe me. I don't think you believe me. I hardly believe it myself. It doesn't make any sense. It's almost easier to suppose I'm going mad.'

'Are you?'

'No.' She paused and stared at the small night-shrouded window. The old crown glass was rippled. Globs of rain reflected light like river water. The silence between them lengthened.

Eventually she added: 'I didn't think I was mad the last time. I thought I was in the psychiatric hospital under false pretences. I felt I shouldn't be taking up a bed at all. Depriving others who needed it. One does not, you know, really suppose oneself to be crazy. However crazy one is.' She moved sharply against the pillows. 'All I can say is that what I told you about the bear and the phone call is the truth.'

She looked at him for the first time. 'I know you

126

don't know that. But I know it. Someone is persecuting me. Why I don't know. All I can say is I really believe I'm quite sane now, at this moment, in spite of . . . well, the panic. But what is happening to me might drive me over the edge again. Probably will if you want the truth.'

'Could you go and stay with someone else for a while?'

'No. My parents are dead. I've a sister but she lives in Australia.' She watched him as he pulled the prescription pad out of his pocket. He was a comparative newcomer to the village, a slight fresh-faced youngster. He seemed anxious and she realized he felt out of his depth.

'I'm going to prescribe some tranquillizers,' he said. 'Just to hold you for now. I'd like to get in touch with a psychiatrist. How do you feel about that?'

'All right,' she said. And then: 'Can you get in touch with Doctor Rainbow at the clinic in Birmingham? He said he'd see me again. I'd prefer that to one of the hospital psychiatrists.' She paused. 'You really feel I need to see someone?'

'Yes.'

'I could lose my job.'

'I'm sure you won't.'

'I suppose I'll lose it anyway if I keep collapsing on them.'

'I am going to keep you off work for a week. Just until we're more sure how things are going. I'll get in touch with Doctor Rainbow tomorrow. I'll try for an emergency appointment.'

Now his decisions were made his anxiety was gone. He was already half-standing. 'Is there someone who can get the prescription made up for you?'

'Drue Lycett-Green. She'll send Mrs Bennett for me. I'll ring her tomorrow.'

'That's fine. I'm going to give you a couple of pills now to help you relax. I'll drop in again tomorrow afternoon. You stay where you are. I'll find you a glass of water.'

She lay listening to the hammer of her heart; in the past it had gone on like this for days. If that happened again she knew she'd become so weak that she wouldn't be able to walk down the village street. Or was that caused by agrophobia? The symptoms of dread – and they were many – crowded about her like waiting vultures.

I can't do it, she thought.

I can't go through it all again.

She could hear the doctor moving about downstairs and the tap being run. He was much better than many she'd encountered when she'd been ill the last time. Most medical men, she'd discovered, didn't have the imagination necessary to really believe in madness. They felt it was a conjuring trick, that they were being bamboozled. The patient was a conjurer; a less than honest man with a less than honest complaint.

But, she felt, Bryan Sanscrit had tried. Of course I've more experience than he has, she thought now. I know I might be going crazy, but I'm not crazy yet. I know that because I know what it was like when I was crazy.

128

I can't face all that again, she thought.

Somehow, in some way, she must move through her terror and reconstruct the ground beneath her feet. She had to get going again; she had to find out who was persecuting her before she was destroyed.

She'd come up against a hard-edged truth she'd recognized before. She wanted to survive.

But now she was listening to that vulnerable heart of hers. It was still pumping terror.

'Here you are.' The doctor arrived with the glass. He gave her two pills. 'Now drink up. There's a good girl,' said this fellow who was at least five years younger than she was. But I mustn't mind, she told herself. He really is doing his best. She was grateful for his tablets and hopeful they'd bring oblivion.

I should have done more for Anne-Marie, she thought.

I should have saved her.

I shouldn't have let her die.

Where did I go wrong?

Charlie had been a believer. 'Into God's keeping—' He'd chosen those words to be written on his child's tombstone.

But what if you were without a god? Into whose keeping could a godless woman commit her child?

In these last days I've felt her so near to me.

'Have you swallowed both tablets?'

She nodded her head.

'Of course I only came to the village two years ago. I never knew your daughter, but she's not forgotten you know. Far from it. People still talk about her. I gather she was an extraordinarily pretty child.'

'She took after her father.' There was no trace of irony in Isobel's voice. 'She was beautiful.'

'I'll be in to see you tomorrow.'

'Doctor—'

'Yes?'

'Thank you.'

After he'd gone she lay and listened to her terrified heart, feeling she would die, but knowing from experience she would not. There was, too, the familiar agitation in her joints and the sweating itchiness of feet which wanted to run away, but had nowhere to run to.

Little by little, though, she felt a drowsiness begin to glue her racing blood together. She adhered to the bed like a frantic fly solidifying in jelly.

She was afraid of the approaching dark, feeling she would meet her daughter there. Was Anne-Marie in the process of becoming something other? My demon, she thought.

My cause for dread.

'Mummy, I'm here.' She saw herself putting the receiver down and turning back to the professor.

Evil, she thought. My child and I are being woven into something obscene.

Now she began to fight the approaching darkness. Nevertheless it enveloped her.

Waking, she was surprised to find peace in herself. Very carefully she examined this state and realized her heart was beating normally again.

Terror had left her.

She wriggled her toes.

She flexed her hands.

Yes.

Dread was gone.

I must make use of this. I must think. I have to find out who is trying to destroy me.

She immediately fell asleep again.

In her dream she was on the threshold of the baby's bedroom in the bungalow, only now the bedroom was in her own house. She couldn't enter, she realized, because in reality this room was the compartment of her freezer and if she went in she'd catch her death of cold.

Someone, she knew, was already in there, but she couldn't tell whether it was Anne-Marie or the second Mrs Maccabee. The cold had turned who-ever it was into an ice cube.

Then, though she was still outside the freezer which was the bedroom in the bungalow, she felt the pain of cold in her hand. The ice cube was melting through her fingers. Soon whoever it was would have slipped away.

She woke with a jolt.

She'd knocked over the glass of water the doctor had left at her bedside. She immediately found herself listening to her heart beat. It was normal.

Am I going to be all right?

I'm going to be all right.

She looked at the clock. It was gone eleven in the morning. Swinging her legs out of bed, she lowered her toes on to the Kalim rug. She pulled on her towelling robe and went to turn on the central heating and make some tea. Every five minutes or so she stopped what she was doing and checked that untrustworthy heart of hers. It was quiet again, wonderfully quiet. And as it was no longer frightened to death, nor was she. She was, in fact, fine. She was hungry.

Eating her tea and toast curled in an armchair in the living-room, she saw the quite unmistakable turban of Drue Lycett-Green passing the window. Behind her, a hand-knitted beret riding on springing curls, was Joan Bennett.

She went to the door to let them in.

'You're up,' grunted Drue. 'She's up, Mrs Bennett.'

'Don't you start gabbling. You concentrate on your walking. If I don't watch you, you'll be falling over giving me more worry and work.'

'One has no intention of falling over, Mrs Bennett. Stop fussing, woman.'

'Rightie-oh, Drue. Leg up. Over we go.'

'It's a step, Mrs Bennett. Not a stile. One can manage a step without a lot of faffing about.'

And she and Joan Bennett huffed and puffed into the cottage. Isobel installed Drue in her armchair, aware as she did so that both women were sizing her up.

'Well, she's not too bad, Mrs Bennett. A good colour. A very nice colour, my dear,' she complimented Isobel.

'You always were an optimist. That's what I say to this new young sawbones who has come to tell his grandmother how to suck eggs. "If Drue weren't such an optimist she'd be dead. She doesn't know when she's beat. That's always been her trouble." Now Isobel. I hear tell of a prescription and who is to go but me? And there'll be some shopping I don't doubt, ducks. I see I've got my work cut out for me today.'

'No rings under your eyes,' Drue was still examining Isobel. 'Well. I don't know what I expected, my dear. But what I didn't expect was for you to be in the pink.'

'The eye's a deceiving instrument,' said Joan Bennett. 'Not to say a downright liar. What could that young sawbones be hopping about for if Isobel weren't badly?'

'I'll get my prescription. It's very kind of you, Mrs Bennett—' and Isobel left the pair of them to their double act. Most of the village now regarded Drue and Mrs Bennett as more of a couple than Mr and Mrs Bennett. 'Of course Mr Bennett has got 'is 'ead screwed on good and proper and leaves 'em well alone. They do say the old lady's worth a mint and it won't be buried with her, will it?' Isobel had been told only last week when she'd bought her small harvester loaf in the Bessie Bunn bakery in Main Street.

After Mrs Bennett had been despatched on her errands, Isobel told Drue what had been happening.

'You're not to mind, my dear, but I'm going to interfere. I was on the bench a good few years as you know and I've still got some jolly good contacts. I'm going to ring up Superintendent

Entwistle. I've nothing against Doctor Sanscrit – well, nothing that a few more years won't cure. But the chap is still wet behind the ears. You're as sane as I am, my dear. And I'll let you in on a secret. I'm horribly sane. The nearness of my end seems to have sharpened up all my faculties. Instead of going dim of eye and weak of head, things seem to have got clearer and clearer until they're almost unbearable. I've never seen straighter – and I can perfectly well see there's nothing wrong with your sanity. The only thing you're in need of is a bit of help from your friends. I'll get on to Superintendent Entwistle and you won't dissuade me from doing so. It's time we started to do really sensible things.'

'Do you really think we should call the police in?'

'Don't be ridiculous, my dear. They should have been called in at the beginning. But leave it to me. I'll do it. I know the right people. And that's always an insurance for a more comfortable life, my father used to say. Though I have to admit some of the right people wouldn't know him. In those days being in trade was rather looked down on.'

'I suppose you might be right about the police.'

'I know I am. What worries me is how long you – or anyone else for that matter – can stand up to this sort of pressure.'

'Not long, judging from what happened yesterday.'

'Quite. And just having the police ask a few questions might stop it all.'

'I did a bit of law-breaking myself,' said Isobel and told her of her visit to Blackpool. 'I felt quite dreadful about it later. Her baby's room, you know.'

'Did you find out where she was?'

'No. I assume she's staying with her parents. They live nearby in St Anne's.'

'I still wouldn't rule her out,' said Drue. 'Grief can make people very angry.'

'Bruno Seuret found a few of Anne-Marie's toys in their stable. Anyone could have stolen some of her things. I suppose I must do something about the rest of them. But I don't even want to think about it.'

'You should get rid of them.'

'Yes. I suppose so.'

'And when someone from the police does come round, try and be sensible. Don't mention all this psychiatric business. The object is to get someone off his backside. One wants something done about it.'

'But they're bound to find out, Drue.'

'No doubt. By that time, though, they could have got moving. They might scare off who is actually doing this. They could even find out who the culprit is. Please don't get on your high horse about this. You can be so jolly unreasonable you know.'

'I'm not going to get on my high horse. I think I pretty well know the score. The trouble is that, however truthful you're being, if you don't expect to be believed – well, people don't believe you.'

'But I believe you, Isobel.'

'Yes. I know.'

'You make things very difficult for most people

you know. The real trouble is you've no belief in yourself. You don't trust yourself.'

'I don't suppose I do—' Listening to herself again; the untrustworthy heart of the matter.

'If you've no faith in yourself, how can people believe in you?'

'It was all that happened I suppose. Anne-Marie and Charlie . . . I lost faith.'

'Most people have a quite false idea of themselves, but at least they believe in what they think they are and they usually manage to convince a lot of others into the bargain. You seem to have no idea of yourself at all.'

Isobel smiled. 'I'm a bit tentative, I agree.'

'But you got going again. You made a new life for yourself.' Drue was considering this.

'Sheer bloody cussedness.'

'I did look at your Tarot. And your talismen turned up as always. The lightning-struck tower. The wheel of fortune. And the empress. God knows what it means.'

'A fine fortune-teller you are,' Isobel laughed.

'You're such a jolly unquiet spirit. A will-o'-the-wisp.'

'What does the vicar think of all this dabbling of yours?'

'What should he think? It is, after all, based on the teaching of the Gnostics. The truth to tell is that the clergy aren't too bright. They must go down straight and narrow roads nose to tail, nose to tail. Most don't even have enough imagination to be good.'

'What does Simeon Kelso say when you tell him that?'

Drue winked and straightened her turban. 'I keep mum, my dear. I wouldn't upset him for the world. I have every intention of being buried in Simeon's churchyard. And I want a very enthusiastic funeral service too. No whey-faced pap. So I butter the man up like mad. Anyway, one should never lay one's cards on the table with a vicar. He might take it into his head to try and save your soul. Then things can get frightfully sticky. Thoroughly off colour.'

They both turned and looked at Joan Bennett's woolly beret as it passed the window.

'She's not having my diamonds.'

'You're not dead yet.'

'Quite so. And I'll get in another five years if I can. That really will be one in the eye for the Bennett tribe.'

TEN

Bruno Seuret backed his blue Volvo into a vacant space in the car park behind Woolworths. Isobel turned up her jacket collar before getting out. It was a very windy night. An agitated moaning came from the branches of trees which lined Minster Pool a short distance away. On the farther bank the floodlit edifice of Lichfield Cathedral reared into a starless moonless dark.   •

'I don't think it's quite cold enough for snow.' Bruno's raincoat tails flapped as he bent to lock the car.

'B-r-rrr-rh—' said Isobel and was taken by surprise as he caught her up and took her hand in his. They hurried through the car park and down a side alley which separated a chain store from a block of small shops in Market Street. Paper bowled along on currents of air; puddles surged and shifted.

'I feel terribly guilty, you know.' They'd hesitated before crossing a pedestrian precinct. 'Sneaking off to dinner with you when I'm on the sick list.' His hand tightened on hers. They hurried to the other side and went down a shopping arcade. Facing them was a line of Tudor and Georgian

138

buildings which had been turned into business premises; estate agents, dentists, cafés, shops, building society branches. Criss-crossing from one side of the street to the other were wires from which unlit bulbs dangled, jiggling in the wind. 'They'll soon be switching on the illuminations.'

'You make much more of Christmas than we do in France,' he said. 'We never go out to buy presents until Christmas Eve. Things don't really start moving until the night of Christmas Day. Then everyone stays up and makes a terrible din. We need St John's Street, don't we?' He'd suggested they go to a Chinese restaurant located there. 'I've never managed to acquire a taste for Indian food,' he'd told her. 'Of course we don't have Indian restaurants in France. I suppose all this Tandoori chicken is a leftover from the British Raj. We're stuck with couscous. Lamb and semolina. A legacy of our African days.'

'There's English,' she'd said.

'Yes,' he'd said.

'Chinese then,' she'd agreed.

The restaurant he'd chosen was in the old part of the city. There were stone flags on some of the floors and – across from the new bar with its Chinese lanterns – a row of small Gothic windows. One of the kitchen walls was plate glass so those customers who wanted could watch the Chinese cooks choreographing woks and flames.

'The awful thing is there have been no re-occurrences. No more panic attacks. I shouldn't be off work at all. Perhaps the very thought of seeing a psychiatrist again has put me back on track.'

The beer they'd ordered with the meal came and as the waiter arranged it on mats, Bruno asked: 'Will you still go?'

'Yes.'

'That's very positive.'

'I'm terrified of going over the edge again. Seeing Doctor Rainbow – well, it's a bit like taking out some insurance.'

'Someone to hold your hand?'

'Yes.'

'Won't friends do?'

'Friends are great, but some have difficulty in coping. At least, that's my previous experience. Someone uninvolved – someone you don't have to worry you're putting too much strain on – well, that's good.'

'It's a bloody awful business,' he said. 'Obscene.' The waiter had come back and was clearing a place for hot plates and finger bowls. 'Earlier you were saying something about Drue Lycett-Green?'

'Oh, yes. She got in touch with a police superintendent friend of hers for me. I was expecting someone very grand to come round. In fact two plain-clothes constables turned up – a woman and a man. I must say they were very conscientious. The policeman did a quick check of doors and windows. Apparently I'm reasonably secure.'

'The police *are* going to do something?'

'I honestly don't know.'

'It strikes me that anyone who goes to the lengths of breaking and entering a house twice is a pretty determined character. For most people that takes a lot of nerve.'

'I don't think you have to be that determined.' Isobel was thinking that she'd found it all too easy to break into Sandra Tiptree's bungalow.

'I'd like to get my hands on him,' said Bruno; his muscles had tightened.

Isobel realized with a sense of shock that she'd acquired a knight errant. I hardly even know the man, she thought. I don't even know if I like him. Yes. I know that. But I'm not ready for a love affair. And he can't be either; he's not divorced his wife yet. She said: 'I've been thinking what to do about the things you found in your stable.'

'Do you want them?'

'I think it would be best if you destroyed the toys.' She paused. 'I wish you wouldn't tell me how though.'

He looked at her.

'What point could there possibly be in keeping Anne-Marie's things?'

'No,' he said. 'No point.'

'Do you mind getting rid of them for me?'

'Not at all. I've a lot of stuff to clear out before I leave.'

'Was Caro with you last Christmas?'

'No. She'd already gone. I went back to France. But this year I'm staying. The house is sold and there're a lot of things to do. I'll be moving in with friends when the contracts are exchanged.'

'When will that be?'

'Towards the end of January.'

'So it will be your last Christmas. Where do you come from in France?'

'North of Paris originally. But my father suffered from arthritis and eventually we moved south to Menton. It's on the border with Italy. Too far east to be the Côte d'Azure, but there are plenty of old ladies clanking gold chains and walking little dogs. It's all toffee pink *fin de siècle* and shades of Katherine Mansfield. My father bought a bookshop there. It's hard work, but it does well.'

'It sounds wonderful. Why on earth did you leave?'

'Far too provincial for an eager young man with intellectual pretensions. Now I'm middle-aged and I've acquired the English disdain for intellectuals. But anyway I must go back or the bookshop will have to be sold. My father's dead now and my mother can't manage the business on her own.'

'The only thing that surprises me is that Caroline didn't drag you back across the channel by the scruff of your neck years ago. Most people would love to live in the South of France.'

'Well, Caro has her design business. And she made it quite clear she wasn't going to leave it. I could hardly blame her. She's worked very hard and it's all paying off. On the other hand, teaching kids French can get grindingly repetitive after a few years. I won't be sorry to start a new career.'

'I'm just hoping to cling on to my job,' she said.

'Things a bit tough there?'

'Well, it's always been a case of dog eat dog. I'm

afraid it does tend to bring out the worst in people. I don't think broadcasters are more awful than anyone else. But if you always feel you're next in line for the firing squad it does make you a less than happy soul.'

'It can't be that bad.'

'I'm afraid it is. Most of us are on short term contracts or free lance. Here today. Gone tomorrow. Actually I don't mind that much. I sort of fell into the job. I'm not even sure I want to be a broadcaster.'

'It sounds a wonderful life to me. You should try teaching some of my kids what an infinitive is!'

And now, suddenly she was looking at him. Their glances met in that slyly gleeful way which revealed much which she would rather hide. She twisted her wedding ring only to find the ring no longer there.

The waiter, bearing the first courses of their meal, came between them.

Later, when he drove her home, she worried that she'd given him cause to suppose she'd welcome his advances. And this agitated her. Ever since Charlie she'd feared intimacy. Now she edged a little further from him and answered him abruptly. She wanted him to understand that this had been a pleasant evening and she'd enjoyed herself, but that it would end with her door closed against him. She couldn't, of course, tell him this for he hadn't done anything except hold her hand on the way to and from the restaurant. What could be more chaste? More ridiculously old-fashioned?

Nevertheless she moved even further from him, dragging her knees together.

As he swung the Volvo into Main Street he said: 'There's no need to be nervous. I'm not going to leap on you. I want to, but I won't. I'll be entirely honourable and drop you at your front door.'

'I'm not nervous,' she snapped.

'Aren't you?'

'Just tired.'

'Tired?'

'I hardly know you.'

He stopped the car in front of the alley. 'But you don't mind if we become better acquainted?'

'No.'

'Good.' He leaned over and kissed her. She knew straight away that what she'd suspected was true. He was her kind of man. Just like Charlie, she thought, still alive to the crackle of feeling which had passed between them.

He pulled away so he could look at her. 'I won't say anything,' he said. 'I'm afraid you'll run for it.'

She wasn't at all sure she could stop herself from crying. She fumbled with the door and got out. 'Good night.' She was a little unsure on her legs, as if she'd just stepped on to dry land after a long sea voyage.

'I'll give you a ring,' he said.

She stood and watched him drive away. 'Damn,' she muttered as she turned to the cottage.

She opened the front door, listening out for the tick of the grandfather clock; tonight it didn't seem as welcoming. It reminded her she was getting older.

There must be something wrong with him, she thought, or Caro wouldn't have left him. And then she thought, perhaps he wonders why Charlie left me?

She took off her jacket, made herself some tea and carried it up to bed with her. After undressing she went through the study to the bathroom. On her way back she saw that the rocking-chair was caught in a pool of moonlight. It was a very ordinary nineteenth-century rush-seated chair. Charlie had bought it for her after the birth of their baby. The lower rails of the back were divided from the upper by a stout cross bar; one of the rockers was slightly different from the other because at some time it had been replaced. There was a poker-work Victorian cushion on the seat and a small matching cushion hung down from the top rail.

Isobel found herself drawn to the chair, as if in resting in those arms, in filling them, she could become all that was missing. She gently set the rockers in motion, her flesh moulding itself to accommodate the child sucking at her breast.

Rock-a-bye

Rock-a-bye

Cloud bowled across the moon.

When all the light was gone she got up.

What do I care about a Frenchman? she thought. Or my job? Or anything?

When she went to bed she became conscious of her unshed tears; they were a weight behind her eyes which seemed so heavy that they would topple her head. She was so used to her grief that for most of the time she was unaware it was there, so near the surface and yet usually hidden even from herself.

She then remembered that for some inexplicable reason she'd felt like crying after he'd kissed her.

She listened to the howl of wind in the chimney and after a while laid herself down to sleep. It is easy really, she thought, you simply have to go on. One foot goes in front of the other. Go on.

In the morning she could recall sitting in the rocking-chair, but she'd no memory of unshed tears.

It was so dark she ate her breakfast with the light on. The phone rang just as she was about to put her anorak on and go down to the bakery for a loaf.

'Hello, duckie,' said Fanny Wragg. 'How are you? I do hope you're feeling better.'

'I'm fine. I've to see the doctor again on Monday and I expect to be back at work on Tuesday.'

'Velma told us you'd be in next week. Vernon's not pleased of course.'

'He's doing my show?'

'The big dick. But the real news is that Jacko Marshall's got the push. They've got some guy in from Wrekin Radio.'

'Poor Jacko.'

'Trust you to miss all the fireworks. You should have been there yesterday. Talk about the smoke of battle. Still, I expect Jacko will survive. Apparently he knows someone at Sound Sounds. There'll always be a bit of free-lance work going somewhere if you're lucky.'

'When does he leave?'

'His contract's got another couple of weeks to run. This new guy Adrian starts on Monday. Vernon reckons he's very good. By the way, Vernon's somehow managed to get an interview with Evelyn Waugh for the arts show. He keeps running into Hilary Winstan's office to tell him.'

'That should make interesting radio.'

'Vernon's cock-a-hoop I can tell you.'

'Fanny, Evelyn Waugh's dead. Didn't they teach you anything at Cambridge?'

'Dead?' Fanny giggled. 'Whoops. But it's a writer called Waugh. That must be good, mustn't it?'

'I expect so.'

'Anyway, I read economics,' said Fanny.

'Would you do me a favour? They wouldn't let me drive home so my car's still down at the broadcasting centre. Can you pick me up on Monday morning and take me in? I want to collect the Golf. I know it's a bloody nuisance, but if the doctor signs me off I've got to have my car for work.'

'Of course, duckie. You know you gave us all a frightful shock. Vernon thought you were about to drop off the perch. What went wrong?'

'I'm not really sure.' Isobel had no intention of letting anyone at the radio station know what happened. If she did, the management might think she'd have a panic attack while she was on air. 'My GP is arranging for me to see a specialist.'

'A heart specialist?'

'A physician. I don't think my GP expects him to find anything.'

'You went an absolutely ghastly colour before you passed out. I'm so glad you're all right really. See you Monday.'

Putting the phone down, Isobel felt thoroughly upset. Of course, lying to Fanny was despicable and she hated the idea of Vernon taking over her programme in her absence, but it was more than that.

Appalled, she realized that when she'd picked up the phone she'd been hoping to hear another voice. Her daughter's voice.

Isobel put on her anorak, her nerveless fingers fumbling with the zip. Collecting her basket, she shut the front door of the cottage and walked down the street to the bakery.

Though it was mid-morning, the gloom was so thick that electric lights shone from many village living-rooms. When she passed the War Memorial at the top of Post Office Road she noticed that Remembrance Sunday wreaths were still piled high on the railed-in triangle of grass. She recalled with a start that when she'd heard the scout band on that November Sunday she'd not yet found the Paddington Bear. It seemed so long ago it was in another lifetime. Now her world was so much darker, as if all colour were draining away. She found herself afraid for she thought it might get darker yet.

She didn't consciously decide to visit Anne-Marie's grave. After she'd bought her loaf she found that, instead of turning back down the alley, her feet moved on up and over the hump-backed bridge which crossed the canal. It was only then that she knew she was going to the church. Along the south wall, near the porch, were grooves where men had sharpened their arrow heads before practising archery in the adjoining Butt Croft. The squat twelfth-century tower, dark against the twilit day, rose above two south-facing thatched cottages. On the other side of the twisting lane were more cottages and the old village school, now an out-door pursuits centre run by the county council. Though the land lay leafless and barely breathing it was full of bird song. A shaft of yellow winter jasmin glowed eerily in the half-light of a sodden garden.

Isobel entered the oldest part of the graveyard by the lych-gate. Here the head stones had been taken up and arranged around a perimeter wall; one of them noted the passing of Matthias Samson, the Victorian tailor who had renamed the cottage in which she lived. For over a thousand years Alrewas's dead had been buried under this turf, though few of the rearranged headstones dated back more than two hundred years for that was when markers had become fashionable. Beneath this grass lay the bones of the village's Doomsday Book inhabitants, twenty villeins, six bordars and a priest, the one hundred local victims of the Black Death, three-year-old Rudolf Bailey, who fell into a pool and died on the night of 24 August 1625, Joy Durham, horribly done to death by her husband John in 1639, Humphrey Swayne who met his end after being bitten by a mad dog and Thomas

Dagley Junior, who drowned in the River Trent in 1752. They were all here, recorded not for the most part in stone, but in the Parish Registers.

The headstones in the new graveyard were planted above their owners; this was a field of flowers for the villagers cared for their dead. Isobel herself had never visited here since Charlie had left but she knew, almost through a process of osmosis, that the village looked after Annie's grave too. It had been Charlie's wish that their child be buried here. His family, originally Jewish, had converted to Christianity in Victorian times – mainly for social reasons, Charlie had told her – and much to everyone's surprise they'd produced an Anglican bishop. Charlie himself, though not sentimental about women or animals, had been apt to shed a tear when unexpectedly hearing the strains of 'Jerusalem', or 'Oh come all ye faithful'. He'd had Anne-Marie christened, taken her while still a babe in arms to church services and later enrolled her at Sunday School. 'Your mother's a heathen,' he'd told the child. 'But we're going to be good, aren't we?' 'Oh, yes, Daddy, yes—' and the inky eyes – Isobel's eyes – had implored her father. 'Oh, yes.'

Thinking of this now, Isobel realized that if Charlie had loved anyone more than himself, then it was Anne-Marie. She had, and she knew it, sometimes been jealous of the way the child had so completely commanded his attention. For much of her marriage it wasn't she who'd kept Charlie at her side, but their child.

She found, to her shame, she wasn't quite sure in which row her daughter lay. And when she first saw Anne-Marie's grave she didn't recognize it. It was only one of a handful which had turned earth on top for most were turfed over. The soil had been recently dug. Not one weed showed above the tilled surface. She had, almost at once, the intuition that the grave had been desecrated in some way and yet at first she didn't know how. Then she identified the flower in the small offering jar; white heather. This symbol of benign fortune smiled up from her child's bones.

Good luck.

Bon voyage.

Happy landings.

She snatched out the heather and took it to the compost heap behind the hedge. Here the graveyard overlooked the canal and as she let the bunch of white heather fall, she saw she was watched by a startled fisherman.

He's as shocked as I am, she thought, as she turned hurriedly away. Who would wish a dead child luck? Another child, not knowing, might. Who had dug and weeded the grave? Well, she knew, didn't she, that Annie had been cared for in the four years she'd lain here? Looking across the graveyard she couldn't see one grave which wasn't tended. The village looked after its own. In fact there was now only one grave without flowers, that of her child. She found that this in some obscure way satisfied her. She didn't want her daughter to receive gifts. She had, after all, not been a good child; she'd died. And she shouldn't have. She shouldn't. She shouldn't.

Isobel, looking again at her child's grave, couldn't cry. But nor could she decipher the words Charlie had caused to be put there – 'Into God's Keeping'. The golden lettering was an incomprehensible blur; anxiety squeezed her heart. She half stumbled as she turned away.

ELEVEN

On the morning she was due to go back to work, Isobel woke very early. The room was dark. The air was hushed. Isobel's eyes were opened to an enormous feeling of expectancy. Expectant joy, she realized. I've been invited to a party, she thought. But there was such a strong sense of having to do something before being allowed to go, that she found herself up and out of bed so she could do it.

Do what? Suddenly she was wide awake. Why am I standing about in my bedroom getting cold?

It was only when she'd climbed back into bed that she realized she was expecting Anne-Marie to call her. And the thing she had to do was not to cut her daughter off as she had last time.

She had to answer her.

No, she thought.

No, no, no.

That way madness lies.

Suddenly she was back in hospital on that very first day. She'd had her knees knocked by the houseman, she'd had the contents of her handbag examined by the ward sister. She'd walked between beds, each and every one of them empty of a suffering body and then escaped from the ward into the washroom.

A thin girl with a halo of bright red frizzy hair had come in. She'd smiled at Isobel and then turned to look in the mirror. She'd licked a finger and brushed back an eyelash. 'I forgot my mascara. I'll have to get Clay to bring it in. My eyes – well, they're no bigger than a pair of pips. They need a bit of something. Know what I mean?' She'd turned back to Isobel. 'Sister James sent me for you. Thought someone had better show you round this dump. Well, this is the lavatory and the washroom as if you didn't know. Through here are the showers and a couple of bathrooms. By the way, you are Isobel? You are the new one?'

'Yes.'

'Rita. Just call me Reet. Most people do.' Rita lit a cigarette and then offered her one.

Isobel shook her head. 'Not at the moment,' she said.

'Christ. I know it's bad for your health. Being a schizo isn't that healthy either. So I think – why worry?' She put the packet back in her patent leather handbag and swung the bag by its gold chain. 'I come in here for a bit of peace and quiet, see. A rest from my old man and the kids. If you've any common you learn the ropes fast, kid. Work the system. Before it works you. I'm a schizo, see? A bona fide nut. Get me? Well, at the start I was innocence itself. They used to slap me under section and pump me so full of bleeding haloperidol I really didn't know whether I was in the middle of next week. Then I got wise. Believe me. You've got to work the system, kid. Now I go off my fruit and nut when it suits my book. When I'm fed up to the back teeth with the kids and Clay and the house-work. When I want to shut off the whole business for a while, see. I act up – back in the old routine – la, la, bleeding la – and wallop! I'm in here and having my meals made and some other poor sod's doing the hoovering and polishing the floors and no kid's hollering down my ear 'ole for its fish fingers and bleeding baked beans. I mean, kiddo – well, you can have too much of that kind of thing. Oh, they don't like you using the baths. They're usually kept locked.'

'Why?'

'Drowning.' Rita opened the door, striding along in bright pink jeans and purple flatties. 'On this block – it's the acute unit – there are two dormitories for the women, two for the men. Nine in each dorm. When they're full, one or two of us get shoved down into the cells. They're behind the sun lounge. They were used in the old days for the strait-jacket types before the major tranquillizers came in. Of course, now they can flatten you so fast they're redundant. Whoever heard of being violent while unconscious? So they decked out the cells with a bit of chintz and pictures of boats and sheep grazing – that kind of thing. They still look like cells. Funny, that. Anyway, you start in a dorm downstairs and when they think you're get-ting a bit better, they transfer you up the apples and pears.'

'Where is everyone?' asked Isobel as they walked down the empty ward, beds made, lockers neat, rows of flowers without owners.

'Occupational therapy. That kind of thing. You never have a minute to yourself in this dump. They keep you as busy as they can. I suppose it's to take your mind off your troubles. Encourage you to be sociable. That kind of stuff. It's a bit like a school, really. There are written rules and unwritten ones.' Rita opened another door. 'This is the room where we do our washing and ironing. They like us to keep our hand in. There's always a queue for the tumble dryer. Why have three washers and one dryer, I'll never know. Don't leave anything of value lying about. It'll get nicked. Anything from knickers to watches. There're always one or two with light fingers. And they've got a copper-bottomed alibi. They're mad. No-one mentions madness, by the way. Generally tends to get people's hair off. In for a rest is OK. Nervous breakdown's fine. You can be depressed, schizophrenic, manic or hypomanic, even plain psychotic. But no-one's mad. Get it?'

'Yes,' said Isobel.

'Well, don't forget. People can be very touchy, I can tell you. Jeez, these shoes are killing me. I bought them in the sales. I thought the buggers would stretch.' She took one off and rubbed the ball of her foot. 'No. Don't mention the word mad, kid. People are even touchy about their sanity when they're not crazy. By the way, everything works in this place as if we're sane down to the last man Jack. But the food's not bad, kid, and of course this dump is out in the country. If you like the birds and the bees and that kind of thing you're well away. Bingo. Darts. A disco now and then. Contrary to what you might hear, most of us don't want to leave. It beats Butlins any day. Some spectacular breakdowns have occurred on the eve of departure. A couple of years ago one of the male patients brained a nurse who was helping him pack. But we all pretend we want to go home and wash the dishes or make cardboard cartons at Barcroft Tapes, because that's what the shrinks want to hear and you have to have lost all your marbles – I mean right down to the last bleeding one – not to keep your shrink happy. They can make your life very unpleasant. Believe me, kid. Always be kind to your shrink, and then maybe he won't stone you out of what mind you've got left. If you take my meaning. And you're speaking to an expert. I've been in and out of these joints all my life. This way.'

'This is the sun lounge. If you want to play darts you've to get them from the sister. Not everyone can play darts you'll be happy to hear. Ping pong. Cards and games in the cupboard. We do bingo in here, too. There's a piano, but it's locked at the moment. We've got a manic in. As I was saying, never cut up. Not if you know what's good for you. Still, you don't look the sort who'd cause trouble. You look like a depressive to me.'

'I don't feel a bit depressed,' said Isobel.

'You don't have to feel depressed to be depressed.

157

This is the dining-room. Gets as cold as brass monkeys. All the glass I suppose. You'd think they were cultivating peaches not nuts. We go on a rota for laying tables and that kind of thing. The rota's pinned up by that door over there. You're supposed to check each night to see if you're down for duties next day. You'll soon get the hang. They let you off for the first couple of days, while you're settling in. The main thing is not to let anyone get you down, kid. Style. It's a great help. Though I've never met a depressive yet who had any sort of style. Miserable buggers. Present company excepted,' she added hastily.

She touched a plastic-topped table. 'Of course it's nothing fancy. No tablecloths or anything like that. You know I can't really say me and my mum got on, but she had style. I'll say that for her. On her deathbed and what did she do? Get my old glad rags, she says. I'm going out in style. And her hardly able to talk, let alone anything else! All of us whining around, but you could see she wasn't about to die in a brushed nylon nightie. Wanted the things she'd worn in her heyday – when she was young and fancy free. Still got half a wardrobe of them too. Never parted easily did my mum.

'Anyway, she wanted her old hobble skirt and a pink jersey with bat wings. Me and my sister got her decked out – wanted her paste, too, her bit of diamante. Dad was in the next room howling like a dog. Thought she'd go straight to the Devil, all tarted up like that. I may not have arrived in style, my mum said. Back Southern Street was never any sort of address. But by Christ, she said, I'm going out in style! And if the Lord God Almighty doesn't like it, he can piss off, she said. Her very last words. I hadn't finished painting her finger nails. Our dad, he was mortally offended. Thought we were all in league with the Old Sod. A bit hot on religion like. Came out when you least expected it. But I remembered, see. They kept telling me I was a schizo. A nut. Bleeding bonkers. Well, I thought, if you're a lunatic you'd better do it in style, my girl. They can't really touch you if you've got style. No-one can. Not bleeding God Almighty. This is the kitchen. We come in here before lights out to make cocoa or what takes your fancy. Three of us do it. That's on the rota too. The day-room's through here.'

'It seems such a big place.'

'Oh, you'll get your bearings in no time. But you'll have to watch it with some of the patients. A few try to be crazier than the rest. They like to shine at what they're good at. If you get my drift. In here the craziest of them all thinks she's queen of the roost. Take it all with a good pinch of salt kiddo. Or you'll be taken for a real ride, believe you me. I don't say I don't have my moments, so to speak. But if you ask me it's abnormal to go through life without slipping off your trolley now and then. Unless you're blind, deaf or stupid . . . well, you're bound to go bananas some time. It stands to reason. Quite nice, this room. Lovely views. If you go in for that sort of stuff.'

Isobel looked down the wide room to the long windows at the bottom. 'Oh, yes.'

'There are hair dryers and rollers and things, and we do each other's hair. We'll have to get our skates on. I'm supposed to have you back at Room 9 by eleven. The big white cheese is coming. You're up for case conference. They look you over when you first come in and two or three times while you're in here. It's him and his hoppos and the psychiatric social worker. She's poison. Some of these types feed off your flesh. But you don't say that, kid, no, or nothing like it. They'll think you've delusions about being eaten by cannibals or some such rubbish.'

She broke off as one of the chairs in the Day Room moved. A large figure rose and turned in their direction. Her nostril on one side was bigger than the other, and there was a livid scar on the nose itself. One eyelid was swollen. The woman absorbed them into the infinity of her blue gaze. She turned, a film in such slow motion that her movement in reality was a miracle of balance. She progressed towards the long windows which overlooked the park.

'Marigold!' Rita called and to Isobel: 'She should be in OT. Still, someone will come along and jolly her up a bit, I expect. Marigold!'

'She moves so slowly it seems impossible she should move at all. I mean, without falling over herself.'

'Retarded depression,' Rita said. 'They used to give them ECT at one time, but Dr Maude's not so hot on ECT. Give me a nice hypomanic any time. Just looking at her is enough to give you the willies.

They say she shot herself with an air pistol. The pellet went right up her nose – God knows how – and before you know it it's in her eye and the retina's detached. She was brought in here from the Eye Hospital. Well, come on or you'll be late for your appointment with God.'

They turned and saw they were being observed by a nurse. 'Hello, Rita. Who's this?'

'Isobel. She's new.'

The nurse nodded and moved briskly across the Day Room to Marigold.

'Oh, I know what she's thinking,' said Rita. 'That Reet. Yak, yak, yak. Talking more than's good for her. Too excited. Better keep an eye on her. Better watch out. A few more twists and, hey presto, on cloud nine before we know where we are. I know what they're thinking before they think it, kid.'

'I'm sure she's only bothered about Marigold,' said Isobel.

'Bit of a queer one, all right, Marigold. What kind of lady is it that goes round toting a pistol? Even if it is only an air pistol,' said Rita. 'Oh. You certainly do get 'em in this dump. Well, come on. I'd better deliver you—' and Rita moved in front of Isobel, her flatties fairly flying over parquet floors.

Isobel found herself at the top of a long corridor. Men and women were gathering at the other end, some sitting in the chairs which lined both walls.

'Getting ready for inspection,' Rita said. 'You just keep your head down. Don't do anything batty. Once it's down on report it's down forever. And the next time you come in, it's taken into account. And the time after that. They're an unforgiving lot of bastards.'

'The next time?'

'People always come back,' said Rita. 'This is our own little niche. I mean, kid, this is what the likes of you and me are good at. Believe me. Not everyone can be mad.' Rita swung the gold chain over her shoulder. 'It's not such a bad little number.'

Isobel looked at the drugged patients shuffling on to their chairs.

'I'll never come back,' she said.

'Some hopes,' said Rita. 'Well, we all have hope don't we, kiddo? At some time or another.'

Isobel, now lying on her bed in Samson Cottage, suddenly found memory scattered into splintering fragments of bird sound. Though it was still dark, darker than it had been for the moon had waned, the dawn chorus had begun.

She turned, comforted by she knew not what, and prepared herself for sleep. Ah yes. 'I'll never come back.' She'd forgotten she'd said that to Rita.

It was a promise, wasn't it?

A promise to herself.

The prayer of her soul.

She turned again and fell into a deep sleep.

TWELVE

Though huge panes of glass ran along the south wall of the production office, all the neon lighting was on. From the ceiling, lines of Christmas cards were suspended on strings. In a corner a large inflated Santa Claus was propped against shelves of archive tapes. Round his neck, on a ribbon, the station's Christmas schedules hung; weeks 49, 50, 51 and 52. Outside was a clammy greyish gloom. Morning was here, but not the light.

'So this is the dark Isobel,' said Adrian Turk, sitting in Jacko Marshall's chair at Jacko Marshall's desk and putting down Jacko Marshall's phone. 'The lady of the arts.' He was wearing his great grandfather's three-piece tweed suit and a shirt his ancestor would never have approved of, navy blue poplin with a white detachable collar. His bow tie was soft toffee pink. He rose, a small slender figure. 'I would kiss you, but one does so worry for one's health these days. One simply never knows where people have been. However, I feel one could risk a shake of the hand.' He held her fingers only and waved them up and down in a parody of a limp-wristed fashion, but there was – of this she was quite sure – nothing limp wristed about Mr

Adrian Turk. A pair of very pale, very intelligent and very cynical eyes were studying her. 'I used to do an arts show myself. I invariably found it amusing. I might like to have another basheroo. Doesn't Birmingham possess dear Simon Rattle? I do so admire his hair.'

'I thought you were presenting Jacko Marshall's late afternoon show.'

'No, no. Oh no. How could you accuse me of such an impertinence? I present *Turk's Teatime Treat*. Jack-my-lad has done a bunk. Gone off in a huff. The naughty boy's broken his contract. His master's voice is none too pleased, I can tell you.'

'Are you really going to call it *Turk's Teatime Treat?*' asked Vernon.

'We all have our foibles. I adore edible sounds.' He looked at Isobel again. 'Naturally I might want to do other things as well. One is not averse to gobbling up one's neighbour's little morsels.'

Was he teasing or was he in earnest? Isobel didn't know him well enough to guess.

'Fanny Wragg's producing his show,' Vernon told Isobel. 'He and Fanny are in their honeymoon period and we must not disturb while they scratch each other's eyes out.'

The Turk ignored Vernon. He said: 'Our Isobel has such an interesting face, don't you think?' And though he was at least ten years younger than she was, he contrived to sound as old as Confucius. 'Fined down. Cerebral. Almost other worldly.'

'Which world might that be?' asked Isobel.

'Ooh. It can bite too, Vernon.'

Hilary Winstan's head grew round the production office door, long and white, like an invasive root. 'Isobel. Good, good. Quite well again? Can you spare a moment?'

Isobel pushed her tottering pile of post further on to her desk and followed him into the corridor. 'What's been wrong?' he asked as he loped along in a waft of aftershave.

'Women's problems.' As she hadn't been away for over a week no sick note would tell another tale.

'All under control now?' Hilary's left nostril had risen a fraction.

'All battened down—' and she skipped out of the way as a Radio Brum news hound bounded by. I could ring Sandra's parents, she was thinking. I could make sure she's with them. Driving to work, Isobel had suddenly remembered that the donkey in the second Mrs Maccabee's garden had sported paniers full of heather.

They turned a corner in the corridor and went into the programme organizer's office. As they did so a body which looked remarkably like the inflated plastic Santa Claus in the production office, but which was undoubtedly made of flesh and blood, crashed by the window. He clung to a bright yellow umbrella.

'He was falling off the roof half of yesterday too,' Hilary complained as they strolled over to the window. 'The television people are doing some kind of spectacular.' Below were cameras and a huge heap of balloon-like objects through which Santa's boots were now slithering. Hilary's teeth jarred. 'I do wish they'd stop it.'

'It's a wonder he hasn't broken his neck,' said Isobel.

'If only they'd do it on the other side of the building. They've turned the courtyard into a snow scene. Last time they did that the stuff they used killed off the grass. I don't know why they keep all the pretence up. After all, when did it last snow at Christmas? Not, I should wager, within living memory. And a very good thing too. Plumbers won't come out at the best of times.' He sighed. 'Christmas is enough to give anyone the willies. Do you like Christmas?'

'No.'

'Nobody does.' They watched Santa drag himself clear of the still wobbling landing zone. 'Well, he's not broken his neck yet.' He turned to her. 'Vernon will present *Brum Arts* tonight of course as he's put the show together. You take over from tomorrow. You also did quite a lot of stuff for Jacko's show too, didn't you? Well, I'm taking you off that. At the moment Fanny and Adrian are working things through together. Finding their direction. You know how it is. But I have a job which Jacko should have wrapped up. *The Spirit of Christmas Past*. A look behind our traditions, how they came into being. You know the sort of thing. We've got Professor Malahide coming in at eleven. We're looking at thirty minutes. I'd like more than one voice. Music. You know the drill.'

'Who is Professor Malahide?'

'University bod. Anthropology I believe. We've had him before. He's as good as gold. By the way, your last *Brum Arts* went down to the review board. The L.S. Lowry piece was particularly liked. But the rest came in for some favourable comment as well.' He offered her, and she accepted, a polo mint.

'That's good. Isn't it?' Was he telling her that her show had been saved from the lurking blade of his axe?

He said: 'Perhaps worth a brownie point.' And then his lips were hauled upwards towards a smile. 'Yes. Worth a brownie point.'

Feeling much better – she'd not realized how much she'd feared losing her show – she felt strong enough to tackle more pressing problems. She went upstairs to the newsroom to get the phone number of Sandra Tiptree's parents.

'I've got a super programme tonight,' Vernon told her when she bumped into him on the way down.

'Fanny said you'd an interview with Evelyn Waugh lined up.'

'God save us from a decent education,' said Vernon, who'd got his degree at Scunthorpe Poly. 'It's a guy doing a one-man Waugh show that's coming to Birmingham in the New Year. Wonderfully good. Lots of stuff from the letters. Do cock an ear.'

'Of course I will. What do you think of our new man?'

'My dear. The Madame Tussaud's suit. And he's

got more than one. We also wear a charming little post-Crippen number.'

'What really happened to Jacko?'

Vernon shrugged. 'Retired hurt. You know how it is, darling. But it's nice to see you back with us. Fanny had quite given you up for dead. But then she thinks anyone over thirty-five is on the way out.'

'What a comfort you all are, Vernie,' said Isobel.

Fanny had entered the production office in Isobel's absence. She'd a different hairstyle, a riot of curls swept back into a knot on top of her head. She wore a new pair of yellow harem trousers with her great grandfather's pin striped waistcoat. Her bow tie was black. 'The guy from the hippodrome is coming in at four thirty,' she was telling The Turk. She was looking at him as if she'd just discovered Africa. Isobel, who was fond of Fanny, felt sorry for her. She supposed she must have looked at Charlie just like that in the days when she was strong and young and beautiful.

'What's the guy's name again?' asked The Turk. Though his back was to Fanny he was seemingly aware of her gaze of wonder; with a fine display of long fingers he preened his hair.

Isobel sighed and dialled the St Anne's number.

'Helen Tiptree,' the woman who answered the phone said.

'May I speak to Sandra, please?'

'I'm afraid she's in America.'

Isobel was silent. And then she said. 'I'm sorry. It's a bit of a surprise.'

'Oh, it was a last-minute decision. She's staying with a friend over Christmas. She needed a complete break you know. She's had a very rough time.'

'Yes. I heard. That's why I was ringing. Do you think you could give me her address? I'd love to send her a card. Just to say . . . you know, thinking of her.'

'That's very kind. Hold on a minute would you?' And: 'It's 1082 Smith-Hartington Highway, Apartment 92, Crystal City.'

'Who should I send the card care of?'

'Sally Bird. But hasn't the last Christmas post to America gone, dear?'

'I'll send it right away. Thank you, Mrs Tiptree. By the way, how long's she been gone?'

But Mrs Tiptree had already put the phone down.

Well, that seems to be that, she thought.

The phone began to ring. It was reception. 'Professor Malahide has arrived.'

She went down to collect him. There was an air of bewilderment about him which vanished as soon as he entered the studio. Scattering hat, scarf, grubby string gloves, the little-boy-lost was found. Unbuttoning his raincoat, he homed in on the microphone.

'I'm afraid Jacko Marshall has left us.'

'What did you say?' He'd taken off his raincoat, sat himself down and was in the process of unbuttoning his waistcoat.

'The man who was going to do the interview

with you. I'm filling the breach, but I've had no chance to bone up, I'm afraid.'

The professor was rolling up his shirt sleeves. 'Don't worry that pretty little head of yours. I'll just tell you the answers. You can make up the questions later. Worse things are always happening at sea. Are my thing-mi-bits switched on? Just say the word and I'll get cracking.'

'Hang on a moment—'

'Ready then?' He was rubbing his hands together. Then, mindful that the noise they made might ruin his tape, he rested them in front of him.

'Off—' The tape began to run.

'Long before the birth of Christ people all over the earth celebrated at Christmas time. This happened, as it does today, at the point in winter when the sun stops going away from our planet – or so it appears to the naked eye – and starts to return. The coming back of the light has always been a cause for great rejoicing.

'This is the time of the winter solstice. The rebirth of the sun. Christmas.

'From time immemorial it has been honoured as the birthday of the sun god. The luminous child of light. Jesus follows in a great tradition of divine births.

'And, like the sun arising out of the depths of darkness, these divine children were born at midnight. The darkness they were born in was the depths of the earth, reeds, a cave, they came out of a rock or a manger.

'Often these divine children of light were born of

170

Virgins. One of the oldest pictures of the Virgin Mother – the sun child on her knee – comes from Mesopotamia in the third millennium before Christ.

'The star which we associate with Jesus's birth was Sirius to the Egyptians of Alexandria. This is a binary star and the brightest in the heavens. It is twinned – symbolically enough though the ancients couldn't know this – with a white dwarf. The old year and the new?

'Every year for hundreds of years, the Egyptians stayed up all night to watch the rise of Sirius. When it broke the horizon, seemingly coming out of the earth itself, the sun god was born. He brought both life and eternal life to the people.

'On the eve of that day it was the custom to sing and attend to the images of gods. At dawn a descent was made into the burial chambers and an image brought forth – the divine child. It was carried in procession and there was great rejoicing. In the place of darkness – of death – the Maiden had given birth to the god.

'This is the Festival of Kore in her temple at Alexandria—'

Jerome Malahide spoke for twenty minutes, never hesitating, never repeating himself, each word clear, each sentence short. He moved easily from ancient to modern and he allowed himself only two jokes and three opinions.

Isobel, when she stopped the tape, had absolutely no doubt that one day this man would have his own television show. Her only astonishment was that it hadn't happened already.

'Will that do?' he asked, beginning to button himself up again.

'Do? You're a wonder, Professor Malahide.'

'Well, my dear, that's jolly nice of you to say so,' and his skin suffused pink. 'I fear I'm getting a little weakness for hearing myself on the wireless. So foolish d' y' see? Mrs Malahide shouldn't encourage me. The trouble is I've always been too fond of the sound of my own voice. We teachers are, you know. But, it's all a bit of fun really, isn't it? My little song and dance act.'

Isobel showed him out of the studio complex, collected the tape off the machine and went back to the production office to tackle her post.

'. . . price of kissing is going up and up,' Fanny Wragg was dictating to The Turk who was banging away on a manual typewriter – the organization being of the belief that only secretaries were bright enough to use the latest electronic miracles – 'and that's because world supplies of mistletoe are getting scarce. This year Britain will import 150 tonnes of the kiss-me-quick plant . . . and that is 30 per cent less than last year . . . And the price of a kiss? Market traders predict this will set you back £1.20—'

Isobel waded into her post, slitting jiffy bags, piling up press releases and Christmas cards.

At first sight the bright red card looked no different from the rest and then she realized it was handmade. 'A season's greeting—' appeared to have been cut from another card and pasted on. Below was a cut-out Paddington Bear. This one had his hat on and sported a yellow and red striped scarf.

Isobel could feel her heart begin to thump. Taking care, for her fingers had grown large and clumsy, she opened the card.

The writing was in thick yellow crayon.

MUMY, I AM COMMING

That was all it said.

She looked at the envelope. The card had been posted in London five days previously.

Like a nurse, she took note of her vital signs. Her heart was certainly thumping, but not thudding. She wasn't panicking. She was getting hotter, but there was no burning agitation in her joints.

Another part of her, a serpent's cranny, was hissing.

MUMY, I AM COMMING

Now the words sang in her head, a soaring carol of good tidings.

She curled her fingers and deliberately buried her nails into her palms; perhaps pain would bring her to her senses.

Her eyes smarted.

She immediately picked up the phone and got through to the international branch of the directory enquiry service.

Fanny was saying: 'Most of our Christmas mistletoe comes from France and grows on apple trees. It's cut by gypsies who climb the trees—'

'What a load of crap,' said The Turk.

'That's what the Fresh Fruit and Vegetable Bureau say. It's true—'

'What have you got for a brain? A left foot?'

Momentarily Fanny Wragg's eyes met Isobel's. Both saw the glisten of unshed tears in each other.

'Oh, fuck you,' Fanny told The Turk and she flung out of the production office.

While she was still within hearing, Adrian Turk told Velma: 'I can't stand females who swear. Apart from anything else, it shows a complete lack of imagination.'

'Stick it up your arse,' said Velma, normally the most polite of secretaries, 'and light the fuse.'

Isobel, now with Sandra Tiptree's American phone number in front of her, asked of nobody in particular: 'We're five hours in front of the Eastern Seaboard, aren't we?' And she began dialling. 'I make them about seven o'clock.'

The Turk drowned her in playfully amorous looks. 'The dark Isobel wouldn't swear. I'll swear to that! She's a goodie-goodie two shoes. Oh, I do so love goodie-goodies. Goodie-goodies are my very favourite type of cupie doll. You can take them anywhere.'

Isobel heard and understood The Turk, but what she really heard was something coming from her loins, a dread delight which rose, choking her. 'Mummy, I'm coming.' And in her ear the metallic pinging of the satellite as she tried to connect with the second Mrs Maccabee.

'Hello,' said a voice three thousand miles away.

'Am I speaking to the second Mrs Maccabee?' Now why did I say that, she wondered in dismay. I should have just said Mrs Maccabee. It must sound very odd.

'I'll get her. Who shall I say?'

'It's a call from England.' Isobel hoped the woman would suppose she was someone's secretary.

'Crap,' Adrian Turk was saying as he ripped Fanny's dictation out of his machine. 'Craperoo—' and he balled the paper and lobbed it into one of the grey steel waste-paperbaskets. He tilted his chair back and began to whistle.

'Hello. Mrs Maccabee here.' The unmistakably English voice had a tone so bell-like that Isobel knew it would carry without difficulty from one side of a hockey pitch to the other.

She put the phone down. She was aware that her legs were trembling a little and she listened in carefully to the beat of her heart. She couldn't hear it at all. That was because of the great shout being ripped out of her flesh.

MUMY, I'M COMMING

A scream of joy.

I'm going crazy, Isobel thought when it had subsided.

'Why, our dark lady is smiling to herself,' The Turk said. 'That is the ghost of a smile?'

THIRTEEN

Isobel began to wake. She was smiling, that small, secretive, joyous smile of a woman with child. Under the duvet she stretched, her back arching, limbs tautening, toes curling and then she relaxed again. Flesh shuddered delightedly on bone.

She looked at her bedside clock.

It was after ten.

With a shock of dismay she sat up.

It's all right, she remembered. It's Saturday.

She slid down under the duvet and lay listening to her body. Ever since the card had arrived she'd snatched odd moments to monitor her vital signs. At first she did it to get advance warning of another panic attack. But there were no panic attacks. What she did detect was a quickening.

MUMY, I AM COMMING.

Her flesh, unlike her bleak spirit, believed in miracles. And out of the light of consciousness blighted landscapes began to swell, to bear forth.

'Glad tidings I bring,' sang the carollers and her flesh sang with them.

She found that at times she hardly dared breathe for fear of halting the miracle that was happening. She was coming back to life after a terrible

176

catastrophe had struck, leaving in its wake burnt out and blackened ruins.

This was her secret existence in the days of Advent.

In her outer life she did her job, she baked a Christmas cake for Drue – an annual custom – she bought and despatched her cards, she laid in a stock of Christmas drink, she wondered who she could get to make her a pan rack and she bought a bright red woollen dress with winged sleeves to wear for the festivities.

She didn't get in touch with the police to find out what, if anything, they were doing. She thought they'd probably discovered her earlier psychiatric history and decided to take no further action. This both displeased and pleased her. It was unjust because she'd told them the truth. She felt relieved because it absolved her from the necessity of telling them about the card she'd received, or anything else that might happen. She was, she knew, on dangerous ground; she'd left herself unpoliced. One more tie which bound her into the reality of her situation had been broken.

Nothing was impossible if one by one all possible constraints were removed.

She was clearing the way, making it easier for her daughter to come to her.

And yet all the while Isobel was conscious of the fact that her child was in the graveyard. She never lost sight of that. The two systems of thought, one rational, one non-rational, seemed to act completely independently.

Weren't the coming twelve days of Christmas the time when all natural order was turned upside down?

Professor Malahide had spoken of this in *The Spirit of Christmas Past*. He'd said these days marked the Roman festival of the Saturnalia; during this celebration the world was inside out; slaves were waited on by masters, the pauper was king, all that was illicit was licit, that which was buried brought to light.

Even today a pale reflection of this ancient celebration was enacted by the organization. After the cooks had made Christmas lunch, it was the bosses who waited on employees in the canteen. Axe men with jolly smiles on their faces and plates of turkey in their plump hands.

And so Isobel stretched and flexed and sometimes smiled as her sense of expectancy grew.

Christmas is coming . . .

The goose is getting fat.

But is it my goose which is going to be cooked, she wondered, never entirely lost to reason.

I must not think of my daughter's hair.

I must not think of her stubby thumb.

I must not see her hand in mine.

Rock-a-bye.

Rock-a-bye.

She climbed out of bed into the twilit world of the mid-winter morning. And in the non-light she glided past the rocking-chair on her way to the bathroom.

Rock-a-bye.

Rock-a-bye my darling, crooned her flesh, never going so far as to let the lullabye rise into words, never giving voice to that which could have no voice within reason.

She'd just finished her breakfast when the door bell rang and now her song was so deeply hidden that even her limbs no longer glided to the rhythm of her tune.

Putting her cup down, using her fingers in lieu of a comb to run through her hair, she went to the door.

Bruno Seuret was on the step, blocking all her light. 'Hello. Come in—' catching something disturbed about him. Not quite anger, not quite pain.

'I'm on my way to Lichfield,' he said. 'But I called by to ask if you'd come to a party with me.'

'Oh . . . well really . . . I don't think . . .' and then, aware of the pull of skin on his face, the shiny stretch of strain '. . . well perhaps. I mean . . . yes. When is it?'

'Oh Thursday evening. At the Latimers. I think you might know him. He was around in Charlie's time. He's head of the science department. They're a very nice couple.'

'Come and have some coffee. You look – tired. I can't place him. Latimer? Perhaps it will come back to me. Has anything happened, Bruno?'

'No. Not really.' He followed her into the kitchen. She slid a stool in his direction. 'As a matter of fact Caro rang last night. She told me she was going to get married again.'

Isobel, her back to him, turned on the coffee

perculator and got out another cup. She didn't answer. She gave him time in which to decide whether he wanted to tell her more.

'I don't know why I'm so upset about it. The truth is Caroline and I had drifted apart long before the split came, but all this business . . . jumping through legal hoops – No, no. It's not that. Every now and then I get this feeling of absolute failure. You really put everything into your marriage, don't you? It's a great project and you have utter faith and belief and love and know it will turn out right because you'll make it.'

He was thinking about it. 'It's ridiculous. I don't feel sadness. I don't feel any more like the rejected lover because I was no longer in love with her when she left. But her marrying again. That's it, isn't it. Really the end of our dream. I've this terrible sense of failure. Every now and then I feel as if I've been hit hard in the stomach. Sick with failure. I wish I could get angry with her. Or myself. I have been furious. Furious in a ridiculous way. I raged when she wanted the pair of armchairs. I tore my hair out. But now I seem to have gone beyond all that. At least for the moment. What's wrong with me? That's what I keep asking myself. Why have I failed so badly? How could I be such a failure? I feel – shrunk. I feel literally smaller. A man of no account.'

She turned and handed him the coffee.

'I'm sorry. I didn't mean to say all that. I really did come to ask if you'd go to the Latimer's party with me.'

'I know.'

'I don't suppose it was quite the same for you. I imagine, in fact, it must have been worse. You were in love with Charlie when he left you, weren't you?'

'Yes. But I did feel much the same as you. A failure. Not up to scratch. Not good enough. Not pretty enough. Not, not, not . . . it's all not.'

'And now?'

'Now I don't give a shit about him,' she said. 'The Charlie thing is over and done with. He's dead anyway.'

'That was the other reason I called round. Before Caro mentioned her future plans I asked her what she remembered about Anne-Marie's toys. She said she started to take boxes of them down to the hospice shop and then something intervened and a couple of boxes got left. I actually found one box. She said she thought she inadvertently sent one back to Charlie. When he left you he dumped some hi-fi equipment and other stuff on Caro and she stored it for him. Sandra later collected it. Caro noticed that one of the boxes of toys had got mixed up in the stuff and she worried about it for a bit, but she never heard from Sandra or Charlie.'

'Sandra's in America. I got her on the phone on Tuesday.'

'Oh well. That appears to be that.'

'Do you think Charlie and Caro were ever . . .'

'I don't know. Not long ago I found myself looking round the staff room at school and seriously wondering if she'd had it off with all the men there, including a couple of sixty year olds.'

'I used to look at all my women friends and wonder,' said Isobel.

'You really think Charlie and Caro—'

'After he'd gone I thought Charlie and everybody.'

'Same here.'

They found they were tentatively smiling at each other.

'It's a bugger, isn't it? Oh well, for me it's been over for a long time. I don't care either way now. For a long time, though, I found it hard work meeting many of my women friends. I felt humiliated. Shamed. Tarred and feathered.'

'Tarred? Feathered?'

'Ashamed.'

'I have wondered about my motives in going back to France. Am I running away? After a rout that's what people do. But then I remember I wanted to go back before the split.' He pushed his fingers through his hair. 'I believe the worst of myself. I put the worst construction on anything I do. I've no faith in myself.' He gave a shrug, hunching and loosening his shoulders as if sliding off a great weight. 'As you say. Bugger it—' and he toasted her with his cup of coffee.

When he'd gone she noticed he'd left his gloves. Looking at them she felt curiously cheered. It was a long time since she'd had anything belonging to a man in her house.

She zipped herself into her anorak and collected

a couple of shopping bags. Earlier it had been raining and water still dripped off the overhang of thatch. The roof was constructed in such a way that there could be no guttering to carry water away. Shutting the door behind her, she hopped over a puddle.

He never called Caro a bitch. He didn't even blame her. She was thinking of Bruno's attitude to his wife and finding it pleased her.

She swung into Main Street. It wound down Alrewas like a worm through soil. It tracked the line of fields worked in medieval times. They'd curved in an S formation to allow oxen and plough to turn more economically on wide headlands. Each great field had been divided into thin curling strips, one holding separated from another by an unploughed ridge; several of these, including the one she was walking along, had become the village's streets. Buildings huddled low in a landscape so flat that most of it was cloud. Even in the depths of winter the shining pewter air was full of song. The birds like the remnants of the village's old orchards, they liked the berries on the hedgerows by the canal and river, even the pickings to be had at the fish and chip shop in the 1960s block halfway down the street.

As she walked along, Isobel could see illuminated fairy lights strung on trees in village livingrooms. Christmas wreaths were appearing on doors. Three balloons had been tied to a skeletal cherry tree. Holly was taped to the rim of the driving mirror in a parked car.

Though it was still over two weeks to Christmas

183

Day, she ordered a small turkey from Oates, the butcher, then went to the grocery store next to the fish and chip shop. Among the things she bought was a box of jelly babies.

Joan Bennett began to wave frantically and beckon at the window as she walked past Mickleholme Villa. She opened the front door as Isobel pushed back the wrought-iron garden gate. Knitted hat on head and hand brush held like a gun at Isobel's chest, she said: 'How can I get on with what's to be done and her down in the dumps? It's not as if she's been short of company. By all accounts the vicar were here last night. Such a nice clean fellow, Mr Kelso. Not one to disturb a bathroom. Nice habits. And her with a shovel instead of a mouth arrived yesterday afternoon and polished off all my short bread. Her that does antiques and has her hopes pinned on some of Drue's old rubbish I shouldn't wonder. How are you, ducks? Perking up a bit in spite of the weather. It's gone quite unnatural warm. It's that there greenhouse effect—' and she preceded Isobel down the hall. 'They're always saying the world's a dead duck and 'appen they'll be right one day.' She opened the drawing-room door. ' 'Ere's Isobel to see you, so you get out that smile even if it kills you. Well, I'd better put my skates on or I'll never be done by lunch.'

Isobel saw that this was not one of Drue's good days. It was an effort for the old lady to find the energy to pull her spine off the back of her chair and lean forward to greet her.

'Rotten?'

Drue pulled a face. 'How are you?'

'Oh, I'm fine.' Isobel dumped her shopping and came to the fire, unzipping her anorak.

'Costive. Mrs Bennett wants to give me some opening medicine. But I jolly well don't have the energy to keep getting up and running to the toilet. The woman's a fool.' The jewels she wore seemed to grow more brilliant as she dimmed so Isobel had the extraordinary impression Drue would soon be transformed into one priceless diamond.

The old lady slumped back. Today her hide was no more than a crumpled semi-transparent plastic bag through which lumps of bone could be seen. 'I dreamed about you.' It was as though fingers had sprung out of that bag of bones and nipped the nape of Isobel's neck.

Drue concentrated on the work of breathing for a minute and then she said: 'I suppose it was sheer exasperation. I've been so jolly well frustrated. Fancy not being able to read your cards. The lightning struck tower. The wheel of fortune. The empress. There they are for me to see. But see what? I don't know what I know. Oh, it's preyed on my mind.'

'What did you dream, Drue?' Isobel found herself asking though she didn't want to know.

'I dreamed I came to visit you. Only you didn't live in your cottage, but in this house. In Mickleholme Villa. I waited in the hall, but Mrs Bennett didn't come to show me the way. No-one came. In the end I got fed up with waiting and set out to find you.

185

'I suddenly realized I wasn't in the villa at all, but in some big important institution. There were those strips of carpet bounded on each side by brass rails.

'I found you in a big room and there was a very good fire in the grate. But you offered me whisky and as you know that is entirely the wrong drink. I'm a gin woman through and through. But I took the drink and sipped it and to my astonishment it tasted delicious.

'You sat down at a small table. It was covered with that small cloth of mine. You know the one, my dear. It has a deep lace border which was worked by my great-grandmother. You've often admired it. It was so placed over the table that it fell in a diamond. Like a star. Very quickly you played a game of patience. They were tarot cards. My cards. But you played just as if you were using ordinary playing cards.

'And when the game had come out you whipped off the cloth and I saw that writing was scored in the wood.'

'What did it say?'

'How should I know?' Drue was, Isobel realized, furious. 'It was written in Arabic.'

Feeling irrationally relieved, as though she'd been let off hearing her death sentence, Isobel began laughing. Suddenly Drue was giggling too. Isobel laughed so much she was in tears. Drue giggled so much it made her false teeth rattle and her aching flesh hurt more.

Beaming, Mrs Bennett brought in a tray of coffee

and biscuits. 'I could hear you in the kitchen. I knew Isobel would cheer you up. Sulking all morning. You should know better at your age. Well, I must get on. Mr Bennett will be wanting his dinner and I'm still not through here.'

'So, there you are,' said Drue after Mrs Bennett had gone. 'Arabic. I ask you. One sugar for me. I don't suppose you know any Arabic?'

'No.'

'Neither do I.'

When Joan Bennett later showed Isobel out, she said: 'I knew you'd bring a smile back to her face. The poor ducks had a bad night. She won't go easily you know. Not her. She's no intention of dying, that one.'

'Is she really that bad?'

'Of course she is. Drue's been that bad for a year or more. There's some go quick and some take a snail's pace. But her. No budging her. Naughty old dear. No good will come of this weather. I'll tell you that for nothing. Whoever heard of primroses in bloom at Christmas? Raining again.'

Isobel put up the hood of her anorak, hoisted her shopping bags and prepared to dash to her cottage.

'Mind how you go, ducks!' Mrs Bennett called after her.

She was just opening her front door when she heard a car door slam. She turned to see Fanny Wragg. 'I've been waiting in the car. I thought you might have just popped to the shops.'

'Don't tell me. You're in trouble.'

'How did you know?'

'You're my third this morning.' The grandfather clock struck twelve as Isobel went in.

'I won't stay if you don't want me to!'

'Don't be so touchy, Fanny.'

'How would you feel if you'd just been slung out of your own house?'

'Oh dear,' Isobel said. 'I'll just drop these bags in the kitchen. Take your coat off and put a match to the fire.'

'He threw me out,' Fanny called after her. 'He pushed me out of the front door and I fell over and he called me a whore.'

Isobel came back in. 'That's awful.'

'The woman next door heard it all. She stopped washing the car and stood there as if it were a show. If he'd have killed me she would have just kept right on gawping. I could have wrung her neck. My jeans are split right across the knee. Look!' Suddenly she began to wail. 'Geoff's not like that. He's never been like that. He pushed me hard. He knocked me flying down the steps. He threw a fork at me too. He could have blinded me. It only just missed and hit the window. It cracked the pane. We can't afford to pay for new glass!' Her hair was standing in wild clumps, tears had made her nose run and suddenly she began to shiver. 'He could have done me in and no-one would have bothered. I thought he might kill me.'

'You've been seeing The Turk,' Isobel guessed. 'Sit by the fire and I'll get you some brandy.'

Fanny's teeth had begun to chatter. Isobel poured out a generous measure and handed her the glass. 'Knock it all back.'

Like a child, Fanny did as she was bidden and then wiped her nose surreptitiously on the corner of her combat jacket. Isobel sat in the chair and stared at her.

'Don't look at me like that. It's not my fault. I didn't ask to fall in love with Mousie. These things just happen. It's not my fault and if we hadn't taken out a joint mortgage and got double tax relief Mr Big Geoff Oh Shit wouldn't even have a roof over his head.'

'But you can't possibly know Adrian Turk. He's only been at the station a week.'

'You don't have to know someone to love them.'

'That's true,' Isobel reflected.

'And Mousie loves me.'

'As far as I can see you spend your whole time rowing.'

'That was in the beginning. You see Mousie didn't want to be in love with me. It made him mad. He was as mad as hell because I was making him fall in love with me.'

'I see,' said Isobel, who didn't believe a word of it.

'And then me and Mousie . . . well, you know . . . at his flat. It's never been like that before for me. Nor for him. It was . . . well, you know . . . I know you know. You loved Charlie, didn't you?'

Isobel didn't answer. She felt like giving Fanny a good shake.

'I've never been in love before—' Fanny had stopped crying and shivering and was smiling a wonderous smile. 'Never. Not in my whole life. And now it's happened.'

'You'll feel differently about it when you come out on the other side,' said Isobel, though she knew she was wasting her breath.

'It was different for you.'

'I hope so.'

'Mousie is just super. He's not the sort of man . . . well, he's . . . he's got . . . Mousie's so kind, Isobel. And he's just bristling with principles.'

'How the hell did you come to call him Mousie?'

'Because you know—' and Fanny pointed between her thighs. 'His . . . well. Just like a big fat gorgeous mouse.'

'Oh my God.'

'I knew you'd understand. That's why I came here. That's how you felt about Charlie, isn't it? Only he was a bastard, wasn't he? Well, I can talk to you. And you see Mousie has gone down to Bristol this weekend to see his folks so I can't move into his flat until Monday. I won't be any bother.'

'You certainly won't. If you're big enough to fall in love you're big enough to sort out all the complications. You've got a roof of your own.'

'I can't go back there. Geoff'll kill me!'

'How did he find out?'

'I told him.'

'You *what*?'

'Well, I didn't know he was going to lose his rag, did I? I mean, we'd always said we'd be open and honest with each other. Ours was a civilized relationship. I mean part of Geoff's salary goes to Oxfam each month. That's the kind of man Geoff is. At least, that's what I thought.'

'Humans aren't civilized.'

'Well, I know that now. But I didn't know it then. It's not even as if Geoff's in love with me. I know he's not. He just thinks I'm part of the property. That I belong to him. He threw a fork at me. I'm telling you!'

'Yes. You said.'

'I never thought—'

'Never thought what?'

'Geoff's so changed, Isobel. I think it's his new boss and all these targets. It's made him – much harder. You just should have seen his face. I'd never have believed it. I thought he was going to do me in. He frightened me to death.'

'It's jealousy that changes people.'

'But I keep telling you. We weren't in love. I mean it wasn't as if the earth moved or anything like that. We'd never have set up home together if it weren't for getting double mortgage relief.'

'Perhaps he wasn't as casual about the whole thing as you, Fanny. Perhaps he's nuts about you.'

'Oh, I'd know if he was.'

'Would you?'

'He felt the same about it all as me. I know he did. Why, he was always going on about some bimbo of a secretary at work. Honestly.'

'That doesn't mean he wasn't in love with you.'

'He pushed me out of my own house. He called me a whore. That's how much he thinks of me! Anyway, I don't give a damn what that pile of shit thinks. I'm in love with Mousie.'

'Listen, you're going to have to come to some

agreement with Geoff even if it's only over the house. I'll get us some lunch and then you can ring him up. He'll have calmed down by then. You've got to work something out.'

Fanny sighed. 'Perhaps you're right.'

'Of course I am. What about some eggs and bacon?'

'I could eat a whole house,' Fanny discovered. 'There's no chance of some chips as well? I was just going to eat my breakfast when he threw the fork. What shall I say to the rat?'

'Just don't mention Adrian Turk,' Isobel advised. 'And don't call him a rat.' She went into the kitchen. The room was so dark she had to put on the light. Between finding the frying pan and cutting the rind off bacon, she unpacked her shopping.

She looked at the jelly babies in astonishment. What on earth made me buy those? she wondered.

FOURTEEN

Hilary Winstan was standing with one hand on the wall, the other on his hip, looking through the window into the yellowish gloom.

'It's only a rough cut,' said Isobel, dropping *The Spirit of Christmas Past* tape into his wire tray. 'I'm short of a bit of actuality. I want some party atmosphere, but I'm going to one on Thursday and hopefully I can get a bit then. And I might tape my grandfather clock striking twelve. Anyway, it needs a bit more work.'

Hilary stuck his head further forward; his nose was now only six inches from the plate glass. 'One mustn't go quite over the top. Nothing too clichéd. One might worry about that.'

Other people might; Isobel, who'd got stuck with the programme at the last minute, didn't feel inclined to.

'I'll have a little listen then,' said Hilary. 'Pop round after lunch, will you?' His breath was beginning to mist the pane of glass. 'Of course they've gone now.'

'Gone?'

'They've stopped shooting on this side of the building.' He sighed. 'Santa ought to have broken

193

his neck, you know. But he just set my teeth on edge each time he slithered through that bloody rubber. The man leads a charmed life. After lunch then.'

'I'm afraid it'll have to be later than that. I'm seeing someone at two.'

'Who?'

'The specialist.'

'A medical item?'

'My doctor arranged it.'

He turned to look at her. Both hands were on his hips, arms pushing back the jacket to reveal a lot of wide red braces.

'You know. I fell ill at the office and was sent home in a taxi.'

'Women's problems.'

'Women have them.'

'I wonder why men don't?' He turned to look out of the window again. 'But you'll be in later? We can have our little natter then. By the way Jack Drummond called from the television side. Could you run off a copy of your L.S. Lowry tape for him?'

'Sure.'

'Didn't you run off something else for him last summer?'

'Only a copy of the interview I did with him. I did a piece on that new programme of his. The one on Henry Moore.'

'*Brum Arts* ready to roll tonight?'

'Yes.'

'Do keep watching out for Hoovers. One can

always disconnect them you know. The essential thing is never to stop thinking.' He turned away from the window. He was looking particularly bloodless today, almost as if he were webbed in a caul. 'Have you been catching Adrian?'

'Most of it,' lied Isobel. 'It's very good.'

'Lovely package on orienteering, I thought. Nice touch. Light touch. Up beat. Steers clear of falling arches and impotence. Cheerful. I know that arts programmes are never cheery, Isobel. Art isn't a cheerful subject. I realize that. But a bit of pezazz never comes amiss. We're not in the Albert Hall, you know. But I'm not being critical. One simply wants to seed a thought. Yes. Well. Leave the door open when you go.'

Isobel did as she was told and emerged into the station's output which washed over the corridor from strategically placed loud speakers. Blow-up photographs of programme presenters stared down from ice-cream walls; there was a grime-edged space where Jacko Marshall had once been. Management had not yet decided to put The Turk in his place.

The production office was quiet. The West Indian who did the station's Sunday reggae show was sitting cross-legged on a desk meditating, Velma Blood was talking on the phone to a secretary in another part of the building and The Turk was swivelling from side to side in his chair. He was still dressed in his great-grandfather's suit, but he'd taken the jacket off and hung it on the back of the chair. He'd also discarded the original waistcoat in favour of a new one in saffron-brocaded silk and he was wearing this with a black shirt. 'The dark, dark lady,' he greeted her sleepily. 'I've sent Fanny up to the canteen for some coffee. I told her to get you one. Aren't I the good boy?'

'Thanks—' and Isobel went over to a vacant tape machine.

'What's this Geoff like? Fanny's live-in person?'

'A karate expert.'

'Very funny. Laughie. Laughie. Oh, what a bore everyone is. Such mediocre minds.' He yawned widely and went on swinging.

Isobel set about editing her tapes. Fanny came in with a tray of plastic coffee cups and The Turk stopped swinging; he watched her with intent half-hooded eyes as she distributed the drinks. Fanny seemed sleepy too, but there was a wag to her bottom which hadn't been there before. Even when she and The Turk were some distance apart the air between them was fraught with sexuality. Mostly unconscious of what they were doing, they preened and displayed themselves, each for the other.

'It'll all end in tears,' Vernon told Isobel over lunch on the seventh floor. 'But, sweetie, aren't you a teeny bit envious? It's absolutely ages since I felt like that about someone. You know. Always sneaking the loved one's name into the conversation. Wearing a bit of his clothing. Having the most naughty thoughts even when emptying the waste-paper bin. Creeping out of bed, saddle sore and weary. Oh, the fatigues of love. Can you remember it all, darling?'

196

'Yes,' said Isobel.

'So surprising when you consider *him*. You could see she was smitten from the word go, but he seemed to take a positive dislike to her. All those darts dipped in pure venom. Oh, it'll certainly end in tears. Poor, poor Fanny.'

'You were envying her a minute ago!'

'I know, darling. But now we're at the beginning. What happens when the gilt wears off Miss Gingerbread?'

'Don't you believe in happy ever after Vernon?'

'Silly sweetie. In the end it comes down to dreary fights over telephone bills and dirty dishes. Though if hope didn't triumph over experience one might as well expire. Really I'm the most romantic of guys. Each time I know that this is it. And when it all ends up I pop again. Like a game birdie waiting to be shot at. I never live and learn. I can't, can I? Well, at least not up to now for there's always been a next time.' He paused and looked at her. 'But there wasn't a next time for you, was there?'

'Not up to now.'

'There! Not up to now. You live in hope too. One certainly has to live in something I suppose, reality being what it is. What about the Froggie with the voice?'

'Bruno. I hardly know him.'

'Much the best thing, darling. Knowing people is such a dreadful disappointment, I always find.'

'As awful as knowing yourself?'

'Ooh. Just like Mumsy. Here we are having a

nice little gossip and then suddenly I get drenched in cold water. You can be fearfully uncomfortably prickly. Far too much like Mummy.'

'I can't be quite as old as that, Vernon. Even in your imagination.'

'Mummy is very well preserved. I do so adore well preserved ladies. Creatures like Fanny aren't ladies at all. The way she will keep pawing. Filthy little thing.'

'You are being bitchy.'

'I suppose it's being exposed to all that young love. There's nothing like someone else's bliss to bring out the worst in one. Quite taken my appetite away as a matter of fact.' He glared gloomily at his syrup pudding. 'Oh. Are you off?'

'I'm seeing someone at two.'

'Did I tell you about Jacko Marshall?'

'No.'

'Working as a casual on Christmas post.'

'Poor devil.' Isobel picked up her handbag.

'Bye, sweetie. Give my love to whoever it is.'

Isobel went down to the washroom next to the production office. All morning she'd been trying to ignore the fact that she was very nervous. After washing and combing her hair, she studied her face in the mirror. That's not an ill face, she thought. What am I doing going to see a doctor? What will I say to the chap?

She suddenly remembered being in the washroom at the hospital. She saw Rita in her pink jeans and purple flatties. What had she said?

'People always come back. This is our little

niche. I mean it's what we're good at. Not everyone can be mad.'

Isobel stared at her image.

When I was mad I didn't recognize myself in the mirror. I do now. I'm sane all right; but in a strange way Rita was right. Madness did have its attractions; among all the horrors there was a certain cosiness in living in a world of your own. When you are out of reach, you were out of harm's way.

She rummaged in her handbag for her make-up. Not too much. She didn't want to look as if she'd needed to put on a brave face.

The car park was muffled in a twilit pall. The vehicles that came and went used their headlights, a moving net of beams. She drove out through gates manned by the security guard and headed for the Pershore Road, passing shrouded figures scurring towards Cannon Hill Park. Nearing the Police Training Centre, she moved over to the crown of the road and turned right by the county cricket ground. The last time she'd been to Underheath Clinic the world had not been cosy. The snowy ground shifted and cracked and disappeared under her feet. She'd put her hands in her anorak pockets and clung on in terror.

She saw just how far she'd come since there. Now she'd enough faith in the world to believe it was there; she didn't step into voids of disbelief. The steering wheel in her hands felt real to her touch, really there. Because it was really there, her body was really here. She didn't have to pinch herself to try and convince herself she had a body.

Suddenly a sweating horror found her out, a dread which rose and shook her by the throat. What if she no longer felt the steering wheel to be there? What if she lost touch again? No longer there. No longer here. Nobody. Nowhere.

She squeezed the wheel and it was certainly there. She was all right. She was up and running. The sense of dread began to ebb.

I must be so careful, she thought, as her headlights picked up the high wall of the clinic. Again she saw Anne-Marie as the demon which could destroy her. And then she saw her child as she'd really been, holes in her jeans and a mucky face, and the feeling of being invaded by something alien left her. She smiled at her silliness.

Though she'd known nothing about Underheath Clinic the first time she'd come, since then she'd been the producer of a show which had run a package on the work done there. It was a NHS clinic, run by the Central Birmingham Health Authority, a teaching authority. There were places for almost fifty in-patients and many more were treated on an out-patient basis. The mansion and its grounds had once belonged to a family of chocolate manufacturers who had given it to the city with the stipulation that it should be used to treat people with psychiatric problems. It was rumoured that the family's interest was a personal one, that succeeding generations had thrown up kin cursed by melancholia.

Parking her car, Isobel walked towards the

entrance. Wearing its shroud of December vapour, the building was as she remembered it, a Victorian gothic horror. Only the steel boiler-house chimney marked it out as NHS property.

Two women, perhaps the same two women, sat behind the glass-fronted booth in the entrance hall. The booth was more like a theatre box-office than a reception area. But there were no tickets for this performance; they marked her name off a list and she went through to the great hall at the heart of Underheath.

She turned round on herself. There was the stained-glass window, the church roof, the huge marble fireplace, the mirrored overmantel now stuck with cotton wool snow and hung about with tinsel. Across the glass conservatory at the west end two-foot-high glitter spelled out *Happy Christmas*. The clock above was just on two.

Isobel crossed the hall and sat on the far side. Opposite her, across an expanse of wooden floor, a wisp of a man slumped in an armchair cried quietly. The woman at his side was knitting baby bootees.

What can I be doing here? she thought in alarm. It was as if the huge boulder she'd been pushing up the mountain had broken loose and rolled backwards to the bottom again, taking her with it.

The feeling of hopelessness had struck her out of nowhere. She lay paralysed, crushed.

She heard the door behind her open and became aware of someone walking past her.

Dr Rainbow turned. 'Mrs Maccabee?'

'The first Mrs Maccabee,' she corrected him. It

was with an effort of will that she pulled her body out of the chair.

He turned and led her through the door into a narrow, crooked corridor, perhaps made when partitioning off rooms. There was a great jangle of keys as Dr Rainbow opened the door to his office. Though this room had a bay window, it was nevertheless very dark. There were two chairs in front of a deal desk; the one he indicated to her was furthest from the door. As he turned a little to settle in his, she momentarily glimpsed the back of his head. His hair was more like that of a twelve-year-old schoolboy than a man of fifty. His face, too, though deeply lined, had a schoolboyish air. It's his eyes, she thought. They look far too young for the rest of him, as though he were right at the beginning of life and up to all sorts of *Just William* devilishness. And all this set in a big stooped, ponderous frame. A knee cracked as he lowered himself into his chair. He made no effort to switch a lamp on; they faced each other in the half light.

'How are you?'

The old question which had always caused her so much trouble. How am I? she wondered. If I say I'm well, which is the truth – at least some of it – he'll wonder why I'm here. Why am I here? Because of dread. The dread of going mad again. And other dread; a fleshy, organic dread, like a disease, like cancer, like malaria, like leprosy, like all the ills of man.

'How are you?' His question re-echoed in her head. 'I'm all right,' she could say. But she knew, didn't she, that she was going all wrong. Do I know that? She was astonished.

She thought further. She didn't want to begin their relationship by lying to him; of course, she may be driven into lies later. If there was a later.

Half concealed in the gloom, which she thought afforded her some protection, like undergrowth, she told him of the panic attack. She then brought him up to date with her life and lastly she began to tell him of finding the Paddington Bear and all that had happened since. She was used to ordering stories. She told him concisely, leaving out nothing. But, she realized, as soon as she'd stopped, the story was only partly told. She'd not said how she felt.

'And the card you received. Did you tell the police about that?'

'No. They haven't been back in touch, you see. Perhaps they didn't believe me. Perhaps they found out I'd been a psychiatric patient. Do you believe me?'

He had pushed out his legs until they were straight in front of him, heels on the floor, ankles crossed. Now he crossed his arms, too. He said eventually: 'I'm not sure.'

She said nothing.

'If I'd have said that to most people they'd have jumped down my throat. They'd be angry with me. They'd try to convince me that what they said was true.'

She found she was smiling; a small, secretive smile.

'You aren't angry? Annoyed even?'

'I've been angry with the police. They might have done something. But part of me is glad they've apparently done nothing.'

'Why?'

'I've told you the truth all right. I realize I'm in a privileged position and that I'm the only one who can know for certain I've told both you and the police the truth. There is part of me though that wants no interference from the outside. I don't really want what's happening stopped.'

'Why?'

'Part of me believes that my child is finding her way back to me. I believe Anne-Marie is coming home at last.'

'But you told me yourself that you visited your child's grave only a short while ago.'

'Yes. That's quite true. She's dead. But you have to understand that in my dreams she's not dead. I'll try to explain. My mother is dead, too, and even if I dream we're walking together and talking to each other – how can I put this? – if I stopped and asked myself in the dream if she were dead I'd know quite well that she was.' She paused. 'In my dreams my daughter is really alive. She isn't dead at all. I even came home from the shops with a bag of jelly babies the other day.'

'For your daughter?'

She didn't answer.

'Your dreaming is beginning to invade your waking hours?'

'I'm full of a kind of expectation. I'm changing. I

feel I'm coming back to life. Something in me is being born again. The coming of Anne-Marie is bringing me back to life.'

'Didn't you feel alive before all this began to happen?'

'I was carrying on, trying to make a new life for myself and succeeding too. But now I see it was a kind of act of bravado. An act of desperation. I was acting as if I were somebody in the hope that someday I would really be that somebody. But really there was nothing there. It was all shell. I was burnt out. It was as if a great fire had raged and the flames had eaten me up.'

'When did you realize you were – as you put it – coming back to life?'

She thought back. 'It was after the panic attack,' she realized. 'I thought I should have more panic attacks, but to my surprise, I didn't. Instead . . . well, something began to happen inside me. I knew I was changing. I was becoming alive again. But it's all wrong, isn't it? Anne-Marie is dead. I know she's never coming back. And yet . . . I feel she is. I wake feeling something wonderful is just about to happen. Nothing wonderful can happen, can it?'

They were silent. The room was growing darker.

'I know she's coming.' As she said it, her scalp wrinkled as she recognized the truth of her words.

He didn't contradict her. He said: 'You introduced yourself as the first Mrs Maccabee.'

'My husband married again before he died. I told you about all that. She's in America.'

'Most divorcees don't introduce themselves as the first Mrs Whatever. I've never heard a woman say that before.'

'Well, I've taken off his ring and perhaps I should go back to my maiden name. When I took off the ring it left me in a bit of a quandary, I suppose. I don't feel I am Mrs Maccabee any more.'

He smiled. 'So who are you going to be?'

'Isobel for now. Isobel who? I don't know yet. Things are changing. I haven't made my mind up about that.'

'The last time you came you wrote to me and said you couldn't come to see me again. Why was that?'

'At that time I couldn't talk to you about Anne-Marie. I couldn't even say her name then. Something seemed seized up inside of me. It would have been no good. I don't have any trouble with her name now. I'm a lot better now.'

'If I set up some appointments would you come to see me this time?'

'Yes.'

'Good.'

She rose slightly before he did. She looked at his desk and for the first time she noticed her file among the books and papers. 'How can you see to read? There's no light.'

'There's light when I need it. Are you going back to work now?'

'Yes. I've to present a show tonight. It's quite bizarre the way my life carries along on the outside as if nothing were happening. Like eating your lunch on a plane while the wings drop off.'

But later she had to admit to herself that now she'd his big bulky figure in the background she felt a little safer.

She realized that, though she'd planned to, she'd not shown him Anne-Marie's Christmas card.

She'd not shown that to anybody though she'd often taken it out of her bag and looked at it herself.

FIFTEEN

The fog came down just before teatime. She didn't leave the studios until ten, an hour after *Brum Arts* had come off the air. When she'd turned on to the A38 she used the red tail lights of the car in front to navigate by, but five miles from Alrewas she lost her guide. Her pace slowed and an ache spread from between her shoulders. Vapours swirled and banked; the light of on-coming headlights drained out of the car.

Dimly she made out the sign to the village and crept off the dual carriageway on to the slip road. *The Happy Eater* roadhouse was in complete darkness, but one or two lights showed in the semi-detached houses which lined the road. The village itself was practically deserted. Sodium street lamps burned phosphorescent holes in the fog, but as she turned off Main Street to the cottage she noticed the one which illuminated the alley was out. Having parked the car, she stepped into a dense moist silence.

All the way back from Birmingham she'd been promising herself coffee laced with brandy; after depositing her bags she made it and carried it back towards the living-room. She poised on the threshold. She caught a whiff of . . . she turned her head, first right and then left . . . something fetid, something dead. But now, her nostrils flared, she couldn't smell it.

There'd been a woman in hospital, Isobel recalled, a depressive, who'd always imagined noxious smells; herself. She shuddered.

Someone has been here, she suddenly thought.

Someone is here.

It's not my imagination.

Her scalp shrivelled against her skull.

Nonsense, she told herself.

She took large gulps of the brandy-laced coffee, looking round the living-room as she did so. Nothing, so far as she could see, had been disturbed.

She knew she would have to climb the stairs and inspect the rocking-chair. Her eye lighted on the poker and even as she was telling herself she was being ridiculous, she put down the coffee cup and picked it up.

Listen.

Can you hear someone?

Something?

Someone is here.

She listened. She listened with her ears, with her skin; her bones elongated to detect better the slightest vibration. The rest of her being stretched too, reaching to the furthermost corners of the cottage.

She could detect no sound other than the steady ticking of the grandfather clock.

Something though . . .

Something fishy . . .

Smelled fishy?

Evil, she thought.

A sense of evil.

What I am sensing is my own dread, she told herself. I'm frightening myself to death.

Fingers clenching the poker, she climbed the stairs. Gently, with the end of the poker, she pushed back the door into the study room. The rocking-chair, illuminated in a flare of light from the landing, was empty.

She found herself thinking of how she'd stood in the doorway of the nursery in the bungalow.

We are almost reflections of each other in a mirror, she thought. Charlie's fruitless, dumped widows.

But she found she didn't feel sorry for the second Mrs Maccabee. She hated the woman who'd taken her husband from her.

And this though she knew Charlie hadn't been taken at all, but had gone gladly. He'd have gone much sooner, too, had it not been for his devotion to his daughter. She remembered quite clearly that she'd once or twice slapped Anne-Marie too hard for a minor offence, in reality punishing her for the ease with which she'd captured and kept Charlie's adoration.

Annie.

Limb of my limb.

Eye of my eye.

Breath of my breath.

She looked at the empty rocking-chair again and then at the poker.

Would she have hit out if she'd found anyone here?

I'd have killed.

Suddenly, shockingly, she was in touch with her fury.

But no-one is here.

I'm furious with shadows.

Shades.

Nothing.

Nothing to hit.

Nothing to murder.

Nothing even to be frightened of.

The feeling of hopelessness she'd experienced earlier that afternoon swept over her again; it silted up her eyes and gagged her mouth. It buried her alive.

When she was able to move, to shake herself free again, she stumbled downstairs. She made herself drink the rest of the coffee, though it was cold.

Drue had once told her that monks believed despair the ultimate sin for it was a sin against the Holy Ghost. This spirit was least easily pacified for its claims were the most tenuous.

Despair, the sin of accidie, spiritual sloth, apathy, indifference.

Missing the mark.

That's what the old lady had said was the root meaning of sin.

People who missed their mark were furious, frustrated, impotent, hopeless. Finally they despaired.

A failed marriage.

A dead child.

How much wider of the mark could she have been?

'I was carrying on, trying to make a new life for myself and succeeding too. But now I can see that it was all show. An act of bravado,' she'd told Dr Rainbow.

But she'd done it. She'd chosen to carry on.

What use is despair to me now? she thought.

It's too late for despair.

And now she'd experienced this burying of her being, she felt curiously relieved; she felt she knew the worst.

She was very tired.

She locked the door, drew the curtains against the fog, switched out the lights and hauled her body up to bed. She fell asleep as soon as her head sank into the pillow.

She dreamed she was on a hill overlooking Alexandria. She'd gone up there to see the rising of a star, Sirius, the brightest star in the heavens. But she'd come too early; nobody else had arrived yet. Her aloneness was such that it was a numbing coldness.

Though she was on a ridge overlooking a pre-Christian city, that ridge was the outcrop on which the church at Wychnor stood and though she didn't turn round, she knew the empty church was behind her. Below, slowly submerging in the canal, was something very white; it dazzled like the star she'd been waiting for.

She slid and tumbled down the grassy outcrop and tugged the star out of the moon-slurried waters. It was the tea cloth edged in lace worked by Drue's great-grandmother. But now it was filthy; it smelled of dead things and dripped with slime. That a star, the brightest star in the heavens, should come to this. Isobel's grief was a terrible grief. She sobbed without restraint.

She sobbed sitting in a chair which was turned slightly away from the trestle-table in her kitchen; this table and her kitchen were in a hot, foreign city, the city of Alexandria. She realized that the star cloth had once covered her table, but had been thrown away by careless people, by vandals, and drowned in the mud.

But she no longer sobbed because of that. She sobbed because she'd spilt something on the table and made a shocking stain on the surface. Many women now sitting round the table, were furious with her for the mark would not come off. She told them she would buy a new table. She wondered if she could afford a new one and realized, to her surprise, that she could. She also knew she was being cheated. She'd buy all the women, who were her mother, this new table and they'd still use the old one. Behind her back, they'd polish the wood so the mark didn't look quite so bad.

And then all the women were gone and she was alone again.

She saw there was a different mark on another part of the table. Writing had been scored into the wood with a biro. To her surprise, the lettering wasn't Arabic. She could read it easily.

It was an invitation to a party.

She was asked by the junior flying corps to come to the celebrations they were holding that night.

Isobel woke from the dream as if she'd seen the light. There was a wonderful feeling of expectancy. Of great things to come.

Oh God.

What was she waiting for?

MUMY, I AM COMMING.

The words taunted her.

She knew the message must be false.

And yet she was again aware of the quickening of her flesh, the pain of dried up and barren places suffusing with returning life. She found herself rubbing her body with her hands to assuage pins and needles.

Am I being tricked into healing? she wondered.

Or tricked into madness?

When she drew back the curtains, she saw the fog had gone. Mid-winter sun had not come, but the quality of the grey air tentatively suggested its imminence.

All through the morning, as she interviewed a group of young potters at the Ormazd Gallery, pictures of the dream kept finding her out. Though she didn't want to view a star which was a sludgy tea cloth, nor a biro message written on pine, these and other dream images jumped from behind her workaday concerns to confront her. She didn't believe, as some scientists did, that dreams were just off-runs from a closed-down computer. All manifestations of life, she felt, had validity; but interpreting that which was unconscious in terms which were conscious, she thought, was trying to turn an orange into a lemon.

Yet the images persisted; it was almost as if they asked to be seen. She began to wonder if this were some senseless activity devised to keep out of mind the untenable position she was in. How could she wait, with ever-increasing anticipation, for her dead child to come back to her?

Was all this hocus-pocus to ward off what was really coming? The hopelessness which would silt up her eyes and gag her throat?

When Isobel got back to Radio Brum she didn't, as she should have, listen to the potters' tape. Instead, she picked up *The Spirit of Christmas Past*. She'd not discussed it with the programme organizer after all, because he'd been tied up when she'd come back from the clinic. He'd put it back on her desk with a note of qualified approval.

She was spooling the programme on to the tape machine when the phone rang.

'Isobel? It's Bruno here.'

'What's that frightful noise in the background?'

'I'm at Euston Station. I'm taking a group of sixth formers to see the Sartre musical *L'Etre et le Neant*. I've been thinking about Saturday morning. I want to apologize to you. I asked you to the John Latimers' party because I hoped I could take you out again. It wasn't an excuse to bitch to someone about Caro. Can you still make it on Thursday?'

'Of course I can. And I didn't in the least mind you talking about Caroline.'

'I do. Caro is over. I didn't want you to think

215

that all I wanted was a shoulder to cry on. I keep thinking about you. I hardly stop thinking about you. I keep worrying too. Have the police come up with anything yet?'

'No.'

'You are all right, Isobel?'

'Yes.'

'Good. I'll see you on Thursday at around seven thirty.'

'I'm glad you rang.'

'So am I.'

'Listen . . . I've some actuality to get for a tape I'm doing. I want some party atmosphere. Do you think the Latimers would mind if I brought a Uher along?'

'A tape recorder? I don't think so. I'll give you the school's number. You'll catch John Latimer now if you ring. He stays at school for lunch.'

She took the number down. 'Enjoy the show,' she said as she rang off.

Vernon asked: 'Your Froggie's a-wooing?'

'How did you know?'

'You went the most delicate shade of pink, sweetie. Suited you, I thought.'

John Latimer knew her. 'I'm afraid I've always been bad at names,' she told him for she'd no recollection of him. 'I'll remember as soon as I see your face.'

'I should think there might be one or two more at the party you'll know. Betty Trumpington. And Ted Hooker-Smith's coming down from Preston. He's an art teacher. He played cricket with Charlie for the Lichfield Corinthians.'

'I do remember Betty vaguely. Plump and jolly.'

'Well, bring along your tape recorder. We'll organize a whole orchestra of clinking glasses and laughter. No names no pack drill?'

'Just a bit of party noise I want to thread through a half-hour programme on the pre-Christian origins of Christmas. I should say the pre-Christian origins of the festivities—'

'Say what you jolly well like,' said John Latimer, 'as long as I continue to get my two weeks of hols. Though I'm not saying that children aren't a good thing in theory. In their absence I sometimes even get quite sentimental about the little horrors.'

Isobel laughed. 'I look forward to seeing you on Thursday.'

'We've laid in plenty of supplies, tuned the piano and invited the neighbours on both sides. What more can a man do?'

Isobel put the phone down and went back to the tape machine. After listening to Professor Malahide again, she sank back in the chair thinking. Perhaps she'd look up this goddess Kore who had her temple in Alexandria?

But wasn't this nonsense? What she should be doing was trying to find out who put the Paddington Bear in the rocking-chair. Who telephoned? Who sent the Christmas card?

I ought to get back on to the police, she told herself. I ought to be doing practical things. At least breaking into Sandra's bungalow, however regrettable, had some *sense* to it. I wasn't in dreamland.

How could she have come to be in such a muddle? Her persecutor had, by some inverse of logic, become the bringer of tidings of great joy. It was not her deliverance she was moving towards but her destruction.

God help me, she thought.

Though as she didn't believe in any god it seemed doubtful that divine intervention would save her. Some kind of practical action might.

Grimly, she took Professor Malahide's tape off the machine and replaced it with that of the potters. Chinagraph in hand, she went through it. When she reached the end of the reel she looked up and saw only Vernon and Fanny Wragg in the room.

'Where is everyone?'

'Most have gone to lunch. The Turk is sniffing round on the third floor. Rumour has it that a major new television series is going to be done from here. *Living Artists*. Some guy thought it would be so much better to interview painters while they're still alive – rather than interview their critics when they're dead. A load of crap don't you think, sweetie? Most artists entirely mistake themselves. They never do what they paint. They're full of God Almighty shit,' said Vernon.

'Mousie isn't sniffing around,' said Fanny. 'Mousie believes in radio. He's radio through and through.'

'Everyone is until they get a chance to be television through and through,' said Vernon.

'You don't know what you're talking about!'

Suddenly Fanny exploded. 'You wouldn't know a piss from a principle! Just you shut up!'

'All right. All right. It's not the end of the world,' said Isobel. 'All I asked was where everyone was.'

'Sorry.' Fanny's eyes began to fill with tears. 'I just keep flying off the handle. I'm having the most awful frightful time. I can't think!' and she tore the copy paper out of her typewriter and screwed it up.

'What on earth's the matter, Fanny?'

'Geoff. My ex live-in. You'd never believe it. I thought he was a real decent guy. Some of his monthly pay cheque goes to Oxfam. Did I tell you that? Listen, this man's got a conscience like a hedgehog. He's up to his ears in principles.'

'What's he been up to?'

'I went to that little shit's house – our house – last night to collect some of my things and I did it ever so nicely, Isobel. I rang up first and I was polite. And when I went I didn't take Mousie with me. I did everything properly. The house was stripped by the time I got there. I've got a Victorian rosewood pole screen which my grandmother left me. It wasn't there. Nor my Rush LPs. Or the microwave I'm still paying for. Not even the kimono he bought me for my birthday. Nothing was there. *He claims the stuff never was there*. That it never existed beyond my imagination.'

'He can't get away with that.'

'He's going to have a damned good try,' said Fanny, 'he's playing this for all he's worth. He even pretended to be indignant. Said I was taking him for a ride and *I* wouldn't get away with it! And he's not prepared to sell our house. He says he is prepared to take over the joint mortgage repayment as long as I make the house over to him. But I get nothing back. That house has risen by almost 100 per cent since we bought it.'

'What are you going to do?'

'I'm going to see a solicitor. It's going to cost me an arm and a leg to get back what's mine. If I ever do. It's not just that. Well, it is that. Of course it is. But it's all so horrid and sordid. I feel unclean.'

'The guy's just trying it on,' said Vernon. 'He simply can't get away with this shit.'

'He called me a cheap little tart,' said Fanny. 'He said he was glad to see my back. I was a dirty little cow who never kept the house clean. It was horrible Isobel. Awful. He said it turned his stomach to see my hair clog up the bath plug,' and now tears were streaming down her face.

'I hope you gave as good as you got,' said Vernon. 'I know I only met the rat once. But you could see straight away he wasn't your type, sweetie. I mean one does so worry about men who must go in for karate. Just what are these guys trying to prove—'

'It's so unjust,' broke in Fanny. 'We had an agreement. He was supposed to do half the housework. But I was the dirty bitch who let it all get dirty. There never seemed time to clean the windows. One can get jolly tired, you know.'

Isobel got up and put her arms round her. Vernon disappeared.

'It's so awful. I never thought anything could be

so bad,' wailed Fanny. 'I couldn't sleep last night. He could have chopped up the pole screen, couldn't he? Mousie just says not to be hysterical. I can't think. I can't eat. Why is he being so unkind?'

'Perhaps he loved you,' said Isobel.

'Shit. Shit. Nothing but shit.'

'Well, it's all right now. You've got Mousie.'

'He's being wonderful really. Even though I keep on droning and droning in his ear. But it's not his house, is it? He's taking me off to London this weekend. We're staying with his brother. Oh, you've no idea how wonderful Mousie is. But he can't understand why I'm so upset, because I've got him you know and the solicitor will sort it all out. He'll settle that little prick's hash. He can't see there's a real problem,' sobbed Fanny. 'But I've never been hated before. Not really hated. It makes me feel so awful. The way he looked at me. I feel mucky all over.'

Vernon reappeared with a whisky bottle and a paper cup. 'I twisted our News Editor's arm,' he said and poured out a stiff drink. 'Come on, sweetie. Down the hatch. This'll make you feel a bit better.'

'No. I couldn't. Honestly, Vernon—'

'Nonsense. Think of my heroic achievement. Since when has anyone else squeezed anything out of those bums in the newsroom?'

Fanny's face screwed like a small child's as she drank the whisky. 'This stuff smells so terrible,' she spluttered.

'You mustn't cry, sweetie,' said Vernon. 'You're

a kid with a lot going for you. A chap from the Pru is no good for a girl like you.'

'He wasn't from the Pru,' hiccuped Fanny. 'His socks smelled vile. I think there was something wrong with his glands.'

'More than likely,' said Vernon. 'That might explain the karate.'

'I'll tell you what. Let's pile into my car and go down to Laure-Michelle's for a slap-up lunch. Treat on me,' said Isobel.

'Oh, I couldn't,' said Fanny. 'I'm waiting for Mousie.'

'Bugger Mousie,' said Vernon. 'Bugger all lover boys. Come out with a couple of pals.'

'Oh, you are terrible. All right. I will. I can't talk to Mousie about it any more. He gets mad at me. He thinks I'm being hysterical. After all, I have him. And I do. I'm very lucky really. I know that.'

'Love is a wonderful thing,' said Vernon. 'Wait for me. I won't be a sec. I'll just return the bottle to the babes in the newsroom.'

SIXTEEN

Isobel, who waited with ever-increasing anticipation so that sometimes she felt sick with excite-
ment, was given no further sign. Her daughter was
so present that now and then she found herself
talking to her. 'It's gone so mild the primroses are
out—' she said as she opened the curtains. 'And
Christmas less than a week away.' 'One, two, three,
four,' she counted as she mounted the stairs so that
Anne-Marie would be able to practise her numbers.

Catching herself out doing these things, the discs
of her spine jarred in shocked distress.

Slyly, reasoning herself out of reason, she put
Anne-Marie's card on the mantelshelf which ran
along the inglenook. It had a place of honour, at
the centre of the other Christmas cards she'd
received.

But there was no further sign.

As nothing happened in reality, she began to
think of the dream again. On Thursday, not long
before she was due to leave the broadcasting
centre, she found she'd some free time on her
hands. She went up to the library on the second
floor and took down a book on mythology, intent
on finding out about Kore, this goddess who'd had

a temple at Alexandria. She took the book over to one of the large pine tables.

Kore – who was sometimes called Persephone – was the daughter of the corn goddess Demeter and Zeus, the ruler of both gods and men. Demeter had at first rejected this great god, but he'd deceived the lady by turning himself into a bull.

In spite of being tricked into pregnancy by an illusionist, Demeter loved her child tenderly. One day though, while Kore was gathering flowers, the earth gaped open and up rose Hades who seized her, dragging her down into the bowels of the earth.

When Demeter heard her child's despairing wails, bitter sorrow surged through her veins. Over her shoulders she threw a sombre veil and then she took wing and flew like a bird over land and sea, seeking her child here, seeking everywhere . . .

Isobel sighed and leaned back in the chair. She was overcome with a feeling of profound relief. It was as if a doctor, on hearing her symptoms, had named the disease she had. She might have come into work day by day and gone about her affairs, but out of sight, out of mind, hadn't she, like the corn goddess Demeter, ranged the whole of the earth looking for her child?

She read further.

Demeter learned that it was Zeus himself, Kore's father, who had given the child to Hades as a bride.

After a long time in the wilderness of men, still

inconsolable with the loss of her daughter, Demeter returned to her temple. Here this Fury, for that was what grief had made of the corn goddess, prepared to kill the whole of mankind.

She would bid the earth be barren. The entire human race was doomed to starve.

Zeus intervened, sending messenger after messenger, but the Fury wouldn't be placated. She wouldn't permit the earth to be fruitful unless she saw her daughter.

Zeus then told his messenger to go to the underworld and command Hades to return young Kore. Hades complied with the will of the great god, but he was a trickster too. He tempted his bride Kore to eat some pomegranate seeds before sending her back; this was the marriage fruit and once eaten made the union of man and wife indissolvable.

Kore came into the light, but she must follow her shadow back to Hades.

Zeus, fearing the corn goddess's anger, decreed that Kore should live with Hades for one third of the year and pass two thirds with her mother. Demeter then set aside her anger. And so it was that winter was the season when Kore slept with Hades in the underworld and all the earth slept too; in spring Kore rose up into the light and the earth came to life and was starred with the blossoms of the harvest to come.

Isobel shut the book.

Was this story the reason why the Alexandrians, worshipping at the temple of Kore, went underground to get their divine child and bring it into the light? Or had many stories tangled together to produce this ritual?

She yawned, suddenly feeling very sleepy. She went down to the production office to collect her coat and bags.

Fanny Wragg had pushed her chair back and was staring intently at her ankles which were propped up in front of her on a desk, 'Do you think I should buy an ankle chain?' she asked Isobel.

'No, I don't.'

'Mousie says ankle chains turn him on. Mousie says ankle chains are very sexy.'

Earlier that afternoon Fanny had been to see her solicitor. When she'd returned there seemed to be something out of focus about her. It was as if, thought Isobel, one now looked at Fanny through a pane of frosted glass. She'd not told them what had gone on at the solicitors.

'It's your party tonight, isn't it?' Fanny asked.

'Yes.'

Fanny turned her ankle to view it from a different angle. 'Ankle chains make me think of slave girls and harems. I think it might be rather fun. I think you're being stuffy.'

Isobel collected her coat and bags. 'See you,' she said.

'You really don't think I should buy one?'

'Of course you shouldn't.' Isobel let the production office door swing shut after her.

As she drove back to Samson Cottage she felt in some strange way clearer, more defined; in naming

Demeter's disease as her own she felt she'd at last some inkling of what had been happening. Of course she hadn't been aware she'd been searching, for in reality she knew just where Anne-Marie was. How could she have suspected that she'd been ranging far and wide beyond her child's grave? But in reading the corn goddess's story she'd also read something of her own.

However reasonable she was, it seemed to her that it didn't stop her being totally unreasonable; she was simply unreasonable behind reason's back. Out of sight, out of mind, she'd thrown a sombre veil over her shoulder and flown like a bird, looking everywhere for her child.

But, of course, she really did know where Anne-Marie was.

Didn't she?

She parked her car and collected her things. Almost immediately she'd shut the cottage door behind her, she became aware of it.

Something fetid.

Something dead.

The stench seemed corporeal; it heaved apart her nostrils to make more room for itself.

Her stomach contracted. Bile rose.

A dead mouse? A rat? Could she smell a rat? Once she'd found a water rat decomposing behind the fridge freezer in the kitchen.

But she didn't go into the kitchen. She climbed to the study.

She opened the door. The smell was so strong her knees buckled inwards. The rocking-chair seemed to be moving in the shadow; it was as if something, someone, had just climbed out of it.

The chair shuddered, as if released from a terrible burden.

She closed her eyes. The thudding of her heart clamoured in her head.

When she opened her eyes again she saw the chair was quite still.

The smell was still there but it, too, seemed to be going. Like some loathsome jinnee, it was plopping back into its bottle.

She suddenly strode over to the window, bent down and flung it open. Fresh air drenched her. It was full of song.

'*Away in a manger—*' sang the village carollers. '*No crib for a bed—*'

Isobel slammed the window shut.

She ran back down the stairs. Bracing herself against the trestle-table, she breathed in deeply, squeezing her frightened heartbeats down to a more normal level. It's all my imagination, she told herself. I must stop frightening myself to death. She poured herself a large gin.

Later, back in control of herself, she bathed and changed. She'd bought some new party clothes; a pair of black silk thirties trousers cut to fall like a long skirt and a black kimono style top handpainted with roses. She'd just finished putting her lipstick on when the door bell rang.

'Just a minute. I'll get my coat and Uher,' she told Bruno as she let him in.

'You look lovely,' he said.

'Do I? Oh your gloves. You left them here—'and she disappeared into the kitchen. She saw the gloves were no longer on the counter top. 'They were just here. I'd swear to it. I must have tidied them away. Oh God. I'm always putting things where I can't find them.'

'Never mind,' said Bruno. 'They'll turn up.'

'I'm getting so absent-minded,' said Isobel, slipping on her coat.

'Got everything?' He opened the front door and switched off the lights for her hands were full.

'*Star of wonder, star of light,*

Star of royal beauty bright . . .' The village singers were now at the entrance to the alley.

They both dropped coins into a large biscuit tin. 'Happy Christmas,' Bruno called as he opened the passenger door for Isobel. And, as he started the car, he asked her: 'Are you all right?'

'Perfectly.'

'You seem a bit . . . on edge.'

'Too much imagination. That's the only trouble with me. Nothing has happened I can assure you. Did you like *Being and Nothingness*?'

'It was wonderful. All the modes of being were Barbie dolls or action men. My Sixth Formers loved them. Bad Faith was a transvestite Genghis Khan who was slowly turning into a fish. There were some great tunes. The set was made up of distorting mirrors and half the time you never knew which was the actor and which was the reflection and which were shadows that looked like somebody who wasn't there! One kid complained it made him feel dizzy.'

'I'm not surprised!'

He drove over the flyover on to the A38. Lichfield lay six miles away, new housing reaching out from its medieval centre. John Latimer's house was in the old town, not far from one which was once lived in by Erasmus Darwin, grandfather of Charles.

Bruno parked his car in a side street and they strolled back to the house, an unlikely building which was two-storey Tudor gabling at the front and three-storey Georgian mansion at the back.

'*Star of wonder, star of light—*' hummed Bruno as he rang the doorbell.

'I'm Daphne's sister. Daphne's John's wife. My brother-in-law,' said the woman who opened the door and who was already rather drunk. 'Poor Dap's in the kitchen. Doing things with mince pies.'

'Do I know you?' Isobel asked as she took off her coat.

'Do you? I expect so. I teach at St Agnes' Primary School. Are you a mum?'

'No.' Isobel found herself staring at the woman in increasing puzzlement; her glance kept returning to a thread of a scar on a very imposing nose.

Down through the years came a voice. 'You really must put his eyes in the right place. It makes a face look so foxy when the eyes aren't in the right place,' the Occupational Therapist had said.

'It is a fox.'

230

'I don't care if it's a kangaroo. Eyes right, my dear. That's the ticket.'

'You made a fox,' said Isobel. Now she saw Marigold as she'd first seen her in the dayroom at the psychiatric hospital; a Rule Britannia on a go slow. Going so slow, in fact, that only some miracle of balance had saved her from falling flat on her face. 'They say she shot herself with an air pistol,' Rita's voice came back to her. 'The pellet went up her nose – God knows how – and before you know it, it's in her eye and the retina's detached.'

'Isobel? Yes, Isobel. You made an elephant for your little girl. You tried to put its trunk on its rear end and its tail on its face.'

'None of us was very good at following the pattern,' said Isobel. And to Bruno: 'Marigold and I met in hospital. She's the first person I've seen from there since I came out. Actually, the elephant was for a neighbour's child.'

'And now you work for radio,' said Marigold. 'John told us you were coming with Bruno, but I'd no idea it was you. The name didn't ring a bell at all. I'll take your coats. You go on through.'

They walked down a wide stone-paved hall. A man in a canary yellow pullover shouted through an open door: 'Old chap it's you. Drinkies! Join the rest. Daphne's still doing miracles of something or other in the kitchen. She'll be through in a minute. And this is Isobel. Just the same, my dear. Just the same trim little baggage. Ain't life wonderful? This is the famous tape recorder. Better do the dirty deed at once. While we're all being very good kiddie-winkies.'

'Thanks. I'm very grateful.' Though in private Isobel was a shy woman, when acting professionally she'd no difficulty in taking charge. With the help of John Latimer, she rehearsed the party-goers. 'Lots of clinking glasses first. One or two isolated laughs. General laughter.' Most of the actuality Isobel taped wasn't actual at all, but stage managed. The trouble with life, she'd found, was that it fell short of good broadcasting standards.

'That's it! Thanks very much folks. You've been smashing—' and, turning to Bruno, she asked him quietly: 'Do you think I could borrow your keys? I'd like to put the Uher back in the car.'

Bruno looked at her questioningly.

'They're all wonderfully upright citizens, but the Uher belongs to the organization. I don't want it to get broken.'

'Or pinched?'

'Well, I'm sure everyone here is all right.'

'No, you aren't. What an untrusting woman you are.'

'One learns through experience,' said Isobel. 'I've reached the stage where I wouldn't even trust the Archbishop of Canterbury. People manage to get frightfully absentminded and do the most amazing things.'

'Are you sure you can trust me?'

'Yes, you goose.'

'Give me the recorder then and I'll lock it in the

boot. And don't run off with anyone while I'm away.'

Isobel, watching him go, couldn't help but feel flattered by the implication of his words. She realized it was a long time since any man had made it plain he found her desirable; it was a long time since she'd *let* any man make her feel like that.

'Oh, Isobel—'

She turned round to confront Marigold. Dressed in purple and silver, Marigold ought to have looked ridiculous, but she'd retained some of that monumental presence which had so awed Isobel when she'd first seen her. Marigold was no laughing matter. 'Most people here – well, they don't know about me being in hospital,' she said. 'Of course some do. But no-one tends to talk about it. I don't suppose it matters in your line of work. Radio and things are liberal minded, aren't they? Of course, I'm not saying that Educational Authorities aren't liberal minded, but they have to think of the mums, don't they? And you know . . . a nod here . . . a wink there . . . I always feel it's so much better to let sleeping dogs lie. If you see what I mean.'

'Of course,' said Isobel.

Marigold sighed with relief. 'Not that it matters at all you understand. But . . . better safe. I mean all it was – the top and the bottom of it – well, I just needed a rest. I mean, it's not as if I were ever . . . well, neither of us were, were we? Honest to God, some of them in there were plain crackers, my dear. They simply weren't like us.'

233

'Did you ever hear what happened to any of them?'

'Little Miss Know-it-all came to a very sticky end. But I expect you know about that. It was in the papers at the time.'

'Who do you mean?'

'Rita, of course. Mind you, I could see it coming. Just a bit of a smart Alec show. That was Rita.'

Isobel was astonished: 'A sticky end?'

'You didn't know then? She hanged herself. Funny when you think about it. It's men who hang themselves. She would have to be different, wouldn't she?'

'Poor little thing.' Isobel was near to tears.

'Well, it's a blessing in disguise really. She never was going to make anything, was she? And to keep people like that in there costs a fortune. You know what I mean, though of course people don't talk about it. I suppose I must sound hard, but a place like that makes you feel hard. A lot of it is plain wool pulling and my eye. Who do these people think they are, my dear? You can be too kind. That's what I've always said. I say, your glass is empty. What's your poison?'

'Gin and tonic.'

'There's Dap! Managed to drag herself out of the kitchen at last!'

Turning, Isobel saw a woman remarkably like Marigold coming through the door. But this woman was very much thinner, more like Marigold's ghost.

'Mind you, credit where credit's due,' said Marigold. 'Daphne's a jolly good cook. She says that's how she keeps her figure. All that cooking makes her sick. 'Ya-ho. Dappy!' and she waved to her sister and mimed the words: 'Finished?'

Daphne put her thumb up, managing to turn this ebullient gesture into something pitiable; a stiff upper lip for God and country while her ship was sinking under her.

'Does too much of course,' said Marigold. 'Runs herself ragged. These women who stay at home always feel they've to prove something, don't they? If our Dap's not baking wholemeal bread she's learning to speak Spanish as well as a Dago or shipping half a ton of blankets to refugees somewhere. Easier to work I say. Apart from the cash, it's so much less effort.'

Isobel saw Bruno come back into the room. Her heart, that trickster at the centre of her being, leapt into joy. He was stopped by Daphne. She found herself extricating herself from Marigold and had almost made her way through to him when she was cornered by John Latimer. He began to introduce her to people she didn't know.

It wasn't until two hours later, when supper was being served, that she and Bruno were alone together again. He was tackling some of Daphne's rollmop herrings, she a pile of *langues de chat* in the hope that the light sponges would mop up some of the drink. Isobel, who'd no capacity for alcohol, had drunk far too much.

'I've got something to tell you,' Bruno said, putting his plate on the carpet and settling down with his back to John Latimer's glass-paned bookcase. She, on her knees, caught the anxiety in his voice and stopped eating. 'I've just heard something extremely worrying about the second Mrs Maccabee.'

Such was her state of inebriation that she almost laughed.

'See that chap over there?' Bruno went on, pointing out a stocky man in his fifties who was wearing baggy cords and a fisherman's smock. 'Ted Hooker-Smith. He left us to teach at a school in Preston—'

'Oh, I know him. He and Charlie used to play cricket together—'

'He's down here with his wife, spending Christmas with his mother-in-law. When Charlie and Sandra moved up to Blackpool, Ted and your ex-husband met up again and kept in touch in a very on-off sort of way.

'Apparently Charlie was off with the ladies, but managed to keep Sandra in the dark—'

'Keep it dark from Sandra,' Isobel said, certainly drunk enough to correct his English.

'In the dark. We Frenchmen have an ear for another language.'

'I think you've had too much to drink too.'

'Do listen, Isobel. I'm being serious. Sandra did find out about one of his affairs. He was seeing this woman called Mrs Turner, a blonde a good deal older than himself. She was married to a Fleetwood bank manager and there were three teenage children.

'Anyway, Sandra took Charlie's cricket bat and

went to Mrs Turner's house and laid into her. She fractured her skull, broke her collar bone and a rib. The thing was all hushed up and no charges were brought. The Turners didn't want the scandal to come out into the open. He'd his job at the bank to think of. And, of course, there were the kids. Hooker-Smith heard about it first from a mutual friend and then from Charlie himself. Both said Mrs Turner was lucky to survive. Are you sure Sandra's in America?'

'I spoke to her. Anyway half killing someone isn't the same thing as what's been happening to me. It's losing control of yourself. Whoever put Anne-Marie's bear in the rocking-chair and phoned me up . . . well, that's so cold blooded.'

'It might be cold blooded, but it's still an act of rage,' said Bruno.

'It always comes back to why Sandra would want to do such a thing. Hitting Mrs Turner was a reaction to something. In my case there's nothing for Sandra to react to. Whichever way you look at it – and if you forget all about America – we're still left with that.'

'According to you there's no reason for anyone to do it.'

'That's the truth.'

'Yet someone has done these things.'

'But, Bruno, what can happen in reality? Anne-Marie simply can't come back. However much I kid myself at times. Nothing can happen.'

'No . . . I suppose – no . . .'

'I shouldn't have eaten all that sponge. Sorry.

Oh so sorry. You'll have to excuse me.' Her hand flew to her mouth. 'Where – ?'

'Up the stairs, turn left to the back of the house. Down the landing. Straight in front of you—'

'Thanks—'

Isobel was very sick. Later, blinking back the tears and washing herself, she looked at her whey face in the mirror. Why do I do it? she wondered. I know I can't drink much. I was lucky I didn't get palpitations.

She got out her comb and then repaired her face. When she'd finished she flushed the lavatory again, pulled up the blind and hauled open the sash window. The beam of light flooded on to the lawn.

Trapped half in, half out of the light was a writhing mass. Isobel slowly made out Marigold who appeared to be riding something. Someone. Her knees were digging into the lawn, her bottom upturned, her hands held on to a pair of ears. She was emitting grunts and there was a sucking sound. Suddenly the legs of a second body flicked up, like the lash of a snake. Isobel gradually realized that the prone body was shuffling off half-mast pants. As the last roll of wool-polyester descended to the grass, she was able to make out a pair of rather smart boots. The soles juddered and clicked together like a pair of castanets.

Marigold, taking a firmer grip on John Latimer's ears, bore down more heavily. Her buttocks squeezed fiercely together as if to wring the last drop of life out of the wretched man.

Isobel slammed the window down, hauled the blind back into place and swung round so quickly her shoulder blade grazed against plumbers' pipes. Her cry was lost in Marigold's shout, more a death rattle than a squawk.

Flying out of the lavatory, Isobel felt not so much ill as winded. She clutched at the banisters to support her weak limbs as she went downstairs.

Bruno was waiting for her in the hall. 'Would you like to go home?'

'Oh, yes please.'

'We'll just tell Daphne. She's in the kitchen.' He took her arm and even as her numbed mind was working out how to protest she found herself face to face with John Latimer's wife. This woman, too, was on her knees, but she was pulling out hot mince pies from her oven.

'I'm terribly sorry, but Isobel's not feeling too well. I'm going to run her home.'

Daphne, who'd reached up to put the last tray on the well-scrubbed butcher's block, rose. Her hair had fallen prettily about her forehead and the heat of the oven had flushed her cheeks. 'Oh, that's really too bad. You do look a little pale. I hope it's not going to be flu.'

'I'm afraid it's just a little over-indulgence. Absolutely disgraceful of me,' apologized Isobel.

'Then you must take your Christmas cake with you.' Despite their objections, she took the carving knife from the magnetic strip on the wall, cut two enormous slices, and wrapped them in tin foil. 'It *is* going very well, isn't it? John will be pleased. He works so hard at organizing everything. He does so love it if a party really takes off.'

Coats on, each with cake in left hand, she shepherded them to the door. 'Oh. Just a mo, will you? I forgot.' She rushed down the hall and returned with a collecting box. 'For the starving in Ethiopia you know.'

Trapped in the guilt of holding two huge wedges of cake, both gave extremely generously. Daphne beamed in triumph. 'So good of you—' she crooned and pursued them down the steps as she told them of the hair-raising changes brought about by malnutrition. 'Have a Happy Christmas, do!' she called after them as they finally made their escape.

Hand-in-hand and clutching their cake, they were like a pair of children leaving a primary school party. 'She's a very good woman,' said Bruno.

'Yes,' said Isobel.

'A wonderful woman.' He opened the car door for her. Isobel climbed in. He dumped his cake on her lap. 'You have it. I can't stand the bloody stuff.'

SEVENTEEN

It was the afternoon of Christmas Eve. Isobel had sneaked off early from work. In this she felt justified because she'd to call at Lichfield Library on the way back to get out some books on Anna Seward. She'd been asked to do a *Period People* item by the producer of the breakfast show. 'Honestly, my angel, I wouldn't ask you unless I was really stuck,' he'd told her. 'Everyone and his cat are bogging off for their hols. And I simply can't trust one of the youngsters. I'll have no time to re-package the tape.'

Isobel, in previous times of crisis, had already come up with two notable sons of Lichfield, Dr Samuel Johnson of dictionary fame and Elias Ashmole, the antiquarian who gave his unique collection to Oxford University.

This time she was determined to do a woman, though the eighteenth-century Lichfield intellectual Anna Seward did have one big disadvantage; she was a poet. Listeners quite enjoyed plays about poets' lives – many poets had interestingly scandalous lives – and they didn't mind poets airing their opinions in interviews. They simply drew the line at hearing poetry. Though it was expected that people would switch off arts programmes – after all they were only there to impress licensing bodies and such politicians who'd decided it expedient to care about culture – a main sequence programme was a different matter. But at least Anna had had the good sense to fall desperately in love with an unhappily married choir master, thought Isobel. That should pull in the customers.

She decided that if she stuck to the life and vigorously eschewed the verse all could work out well. She didn't feel too guilty about this as her edition of *The British Encyclopedia* referred to Anna as having 'gained an unaccountable reputation as a poet'. There was plenty of material, Isobel was pleased to discover, because Anna had been a wonderfully gossipy letter writer.

She'd almost finished filleting what she needed from the reference works when the door bell rang. It was Drue, who'd abandoned the turban she usually wore in favour of a head scarf tied in gypsy fashion. Isobel peered round the frail figure. 'Where's Mrs Bennett?'

'At home with Mr Bennett preparing her bird and trifles.'

'You mean you've walked across here alone?'

'And why not?'

'You could have fallen.'

'Why should I fall more easily crossing the road than in my own home? Don't lecture me. I'm old enough to be your mother.'

'What's ruffled your feathers?'

'Nothing. Just you being so jolly cheeky. As if I

can't cross a road. As if I'm no more than two years old. Anyway, I haven't come alone as it happens. I've brought my sloe gin. I fancied a tipple. And why not? It's Christmas, isn't it? But I've not the slightest intention of drinking alone. You've no idea where that sort of thing may lead to. Fetch the glasses.'

'You're on your high horse about something,' Isobel said and went to do as she was told.

'Just that man Simeon Kelso. If I'm to have words on my tombstone he's to vet them if you please. Talk about a free country. I could put anything I liked in a book. But not on my tombstone. Apparently it has to be in good taste. Well, for a start I don't think it's in good taste to die. I just can't see why things couldn't have been arranged better than that.'

'But what did you want written over you?'

'Haven't actually decided, my dear. The vicar and I were talking about it and then he let slip about his having to approve. Really. Who is footing the bill? That's what I'd jolly well like to know. Oh. I'm so vexed.'

'You've upset him,' Isobel surmised. 'Simeon's a very nice man.'

'I told him I'd like something inappropriate. I was only teasing the silly man. Well—' and she lifted her glass so Isobel could fill it from the jar '– sounding him out a little,' she conceded.

'But why do you want something inappropriate?'

'Well, it would jolly up the graveyard a bit. Make the whole thing a little less depressing. If

243

we've got to go – and it appears we've jolly well all got to go – why not try to make things a bit more cheerful. A bit livelier if you see what I mean. After all, if we're being truthful, not a few people will be glad to see the back of me. I mean, I'm worth a pretty penny you know and it certainly isn't going to a cats' home. I don't mind people waiting in the wings to grab it. If I were in their shoes I'd be doing just that. One has to be practical. What I'm driving at is that there's a great deal too much humbug in funerals. I don't like it. I don't like it at all. Oh don't let's talk about it, my dear. Though I must say the vicar made my blood boil. All that pious mewing. What do you think of my brew?'

Isobel tasted the bright red drink and shut her eyes. 'Wonderful.'

'Yes. I really believe we've excelled ourselves this time. We've got plenty more at Mickleholme. I'll leave you the jar.'

'Just what is the secret?'

'No secret. Almonds.'

'You're pulling my leg.'

'I assure you. Layers of sugar, sloes, sugar, sloes and when the pickling jar is almost full you add blanched almonds and, of course, the gin. You ought to try making some yourself.'

'I very well might.'

'I've been meaning to get hold of you, you know. I've heard a very interesting tale about your street lamp.'

'It's out,' said Isobel.

'Well, of course. And do you know what Mrs

Bennett was told by that woman – what's-it who always says that distressing rabbit of hers is silver fox? The one with the son?'

'Mrs Pike.'

'I always remember she's a fish. My trouble is I never can recall which fish. Well. The night of the fog – do you remember that dreadful fog? – the Girl Guides were holding their Christmas do at the village hall. Mrs Pike has a girl, too, apart from that poor lad of hers. The daughter and some other guides were walking to their party down Main Street when they saw a woman with a push chair turn down your alley. The woman mustn't have realized they were there, because my dear, quick as a flash she dives under the hood of the pram, takes out a stone and jolly well chucks it at your lamp.' Drue paused and then looked at Isobel in a curious, rather triumphant way. 'What do you make of it?'

Isobel stared at her. 'I've no idea.'

'Quite. What can anyone make of that? I've a good mind to ring up my superintendent again.'

'Oh, Drue. They've enough to do at this time of the year. It's hardly the crime of the century.'

'You know perfectly well what I'm driving at.'

'Look, you mean well but I'd like you to drop the whole thing. Forget it. Nothing has happened for quite a time now.'

'You're a very stubborn young woman.'

Isobel put another log on the fire and then refilled Drue's glass. To cheer her up, she told her about the dream.

'You can't just end it there. What were the words on the table? In plain English?'

'In plain English the junior flying corps was inviting me to join them at a party that night.'

'Is that all? What can it mean?'

'I've no idea.'

'I think you've spoiled my dream,' Drue said. 'Biro and parties. That's not the same as Arabic at all. Arabic is jolly well exciting and mysterious. Biro.' She was disgusted. 'Whoever heard of one's future being written in biro? No person of taste would use a biro. And don't laugh at me.'

'I'm sorry, Drue. Honestly.'

'You simply aren't made of the right material. Not at all the material prophesies are made of. When the moving finger wrote there was no mention of biro, was there? You're an incorrigible, my dear. All your generation are. You've no feeling for the heroic. No vision of how things should be. Sometimes you make me feel jolly old.'

'Not too old to walk across here with a bumper jar of sloe gin.'

'Well, I expect you will go about things in your own way,' and very slowly she levered herself out of the chair. 'Whist tonight. I must have my nap before then.'

'Now don't you go galloping off. I'm going to take you back.'

'All right. But I've simply no intention of falling. Not until I've beaten Henry Crick in a rubber or two. That man thinks he's a mind, my dear. Mind indeed. Strictly between us two, he's just the sort of

246

fool who thinks everything adds up because two and two sometimes make four. But of course he's a lawyer. That's been the unmaking of many a fine man.'

The afternoon was mild and sunny; Drue's winter jasmine was in full flower, acid yellow against the hard-baked brick of Mickleholme Villa. 'So heartening to see a bit of sunshine in December,' Drue said and Isobel bent so she could kiss her cheek. 'Thank you for the Christmas cake. It was jolly thoughtful. Take care. Do take care.'

Isobel, suddenly in the grip of a compulsion she couldn't explain, took a short cut down by the side of Drue's house to the church. She climbed the steps of a steel footbridge which spanned the canal. A barge was tied up on the farther side. Two fishermen, lines out, contemplated the limpid water.

Reaching the towpath on the other side, she warily rounded an evil-looking drake. A new vicarage of a butterfly-roofed design lay in grounds which shelved to the canal. The church and churchyard adjoined and further along the towpath was the village bowling green. All swam in a misty golden light which, though it was only three o'clock, deepened towards twilight.

She walked through the gap in the hawthorn hedge into the new churchyard. Nearly all the graves had been decorated for Christmas, chrysanthemums, roses, pinks, iris, freesias, all blazed triumphantly in the winter landscape. On Anne-Marie's grave someone from the village had placed a small bunch of snowdrops.

When she got back home she took Anne-Marie's card down from the mantelpiece, tore it up and threw the pieces on the fire. The pain in her heart had spread, stiffening her fingers, making them clumsy; some of the bits escaped and fluttered on to the hearth. Resolutely she gathered them up and fed them to the fire.

Afterwards she felt shocked. She'd no idea what had driven her back to her daughter's grave or caused her to burn the card. Both were spur of the moment actions. And yet . . . now she'd read Demeter's story, now she'd named her disease, it was as if some malignant spell had been broken. She felt free to act in a way which had been impossible before.

Can it be as easy as this?

Her pain told her it could not.

But she had to begin somewhere.

Sweet reason.

Yes.

That was a start.

She felt she was both shrinking and growing, shrinking because she was being redefined in the reality of her loss, a woman without child or husband, but nevertheless she was not all loss for something had remained, some presence in the world; and growing because out of nowhere – out of the unnamed, the unrealized – she seemed at last to be finding enough grace to bear the pain of her loss.

Smoke was twisting off the last edge of card when the telephone rang.

'You are all right for tonight?' It was Bruno. 'Seven o'clock?'

'Yes, of course.'

'Good. I . . .'

'Caro has been on to you again—' she said, detecting a metallic edge in his voice.

He was silent for a moment. 'Yes.'

'Oh dear. Bad?'

'It's not about her.' He paused again and then said: 'Before she rang off she told me that she'd seen Sandra over a week ago. She bumped into her in Harrods. Sandra was in the children's department buying clothes.'

Isobel found she didn't want to hear this. She simply didn't want to know what the second Mrs Maccabee had been up to. It seemed that however hard she struggled to free herself of her past life she was dragged back into it. 'I expect she was buying presents. After all, it is Christmas.'

'You told me that woman was in America.'

'She's obviously come back.'

'We've no idea how long she stayed in the States. It need only have been for a day or two.'

'Look, we've been over all this before. Whatever that woman does or doesn't do, I don't see how it can concern me.'

'I wish I could be as sure,' said Bruno.

'Oh, please forget it,' Isobel begged. 'I just want to have a nice Christmas. See you at seven.'

After she'd put the phone down, she drew a bath. Dressed in a new black velvet dressing-gown her sister had sent her from Australia, she went downstairs and took a small tot of Drue's sloe gin to the bathroom. Slipping out of the dressing-gown, she toasted herself in the mirror. 'Here's to the end of Mrs Maccabee and the beginning of you.'

While she was in the bath it occurred to her that she could sell the rocking-chair.

The audacity of that thought took her breath away.

She could even sell the cottage.

She could, she realized, do anything.

She was hardly dry when the phone rang again.

'Duckie, have I got news for you. What a pity you sneaked off early! You quite missed all the fun. Oh you lucky, lucky thing. Wait till you hear this. Our programme organizer went to a slap-up Chrissy lunch with some of the organization's executive types. And our squeaky-clean Hilary got as drunk as a skunk. Pissed out of his brains. And when he got back he chased the newsroom secretary into the gram library. Do you know, darling, I always thought our Hilary was a queer,' Fanny told Isobel.

'The man's married with three children.'

'Doesn't mean a thing. Not a thing,' Fanny assured her. 'You have to admit Vernon is never out of his office. They're always closeted together. Oh, I'm sure Vernon had hopes there. Anyway, it seems we've pegged Hilary wrong.'

'You did.'

'Listen, will you? He gets Sunita Jones cornered—'

'That I find really hard to believe. Every hack in

the newsroom has spent his life trying to corner Sunita. None of them has managed it yet—'

'Well, it didn't do Hilary a fat lot of good. He got brewer's droop at a very vital moment. Mind you, it might have had nothing to do with the drink. They say Sunita's a look which would freeze the balls in the biggest cannon. And poor old Hilary hardly has a pea-shooter. Anyway, the guy then starts to get maudlin and go on about his wife. She's suddenly become a born-again Christian. I suppose if you're married to Hilary you've got to get your own back somehow—'

'Fanny!'

'Oh, come off it, you know what I mean. Anyway, darling, he then starts to ramble on about the staff. Apparently one of the people at his posh lunch was the producer Jack Drummond. He's going to do this new television series on living artists. Jack wants you to work on the series.'

'What?'

'I know it's all pretty amazing, but Sunita swears to it. And as you know that woman has never got anything wrong.'

'Hilary might have got it wrong.'

'Don't be silly, darling. He'd only just come from seeing the guy. You could be a little more enthusiastic. This is it, duckie. This is your big break. I think it wonderful that someone like you should become a high flyer.'

'Someone like me?'

'Well, you know what I mean. No offence. I mean most people say you have to make it before you're thirty. After that you're practically too old for anything. That's what I was told when I was lucky enough to land myself a job here.'

'Thanks very much!'

'Don't get sore. You know exactly what I mean. I know you know. We're all bound to be over thirty at some time, aren't we? And by the time you've reached that age people begin to wonder why you haven't done anything spectacular. I mean, they're asking themselves what's wrong with you. And then this . . . right out of the blue. Lucky little pig. Listen. I know I'm being a bit cheeky darling, but Hilary's bound to ask you who should take over *Brum Arts*. Would you mind frightfully putting in a good word for me?'

'I don't see why not. That is, if it comes to it.'

'Oh you're grade one, duckie!'

'I wouldn't bank on any of this. I'm not through the door yet, Fanny.'

'Sunita is never wrong. Isn't it wonderful. You can really celebrate tonight.'

'Actually I'm off to a performance of Handel's 'Messiah' at Lichfield Cathedral.'

'Well at least it's seasonal, darling. If nothing else. I must dash. I've got to wash Mousie's hair.'

'And are you happy about it?' Bruno asked her later as they drove to Lichfield.

'I keep worrying that Fanny's got it all wrong so I must be happy about it,' said Isobel.

Bruno laughed. 'Don't worry. *In vino veritas, hein?*'

During the oratorio, she became aware that

Bruno kept looking at her; in the moments when he averted his gaze she found herself turning to study him. Their hands joined and like a pair of children they hung on while the music in Handel's mind rattled the foundations of the cathedral.

But, though she invited him into the cottage for a nightcap, he made no move to stay. He seemed to have a wish to woo her like an old-fashioned white knight. Perhaps the brutal break-up of his marriage, the corroding effects of love's ill will, had given him the need to try and put the pieces back in a different order.

They would, she thought, be tender with each other; neither would love in the way they had before. Yet this – nor any other kind of loving – would save them from the abyss which would gape if one withdrew love from the other. But she was astonished to discover that she must count the gain higher than the loss, or she wouldn't even be having these thoughts.

They kissed goodnight on the steps of the cottage. Climbing the stairs to bed, she had a vision of her life moving too quickly; it was almost as if she were being caught in a whirlwind. She must try to separate out events, think about them.

But she slid into sleep as soon as she drew up the duvet to her chin.

Opening her eyes, she was aware of thinning light, the whey of a waning moon. She was listening to a steady rhythmic creaking. A boat on choppy seas, her half asleep mind pictured. A dipping, bobbing hull with a name on its prow:

Anne-Marie. And a smell. Fish rotting in the hold.

She struggled to sit up; the smell, though noxious, was not overpowering. It drifted in and out of her nostrils, carried on eddying draughts of air.

The creaking was persistent.

The rocking-chair.

Her bones stood out of her skin.

Back-and-forth. Back-and-forth.

Crea . . . eek. Crea . . . eek. Crea . . . eek.

Rock-a

Rock-aahh

Rock-aahh . . . bye

Rock-a-bye baby! sang the chair. Now a song of triumph.

Isobel's legs slid shiveringly together as she swivelled herself off the bed. Her feet found the leather mules on the floor and crept in. One whey-fingered hand reached out for the black velvet robe. She stood and slid it over her head.

Rock-a-bye

Rock-a-bye

Rock-a-bye baby sang the chair.

Hypnotized by the rhythm, Isobel opened her bedroom door. The sound of the hinges sawed through the lullabye. Her knees banged together.

The door became silent. The chair rocked on. The smell, a fetid smell, a pungent mucky smell, made her think of afterbirth.

Isobel, wanting to shut her eyes and yet not able to, put her hands out like a sleep walker and pushed open the study door. As she did so she had a sense of double vision; she didn't know if she were looking at herself doing this or if another pair of equally alien eyes did so.

Though she'd now entered her study, though the creak of the chair was so much louder, she couldn't at first bring herself to look. She walked over to the moon-washed window as if to an exit, as if this somehow provided her with a way out.

Look. Look. Look. The moon was shouting at her.

Glad tidings I bring.

Very slowly, the black robe billowing gently at her ankles, the silver tassles swinging, she turned. As she did so exultation filled her.

Anne-Marie was turned sideways in the chair. There were two grotesquely large red woollen gloves on the hands which clutched the bear. Paddington had a new hat on and wrapped about his neck was a jaunty little yellow and red check scarf. She wore a shiny red raincoat. The hood, lined with Black Watch tartan, obscured her face. Red Wellingtons were pulled well up over denims.

The only pieces of clothing that Isobel recognized were the gloves. They were Bruno's.

That strange moment of exultation was gone. She both knew this was her child and yet was not her child and now tenderness was gutted on spikes of fear. Very slowly, very cautiously, she moved forward, her fingers seeking out the face of this apparition. Sliding under the hood those fingers came into contact with something that felt like dead mouse. She withdrew in shock. As she did so a

255

black coconut-like thing toppled out of the hood and bounced on the floor. It rolled to a stop near her feet.

She stood transfixed; her lips were stretched out, empty of sound, the bottom lip so drawn back that teeth showed. Her prying hands were arrested mid-air, in the act of flying upwards. Her feet arched in the mules, heels leaving contact with the ground.

Anne-Marie moved.

Very slowly something slipped out of the right arm of the raincoat. She saw it was a length of fibula; not an arm at all; but one of the lower bones of a leg even though it wore a glove. When it clattered to the floor the vibration caused the head to roll over. It stopped face upwards.

Though her eyes were stone and could not see she recognized this, her daughter. The child's lips were rotted away to reveal the gap caused by the loss of a milk tooth. The eye sockets, now empty, nevertheless were haunted by Isobel's own inky blue eyes.

Limb of my limb.

Light of my light.

Life of my life.

Isobel would have known Anne-Marie anywhere; she knew her here, acknowledged these rotting remains. She couldn't deny her child.

When she saw she couldn't deny what she'd seen, her heels came into contact with the mules, her hands fell, her eyes were no longer made of stone. Her whole body sighed and shook.

Restored to herself, she knew she was being watched by another. The second Mrs Maccabee.

'As you see,' said the other. 'I've brought her.'

Her voice was clear; in Isobel's ears it rang out like the Lutine bell.

'I've delivered your child.'

EIGHTEEN

She saw the other half of Mrs Maccabee reflected in the cheval mirror. Her blond hair was crew cut. All her war paint was in place. False eyelashes stuck out from the lid of the eye Isobel could see, a green eye encased in kohl. Blusher was worked into a cheek still plump with stillborn pregnancy. Florescent lip gloss.

She was wearing Charlie's wedding ring, his engagement ring and his eternity ring. She also had a gold chain about her neck and from it dangled a cross; perhaps a present from Charlie.

This Mrs Maccabee, Isobel further noted, had very beefy shoulders and not all of that was the padding in her partly unzipped white leather blouson jacket. Her pants were stuffed into cream cowboy boots; the boots were thick with polished steel studs.

It was when the reflection moved that Isobel observed the cricket bat in the right hand. The finger nails were long and green and the grip more that of a rounder's player than a cricketer.

Isobel took all this in as she glanced for no more than a moment in the cheval mirror. She was intent on other things. The second Mrs Maccabee was no more than an intrusive face in the congregation.

There were rituals to perform, observances for her dead.

She went through to the linen cupboard which was next to the bathroom. She selected a white cotton sheet, a pillow and pillowcase and a white lacy tray cloth. She came back and arranged them on the single bed.

Going to the rocking chair, she gently lifted her child. Her arms trembled with the effort of moving the remains in such a way that none of the loosening joints broke away.

She laid the body and the Paddington Bear on the bier. She retrieved and placed the leg bone next to the remains and then she took up the head. She laid it on the pillow which she'd covered with the lacy cloth.

In all this she'd to will her flesh to do the work she commanded of it; she cringed from the feel of dead matter. It was as if she were laying out herself.

When her child was arranged to her satisfaction, she slowly wound the sheet about the body. She looked into shining inky eyes for a moment and could not cover them, could not deny sight. But then they became empty sockets again and, hand trembling only a little, she drew the linen across. The light was out.

She went into the bathroom.

What she had in mind was a large butcher's knife, something to do butchery with. Her search yielded a pair of hair-dressing scissors. She would have preferred to break a glass bottle and use the neck edge, but all the bottles were plastic.

She felt she moved through a dream and yet she was well aware she was wide awake. Having laid out her child, she must now lay out the second Mrs Maccabee. After, of course, killing her.

Her spirit, like Demeter's, had ranged over land and sea; now she'd found what she'd sought. A Fury had returned to the temple of its flesh. The scissor blades opened. They snipped experimentally at air. The blades were not bigger than the gape of a small alligator's jaw.

Her mule-shod feet padded quietly back.

The other Mrs Maccabee was crossing the threshold.

Isobel moved in front of her child.

For the first time the two women came face to face. Sandra was a head taller and four stones heavier than Isobel. She was flexing her shoulders.

Isobel could smell Chanel Number Five and there was another smell, too. The smell of her child was on the other woman.

For the first time she experienced her fury. The veins in her neck pushed out through her skin.

The other Mrs Maccabee, looking into those narrowing inky eyes, read her fate there. She swayed, off balance, as if a hole had opened under her feet. Her hand went out to touch the cross at her neck. She straightened again. She was ready to make her own fate.

Neither spoke.

They rose on their toes. Isobel spread her body, defending the length of her baby. A small sound whistled through her teeth.

The other Mrs Maccabee stepped back, giving herself more room to wield the cricket bat. The blade had only half risen when Isobel flung herself at her. Both hands were on the scissors. She went for the jugular.

Sandra jerked her head. The tip of the scissors grazed skin. The force of Isobel's body sent them both reeling backwards. Sandra cracked her head on the beam above the door jam. Her body sagged and she almost fell.

Isobel, making a cat-like recovery, was back in front of her child.

Dazed, Sandra's hand felt towards her head but she was righting herself. And then Isobel saw her shoulders convulse. The left side of her face was caught in bright moonlight. A tear rolled through the mascara and a dirty blob appeared on the plump cheek. But she took a firmer grip on the cricket bat.

Isobel waited. She knew nothing would get between her and her daughter. She could feel the heat of her rage. Her feet were making small rhythmic dancing movements.

Sandra swayed again as she turned to fully face her. The bright moonlight now united then both in its beam. Another tear made a stain on Sandra's cheek. Her body began to shake. At first it was barely noticeable, but as her grief grew, her arms folded towards her chest. Her hands made a strange upward cupping movement. The cricket bat clattered to the floor.

Suddenly she turned and hurled herself towards the stairs. Isobel ran after her.

They burst out of the cottage into the blackness of Christmas morning. Sandra sprinted down Main Street. Isobel half tripped in her anxiety to grab hold of her. Caught in street lighting, they threw grotesque shadows; the first a bat, the second dipping low on the shade of a broomstick.

Rounding Mickleholme Villa, Sandra bounded down the lane and over the steel footbridge which spanned the canal. She turned right towards Wychnor.

The trailing Mrs Maccabee was distantly aware of pains but couldn't yet understand these gasps of hurt were hers.

Sandra reached the humped-back brick bridge which marked the village boundary. She passed the lock, pounded over the Quarter Miler and disappeared into the vegetation which bordered the towpath on the other side.

Isobel, still so far out of her skin that she was flying over gravel and not on it, nevertheless saw the distance between herself and her quarry widening. She plunged off the Quarter Miler into the rattle of rhizome grasses. Shifting high nets of dead Queen Ann's lace obscured her vision.

I mustn't lose her, she found herself thinking. Her anxiety had sharpened into dread. It was as if half her own body had detached itself and was disappearing beyond recall. She lifted her long skirt higher and increased her speed, hurling herself across the series of footbridges which lifted the towpath above the squelch of water meadows.

Suddenly she shrank back into her pain-wracked

body. Leather had rubbed holes in her toes; her lungs squealed. Silent tears began to course her cheeks for she realized she could run no more.

She saw Sandra through blurring vision. She was partially lit by the sodium lights of the A38, a mile to the right over the fields. The twilit orange figure was limping across the fourth iron footbridge.

Both of them toiled forward.

Perhaps she'll tell me why, Isobel thought. Surely there's a reason. There must be a reason. Something I can understand.

They had given her a reason for the death of her daughter. It had been meaningless all the same.

Still . . . perhaps there was a reason.

After all, she thought, Sandra knows what it's like to lose her child.

And . . . she's just like me.

There's nothing about that woman that's like me, she thought, and now her rage had died the thought saddened her. The two Mrs Maccabees with such similar histories seemed caught in spinning collisions and collusions of shock and loss. Compounding each other's woes. All come to grief.

In her agony she forgot what she was doing in this gusting landscape where dead grasses nodded briskly, where slivers of severed leaf worked free from pretty skeletons.

She kept on moving because she was moving. It was what she was used to doing, putting one foot in front of the other. A blind faith in moving on.

And then, looking ahead again, she saw the other Mrs Maccabee. She'd climbed on to the tubular steel railings of the cattle bridge which crossed the canal at Wychnor.

Shocked that her quarry no longer moved, Isobel came to a standstill.

At first she couldn't make out what Sandra was up to and then she knew. The second Mrs Maccabee was going to throw herself off the bridge.

Isobel must shout out. Stop her.

But she was empty of words. She'd nothing to say to the other Mrs Maccabee. She watched her manoeuvre her body forward from the tubular steel bars.

Viewing the waters below her, Sandra juddered.

She saw herself in my child, Isobel realized.

She saw death.

The other Mrs Maccabee sat back on the top bar, the heels of her cowboy boots hooked over a lower one. The canal was ten feet below her; Isobel calculated that the water at this point was about mid-thigh level.

Committing suicide wasn't going to be easy but this was obviously what Sandra had in mind; mesmerized, she gazed into the water.

Will she do it? Isobel found herself wondering.

Will she take the plunge?

It was certainly not the best place in which to attempt an act of suicide. She would have a much better chance of succeeding at the lock further down towards the village.

She could, of course, hit her head on a rock as she fell. There were quite a few towards the other side of the canal where the water was shallower. The navigable channel was by the towpath, to the left of the bridge's central brick pillar.

Perhaps I could give her a push? Isobel found herself thinking. And when she's in the canal I could hit her head with a rock?

She found she was flexing her fingers.

Oh, how the chattering of the other Mrs Maccabee's teeth got on her nerves. Sandra was certainly taking her time.

Was she made of the right stuff? Did she have the guts?

And then Isobel felt her own body begin to rise a little as Sandra pushed herself upright. The tubular steel rails vibrated.

'Don't!' screamed Isobel.

Sandra, one hand attached to the rail, turned to look at her. And then she made the sign of the cross.

Isobel was dumbfounded.

Is it a sign to ward off my evil thoughts? she wondered.

Is she blessing me?

Blessing herself?

Oh, she's going to do it.

Go. Go. Go. Go.

Go.

Guilt suddenly settled on her, a skin attaching to her skin; she began to mortify beneath it, to decompose for want of goodness.

It was as if Isobel had run off with Sandra's husband.

Isobel had dug up Sandra's child.

The evil eye absorbed and she was rewritten, the villain of the piece. As guilty as sin.

The other Mrs Maccabee seemed to rise in triumph, a white, bonny, bouncing ball of light, the brightest object in the sky. She pitched herself in to the canal. Her body slapped the water. Two great transparent wings spouted and spread themselves in the air.

I must pull her out, Isobel thought.

It's the only way.

I can't let the bitch die.

But in her mind's eye she saw herself, not Sandra, drowning in the canal. The other Mrs Maccabee was certainly enamoured with death; but whose? Those green-nailed hands could rise up and carry Isobel under. And hold her there.

I must pull her out, Isobel thought again and even took more steps along the towpath. I must rescue her.

It was then she saw, through folding wings of water, that something was moving. Sandra Maccabee was struggling.

Struggling to drown herself?

Struggling to not drown herself?

Streaming, a head rose above the waters. It bobbed along the surface.

'Come out!' Isobel found herself entreating.

Hair parted to reveal one eye.

'Please come out!'

Sandra, she realized, must be sitting up in the water; the canal, lapping the top of her spine, severed her head from her body.

She drew nearer the bank. If she leaned over, held out her hand, could Sandra stretch out and take it?

But what would happen?

Would she pull Sandra out or would Sandra pull her in?

'Come out!' she yelled again.

Sandra might have heard her once, but now she heard nothing. The head appeared quite inanimate; it looked like one of Anne-Marie's jelly babies after the child had swallowed the body.

I must get help, Isobel thought. The relief of thinking that made her knees quiver. She turned to the stile and the sweep of grey grass which rose up to Wychnor Church. Pulling herself over the stile, she began to climb the hill. She didn't look back.

The church, a darker black than the sky, loomed before her. Rain splattered intermittently. She'll be dead before I get back, she thought. Now she felt neither glad nor sorry, nor even guilty; she just felt old. She opened the gate at the top of the field and stepped into the lane. She went past the schoolhouse and down to Bruno Seuret's. Her hands scratched and clawed at the catch on his gate.

At first she tapped timidly on the knocker. The sound was shocking in her ears. After a while she knocked more loudly.

In the glint of brass she saw Sandra Maccabee's head in the canal.

Terrified, she banged both fists on the door.

She became aware of a beam of yellow coming through the fan light.

The door creaked.

Like the rocking-chair, she thought.

My baby's dead.

They told me the truth.

My baby has died.

Her hands felt dead flesh and she swayed. The door opened. She collapsed inwards.

He half carried, half dragged her into the sitting-room.

'Sandra Tiptree's trying to kill herself,' she said through the sips of brandy he brought her. 'We've got to do something. I don't want her to die.' Though she did, oh yes, she did. 'No, I *don't* want her to die—' But through chinks in that denial whistled surging hope; hope that the bitch had opened wide and swallowed the canal dry. 'She dug up my baby. My baby's dead.' Her teeth began to rattle against the rim of the glass; she heard Sandra's teeth rattle as she sat on the tubular steel bar.

Far away Bruno Seuret was talking. He gave her another glass of brandy and because her hands were shaking so much he fed it to her.

'Isobel!' He'd seized her by the shoulders.

She stared at him.

'I can't understand what you are saying,' he said. 'Slowly. Tell me.'

She began to tell him though she couldn't tell him all of it; she couldn't tell him about drawing the linen across her child's eyes.

He was talking to her in French. She was horrified. Hadn't he understood her? But his hands

now gripped her shoulders reassuringly. 'Now I'm
going to ring the police. After that I'm going to the
canal.'

'I'm coming with you.'

'Your feet are bleeding.'

'Ring the police. Get me some socks.'

When he'd gone she tried to fold herself into the
comfort of her arms.

My poor baby.

She came back.

Tears ran down her cheeks.

She came back to me.

When Bruno Seuret entered the room she said
through her tears. 'Give me the socks.'

'Isobel—'

'I'm coming with you.'

Getting down on his knees, he gingerly pulled the
socks over her bleeding feet.

'Listen, you're not—'

'I'm all right.'

'We'll go across the fields at the back of the
house. It's quicker.' He helped her up. 'The police
are coming. And an ambulance.'

They went out through the kitchen of Burhay
Lodge, skirting the stables and walking across the
lawn to the gate at the bottom of the garden. As
soon as they were away from the lights of the house,
Bruno switched on a torch. The beam flickered
over rain-sodden fields. Darkness was thinning
toward dawn.

St Leonard's Church was to the right of them,
nailed down to the outcrop of land by tombstones.

Birds squealed round the bell tower. As they came to the top of the rise, Isobel looked down to the canal below. At first she could only make out the cattle bridge and the gleam of water and then she saw something slowly submerging.

She realized she'd seen it first in her dream of Alexandria, something very white. It dazzled like the star she'd been waiting for.

The second Mrs Maccabee, she thought now.

The star of ill omen.

The wind made such a noise, a wind so sharp it stung her ears. She shrank beneath her shell of clothes. 'Did you see that thing in the water?' she asked him as they were halfway down the hill.

'Yes.'

'I really didn't believe she'd do it.'

'It might not be her.'

They reached the long grass at the bottom of the field. 'There should be a gap in the hedge,' Bruno said. 'I often come down to the canal this way.' He took her hand and helped her through on to the towpath. She was surprised to feel the quiver in his fingers.

Why, he's as frightened as I am.

Perhaps he's never seen a dead body before.

His fear comforted her; he needs my help, she thought, just as I need his.

They were now both on the towpath. From here she couldn't see the star-shaped patch. It was hidden by the brick pillar of the bridge. 'When I left her she was sat up in the canal,' she said. 'I could just see her head.'

Coming through the bridge, they both saw water swirling round Sandra's jacket. There was no head.

Isobel groaned.

'Take it—' Bruno thrust the torch at her. 'I'm going in.'

'It's too late. I should have tried to pull her out.'

Bruno didn't answer. He took off his shoes and socks.

'I thought she'd pull me under.'

He rolled up his trousers, twisted away from the waters and lowered himself over the bank. He gasped as his feet plunged to the bottom. Turning, he flattened a path through the reeds and began to make his way forward. He flapped his arms, balancing himself; through keening wind came squelching plops of mud.

I don't want to see her body.

She was beginning to panic.

I can't lay it to rest.

I can't perform the rites.

I'm helpless to do anything.

Bruno was tugging at the jacket. He used one hand and then both. He swayed backwards. A white streak rose above a fountain of water. 'It's just her jacket!' he shouted.

'What?'

'Just the jacket. That's all.'

'She's not there?'

'No. Her jacket got jammed under a boulder. She must have wriggled out of it.'

'She's not drowned.' Isobel saw the door of her cottage. She'd left it wide open.

Bruno, wading back towards her, pitched the jacket to her feet. 'Do you think she could have looked for somewhere else?' he asked her. 'Somewhere deeper?'

'Somewhere else?' Isobel turned round on herself in bewilderment. 'Do you mean the lock?'

He put both his hands on the bank and hauled himself out. 'Jesus. It's absolutely freezing.'

'Would she try twice?'

He didn't answer her. He sat down on the wet towpath and pulled on his socks and shoes.

'Would she really?' Isobel asked again.

'We'd better go back along the towpath to the village.'

'She'll be at the cottage.'

'Why would she go there?'

'Anne-Marie's there.'

Bruno took her hand but soon they had to separate. The towpath was too narrow for them to walk abreast. She gave him the torch and he moved ahead.

Quickly they moved over six of the footbridges and then rounded the bend towards the long footbridge which spanned the crossing of the canal and river. Bruno stopped. She came up to stand at his side.

Far beyond the beam of his torch, but before the Quarter Miler, was a shape like a large boulder.

They increased their speed.

The other Mrs Maccabee was sitting cross-legged in the middle of the towpath. Her arms dangled between her thighs. Her head fell towards her chest. From where they were it looked as if she'd been turned to stone. Stone still, she didn't seem less than human, but more so. She was a primordial god presiding at her wayside shrine.

Isobel, seeing her so formidably there across her path, so immovable, felt an irrational need to propitiate.

But what offering would appease this other?

She'd a dim realization of their fates crossing and recrossing. Demonic partners, each stepping into the shoes of the other. Merging, separating, dancing to hidden music, the music of long lost gods.

But now, though the first Mrs Maccabee still executed her steps, the second Mrs Maccabee sat out. And yet her presence was full of portents. Isobel realized her need to propitiate was founded in the hope that her offerings would induce this other to remain eternally where she was. Stone still.

However, as they drew nearer, she heard the dreadful liveliness of Sandra's flesh. It shook and chattered and made curious convulsive sucking sounds.

Sandra lifted her head. 'Hello—' she said between the rattling of her teeth. Her marbled green eye looked at them through a patch of mud.

'We were afraid—' Bruno stopped.

'Afraid?'

'Afraid you—'

'Well, I'm here, aren't I?'

'We'd better help you up,' said Bruno. 'You can't stay here. We must get you out of those wet clothes.'

Sandra turned her head. She looked at him and then she looked at Isobel. She began to smile. Not at all the rictus of a corpse. A smile that danced to hidden music. She raised her hand and the partner she chose was Isobel.

Across the marshy flatlands came the first peels of Christmas bells.

NINETEEN

Isobel stood at the bottom of her garden watching the canal waters slide by. Her feet were bandaged and she wore soft canvas sandals. It was mid-morning; Boxing Day was a moist pumice-stone grey, tree trunks and paths emerald green with lichen. There was a lot of sound in the air; even in the depths of winter the village sang. Perhaps blackbirds, Isobel thought, and what else? The tunes unknown and yet as familiar to her as the downy, slightly chill breeze on her face. From the opposite bank a drake observed her with his beryl eye. Nearby there was a movement in the reeds. This formed into a water rat.

At times she felt so strange that her skin prickled as though perhaps she'd peeled to a baby softness which was shockingly exposed; she must acclimatize herself all over again to moisture and breeze and the movement which became a water rat.

She'd not cried and not raged; she'd even joked with the locum doctor who'd come to see her. 'Shock,' he said.

'Yes,' she said. 'I'm not myself.' Shocked right out of myself.

She turned back up to the cottage. She'd the

breakfast pots to wash. Small rituals were little strings which were tying her into her life. Keep doing things, she thought, and they'll become the things that must be done; the lines on a canvas which might become my picture.

Last night she'd dreamed of her child. Not the child the other Mrs Maccabee had shown her, but the child she remembered.

She hoped she'd never dream of Sandra; no, she must never dream of her. And yet she'd no feelings about her; being shocked out of herself had shocked Sandra clean away.

Her feet, coated in creams, led her into her kitchen without too much pain. Sergeant Probert, who'd come to see her last night, told her that the other Mrs Maccabee had used the Victorian window in this room as an entrance. It had a catch which locked the two central glazing bars of the sash together. Sandra had simply unscrewed the catch and set it back together in chewing gum.

'She was quite proud of that,' said Sergeant Probert. 'She talked and talked about her planning. You'd think it was the Third World War she'd conducted. She said she supposed you'd change the locks so the first time she broke in – using her husband's old key – she fixed up the window. It's quite clever really,' he said, showing her. 'The catch looks as if it's locked but in fact it lifts up . . . well, I wouldn't say easily, but without too much difficulty . . . and there goes the window. That's one chatty lady. She never stopped talking. If you had a screwdriver – ?'

She found him one. He stood on a chair and removed the gum with his thumb. 'She kept on and on about her husband's cricket bat. She wants it back. She's an Ian Botham fan. There. Stick this in the bin. I'll screw the lock down.'

'She tried to brain me with that bat.'

'Did she?'

'Would you like a cup of tea, Sergeant?'

'Thank you.'

He was a man as young as herself and he'd very pale eyes. Later, when she began at the beginning, he heard her tell him the most outrageous things and he treated them all as commonplaces. Perhaps his work had led him to suppose the bizarre quite ordinary. Perhaps it was his way of rendering safe the wickedness in the world.

She'd found his attitude very disturbing. At times she wondered if he could be hearing what she said. She became so anxious that once or twice she lost the thread of his words altogether. She simply watched his ginger moustache go up and down as he spoke.

She looked at the window he'd secured and then she put away the pots she'd washed. She did this with much more care then usual. It seemed she'd to summon all her concentration to perform the simplest tasks.

She'd put the kettle on when the door bell rang.

'I've been to the police station.' It was Bruno Seuret. He brought the sound of church bells in with him.

'Come and have some coffee. I'm just making it.'

277

In the kitchen, as she set out the tray, she was aware of him looking at her as if she were a stranger, as if this was the first time he'd seen her. She too, she realized, saw him differently. Did she want to continue to know someone who had been part of that night?

Would these changed people even like each other? That was what was in her mind when he said: 'Before I went to the police station I called at the chapel of rest. The funeral director told me they'd moved Anne-Marie to the village church.'

'You went there?' Isobel looked at him again, beginning to like what she saw. 'Simeon Kelso arranged it all. He asked my permission to have the coffin moved. I'm afraid it's instant coffee—'

'That's fine.'

'I find it very strange, but I don't seem able to feel a thing. Simeon was in tears. It made me feel very awkward. The doctor says it's shock. The vicar said that he and those parishioners who'd known her wanted to . . . well, he said – he said they wanted to circle her in prayer until she was laid to rest again. He was very upset.'

'Let me take the tray—'

As they went through to the living-room she said: 'Perhaps you don't know, but I'm not a Christian. Charlie was and Anne-Marie was baptized and went to church and Sunday school. My position – in the days when I thought about such things – was that it was better to have faith, any faith, than none and I wanted the best for my daughter. I suppose it sounds very silly and middle-class. Taking up positions about such things. Most people just slide through. They just get on with it.'

He set the tray down on the hearth.

'No. No sugar,' and she took the cup from him. 'Well . . . when the vicar asked for my permission. Oh, it was quite ridiculous. I felt excluded from her care. But then I remembered I had excluded myself from her spiritual care. So I said yes. There'll be people with her all the time. They'll keep watch over her.'

'What arrangements have been made?'

'It's been difficult because of the holiday. But everyone has been marvellous. They're opening the crematorium early for us tomorrow morning. It's quite irrational of me, but I feel the only safe way is to have Anne-Marie cremated. I simply . . . I suppose my fears are absolutely groundless. But I feel that's what must be done. I'm hoping it will all be finished with before the Press get to hear of it.'

'Who will be with you?'

'At the crematorium? Just the vicar. I must say Simeon Kelso has been wonderful. He's discussed the matter with his bishop and he says they'd like to take the child in.'

'What do you mean?'

'Her ashes will be interred in the church near the altar. In God's eye. That's how Simeon puts it. I asked that there shall be no marker on the spot. We're going to move her headstone into the old graveyard. That's all been grassed over now, but the stones of the village ancestors are ranged round the perimeter wall.'

'You surely don't think Charlie's widow would—'

'She might. Oh, she might. You know that Charlie left her for another woman while she was in hospital having her second miscarriage? The bastard stuck a note behind the clock in their bedroom. He told her he was coming back to me.'

'Why would he do that? You told me yourself you hadn't even seen him for over two years.'

'I hadn't. But do you remember what you told me about Charlie's affair with the bank manager's wife? How Sandra had gone after the woman with his cricket bat and given her a good hiding? I think Charlie was laying a false trail. Covering his tracks. It probably even amused him to set the second Mrs Maccabee on the first. I'm not sure he wouldn't see it as one big joke. Apart from preserving the looks of his new lover.'

'That's monstrous.'

She looked away from him. 'I know, I know.' Then she said: 'Even after that shit had left me I still loved him. I thought he might . . . I couldn't seem to help myself. I thought that somehow, some day, it would be all right. I really used to think we were made for each other. From here to eternity and all that rubbish. Perhaps he was sore that I got the cottage in the divorce settlement. Perhaps that's why he sent Sandra after me. It's terrible to bear such . . . such a colossal burden of ill will from someone you've worshipped. I was a fool. That's the top and bottom of it. I let my heart rule my head. I fell for the wrong man.'

'I know.'

'Civilized indeed. What's civilized about love? The real truth is Charlie has only ever loved one person outside himself and that's Anne-Marie. I used to watch them. He was wonderful with her. He used to put her hand over his own and marvel. Their hands could have been stamped out of the same mould.' She smiled, a small wintry smile. 'If he could have ever guessed what Sandra would do, he'd never have left her that note.'

'But surely if Sandra knew—'

'I told the police it was all nonsense. But will Sandra ever believe that? He was certainly running off with someone . . . and he told her it was me. I must do the best I can for Anne-Marie. I have to keep her safe. I can't tell you how powerful that feeling is. I want her to be in a circle of prayer. I want her to be in the eye of God. As a non-believer I know I'm being ridiculous. How can I be comforted by the thought that she'll be within the walls of the church? After all, I'll be forever outside those walls. But I have to do what I can for her. It's not a duty. It's a necessity. I can't be at peace unless she's safely laid to rest. I have to purge myself and somehow or other Simeon has given me a way of doing this. It seems to need some kind of priestly ritual. It can't be done in any other kind of way. My child was in the cottage long before Christmas Day. Sandra brought her in on the night of that dreadful fog and put her under the bed.' For the first time her horror began to emerge; rising hysteria made her voice sound tinny. 'Something has to be done. Something. Some ceremony. Do you understand?'

'I think I can understand in part.'

'Can you? If it sounds the most terrible muddle that's because it is. I can't be rational about my daughter and what happened to her. And I can't absolve myself. It seems to be a thing of ritual . . . a communal kind of thing. It seems to need ceremony.'

'But why did Sandra do it? What possessed her? Why did she exhume the child?'

'She told the police she wanted to really punish me. She wanted me to feel as terrible as she did. She couldn't think of a worse punishment than that. They're keeping her in the hospital at Burton. They're waiting for her to be seen by a psychiatrist. I suppose it'll get labelled with something like post-natal depression.'

'You don't think it is?'

'I think it very well might be. But I also think when she's not in a post-natal depression she's likely to turn up on my doorstep again. Sane or crazy that woman wants my hide. That's what I feel.'

'Pity she can't have a go at the real villain of the piece.'

'Well, Charlie's dead now and someone's got to get it in the neck.'

He didn't argue with her. 'What will you do?'

'Well, I'm not going to run away from the second Mrs Maccabee. I'm never going to do that. If she does turn up again I'll simply do the best I can. She was going to lay about me with Charlie's cricket bat. And now she's enlisted police aid in trying to get the bat back.' A ghost of a smile hovered round her lips. 'How's that for nerve?'

'But surely she'll be charged with something?'

'She's on a holding charge at the moment. Illegal entry. To be honest I hope it won't come to court though the sergeant seemed to think it might.'

'Why don't you?'

'It'll be a publicity circus. It'll be awful.'

'I hadn't thought of that.'

'Why did you go to the station?'

'They wanted me to make a written statement.'

'I know this must sound absolutely ridiculous . . . but the thing I really dread is dreaming about Sandra. She seemed to be very ordinary when I first knew her. Well, you must have known her better than I for you were colleagues. Charlie's turned the woman into a monster.'

'You said that just you and the vicar would be at the crematorium tomorrow morning?'

'Yes. It seemed best. After all, it's not a funeral in a proper sense.'

'I think you should have someone with you Isobel. I'd like to come. Can I?'

'That's kind of you, but I'll be fine. I'm quite all right—'

'No, you're not. You need someone with you. Let me come.'

She looked at him.

He smiled. 'I'm not going to turn into a monster. I promise.'

'Thank you. Yes. I'd like you to come. I'm being silly, aren't I? I always think I can manage everything on my own. Please come.'

'Good. That's settled.'

She moved, startled, as the door bell rang. 'I'll go,' he said.

He came back with a bunch of white chrysanthemums. 'They were left on the step,' he said.

'Oh dear. I think the village greengrocer must have opened his back door.'

'What do you mean?'

'It's Boxing Day yet all these flowers keep turning up. Not long before you came the vicar was here. He says that people at the church keep arriving with bunches. They're for Anne-Marie.'

'Offerings.'

'Yes.'

'Then when you've finished your coffee we'll take these to the church.'

COME DOWN INTO DARKNESS
by Clare McNally

The house had been empty for twenty years. There were dark stories of murder and suicide told about it. But it was just what Doreen Addison was looking for – big, inexpensive and secluded. It was perfect for her child refuge.

At first it was just a crazy man in the woods and a dead cat on the back porch. But then the children started seeing and hearing a beautiful woman dressed in black and there was a terrrible accident in the cellar. Something wasn't right about this house.

And then the nightmare really started as children disappeared and Doreen found herself confronting an evil power beyond her understanding. Only one thing could save her and the children from destruction: she must discover the secret of the woman in black who commands them all to: Come Down into Darkness.

0 552 13034 6

BLOODLINE
by David St. Clair

HE WAS JUST SIX YEARS OLD . . .
and her only child, yet after the shocking kidnapping and even the horrible identification of his small tortured body, Lois refused to believe her son was dead – *really* dead.

Plagued by strange psychic premonitions and disturbing wide awake visions, Lois became more and more convinced that her child was being held captive somewhere – for some unknown reason – and she was the only one who could save him.

And then the framed engraving arrived . . . the one with the old manor house and the weird little man who moved effortlessly under the glass. He led her to Scotland . . . and a family . . . and the unspeakable horror of her BLOODLINE.

0 552 13323 X

SHOCKER
by Randall Boyll

SHOCKER will give you nightmares!

A serial killer is plaguing Maryville, Ohio.

Jonathan is an all-American college student and football star. After an injury on the field, he lies unconscious – and has a terrible, realistic dream of the killer murdering his family. To his horror, Jonathan recognizes the killer. And the killer sees Jonathan.

Written with incredible power and pace, SHOCKER brings the reader into a terrifying world of murder and mayhem. A desperate young man must somehow find the strength of will to track down and destroy the evil force that inhabits a bloody assassin who will stop at nothing to survive.

SHOCKER is a novel of psychological and supernatural horror that follows in the tradition of Stephen King's *The Shining*.

0 552 13641 7

A SELECTED LIST OF HORROR TITLES
AVAILABLE FROM CORGI BOOKS

THE PRICES SHOWN BELOW WERE CORRECT AT THE TIME OF GOING TO PRESS.
HOWEVER TRANSWORLD PUBLISHERS RESERVE THE RIGHT TO SHOW NEW
RETAIL PRICES ON COVERS WHICH MAY DIFFER FROM THOSE PREVIOUSLY
ADVERTISED IN THE TEXT OR ELSEWHERE.

☐	09156 1	THE EXORCIST	*William Peter Blatty*	£3.99
☐	13641 7	SHOCKER	*Randall Boyll*	£2.99
☐	13034 6	COME DOWN INTO DARKNESS	*Clare McNally*	£2.99
☐	12691 8	WHAT ABOUT THE BABY?	*Clare McNally*	£2.99
☐	12400 1	GHOSTLIGHT	*Clare McNally*	£2.99
☐	11652 1	GHOST HOUSE	*Clare McNally*	£2.99
☐	11825 7	GHOST HOUSE REVENGE	*Clare McNally*	£3.50
☐	13033 8	SOMEBODY COME AND PLAY	*Clare McNally*	£2.99
☐	13323 X	BLOODLINE	*David St. Clair*	£3.99
☐	12705 1	THE DEVIL ROCKED HER CRADLE	*David St. Clair*	£2.99
☐	12587 3	MINE TO KILL	*David St. Clair*	£2.99
☐	11132 5	CHILD POSSESSED	*David St. Clair*	£2.99
☐	13532 1	SAY YOU LOVE SATAN	*David St. Clair*	£3.99
☐	10471 X	FULL CIRCLE	*Peter Straub*	£2.99
☐	13466 X	STILL LIFE	*Sheri S. Tepper*	£2.99

*All Corgi/Bantam Books are available at your bookshop or newsagent, or can be ordered from the
following address:*

Corgi/Bantam Books,
Cash Sales Department,
P.O. Box 11, Falmouth, Cornwall TR10 9EN

Please send a cheque or postal order (no currency) and allow 80p for postage and packing for the
first book plus 20p for each additional book ordered up to a maximum charge of £2.00 in UK.

B.F.P.O. customers please allow 80p for the first book and 20p for each additional book.

Overseas customers, including Eire, please allow £1.50 for postage and packing for the first book,
£1.00 for the second book, and 30p for each subsequent title ordered.

NAME (Block Letters) ....

ADDRESS ....

....